RULES OF ENGAGEMENT

J.T. GEISSINGER

Published by J.T. Geissinger, Inc.

www.jtgeissinger.com

Cover design by Letitia Hasser

Printed in the United States of America

For my mother. Thank you.

1

MASON

Have you ever noticed how versatile the word "fuck" is?

I know, random question, but stick with me. I have a point.

As a noun, verb, or adjective, "fuck" really can't be beat. I use it constantly in all its forms.

For example, right now I'm staring at the naked blonde snoring softly in my bed and I'm thinking *This is fucked. Why the fuck did I take her home from the bar last night? I am a fucking moron. FUCK.*

That last one's probably my favorite.

Just the word all by itself.

In capitals.

Like that, it can mean "wow." Or "life sucks." Or "how did I get mustard on my shirt?" Or even "we're all gonna die!"

Or, in this particular case "why do I keep making the same mistake over and over again?"

My therapist has a theory, but I don't wanna talk about it.

"Mason! *Maaasooonnn*! Where are you? We're late as fuck!"

That Brooklyn-accented voice shouting at me from downstairs reminds me there's another great use of the word—as a unit of measure.

"As fuck." A "fuckload." A "fuckton," which is heavier than a load but different than a "fuckwad," which when used as a noun is a unit of measure, but is better used as an adjective to refer to a person you can't stand.

Like Tom Brady for instance. Yeah, the famous QB of the Patriots.

Don't even get me started on Mr. Perfect.

Blech.

Sometimes my mind gets the best of me and fixates on how many shitloads are in a fuckton, but these are the kind of things my therapist sighs quietly at when I mention and looks down at her hands like she's lost all hope of being useful to society, so I've never gotten a solid answer to that.

Where was I?

Oh yeah. The blonde.

"Mason! MASON! JesusChristonacrutch, *let's go*!"

The guy about to have a stroke downstairs is Dick, my agent. You'd think he'd show me some respect, considering the amount of money I make him, but nah. He treats me like family.

I mean, not *close* family. Not like I'm his son or whatever, but maybe like…a stepson?

Yeah, like a stepson.

Like, he *kinda* likes me? Because he *has* to? If I'm *behaving*? If my mom's in the room and he's pretending to be all kissy-kissy-we're-just-one-big-happy-blended-family until she leaves and he can let his toupee down and collapse onto the couch and yell at me to get him a beer?

Like that.

Like…well, like everyone else treats me, I guess. With kid gloves.

Like, "Holy cow, who brought the Yeti to the party? Hahaha, is the Sasquatch house trained? Joking! Of course we're joking, hahaha!" Stage whisper: "No, seriously—is it house trained? Because we just had the carpet cleaned and it looks like it could really use a potty mat."

Spoiler alert: I'm not known for my social graces.

"I'm coming!" I holler, making the naked blonde on my bed jerk and snort.

But she doesn't wake up. She just burrows down into my fucking (adjective) sheets and does fuck all (noun), so I leave her to sleep off the fuckload (unit of measure) of booze we drank last night before we came back here and fucked (verb, past tense) like rabbits.

Can you see why I'm always so crabby?

Being me is exhausting.

~

"This is a bullshit idea."

"You got a better one?"

"Yeah. Let's stop at that bar on the corner. Get some drinks."

Exasperated sigh. "Mace, it's ten o'clock in the morning."

"Exactly. I need a Bloody Mary." I stare gloomily out the passenger window at the Irish pub we're passing on our way to the meeting with the matchmaker.

The fucking *matchmaker*. For the love of all that's holy.

Dick is driving my car. It's a brand new Mercedes-Benz Maybach. I hate it with the burning heat of a thousand suns. It's too cushy. Safe.

Makes me feel old.

I shoulda bought that vintage Shelby Cobra Super Snake with the 800-horsepower engine I wanted, but Dick screamed about how I'd kill myself in it, blah, blah, so here we are.

That I hate the car isn't why Dick's driving me. He drives me around a lot, because my license is suspended. Two dozen tickets in ten months and the DMV gets pissy.

Also, it's his way of keeping an eye on me. If I get into any more trouble, my ass is grass and I can kiss all my sweet endorsement deals goodbye.

And I *do not* want to kiss them goodbye. Other people might measure happiness by how many friends they have (spoiler: I don't have any) or how close they are with their family (spoiler: don't have any of those, either) or whatever other sappy shit makes them feel good, but for me there's only one measure of success, and that's money.

Which (how many spoilers are we on now?) I've got a lot of.

A shitload, you could say.

Or a fuckton.

Either way, you'd be right.

Yeah, I know what you're thinking: I'm a shallow asshole. Better shallow than poor.

I've been poor—the *poorest* kind of poor, where you have to go to the gas station down the street and stuff your pockets with toilet paper to bring home because there's none in the house and the only cheese you've ever eaten is the government kind that comes in a box and when the power gets shut off you just go without lights and heat and a stove to cook on, because there's no money to pay the bill.

Poor means having to do things to survive.

Humiliating things.

Illegal things, sometimes.

Things that go against your nature or your morals, but it's not like you have a choice. You're powerless. Especially when you're a poor *kid*, because then you're also invisible.

And being invisible is even worse than being poor.

You might as well be dead when you're invisible.

"You don't need a Bloody Mary," Dick says with irritation. "What you *need* is a woman to look after you."

I smirk, thinking of the busty blonde I called a cab for before we left. "Got plenty of those."

"Don't be a dipshit. You know what I mean. And let *me* do the talking when we get there!"

"Stop shouting. You're making my headache worse."

Dick ignores me and keeps right on shouting. "And would it have killed you to run a comb through your hair? You look like you slept in the woods!"

"Good point. Let's stop at Supercuts."

Dick heaves a big, dramatic sigh. "You have to start taking this seriously, Mace. Your entire future depends on you getting your shit together."

He's right. I know he's right, but it still pisses me off that he's lecturing me.

Besides, it's not like I've got a future, anyway. This football thing will be like everything else in my life: temporary.

Nothing good ever lasts for me for long.

I glare through the windows at the sunny spring morning. "Tell me again why I have to go to this meeting?"

"Because you've already been fired by two other outfits who do this matchmaking shit, and we need to have you settled by the start of the season."

Settled equals married.

Shoot me.

"I don't wanna get married."

"Boo frickin' hoo."

I grouse, "You know, this is very dehumanizing. I'm not some slab of beef with no feelings."

Dick hoots with laughter. The asshole.

"I'm being serious!"

"Shut up, Mason. If you could be trusted to choose a good girl on your own, we wouldn't be in this situation. But your taste in women runs from bad to worse, and I'll be damned if I'm gonna let some illiterate, money-grubbing broad with a face tattoo whose ex-husband is a blood relative sink her claws into you. We're gonna get you a *nice* girl, from a *nice* family, who you can settle down with and have a *nice* life."

Nice is the foulest four-letter word in the English language. It's got fuck beat by a mile.

I mutter, "I don't want a nice girl." *Don't deserve one, either.*

"No shit, Sherlock! Hence the matchmaker! Look, we're here. Just be quiet and I'll take care of everything. Try to look earnest."

"*Earnest*?"

"Sincere. Like you're into it."

"Yeah, I know what the word means. But have you seen my face?" I point to it. "The default setting is Fuck You, volume ten!"

Dick pulls into a parking space in front of an office building that was converted from a Victorian house. It's all cutesy, painted pale pink with yellow trim. Lots of dainty pink rosebushes line the white picket fence that surrounds it.

I wouldn't be surprised if Bambi and Cinderella skipped out the front door. The place looks like Walt Disney threw up all over it.

The heart-shaped sign out front reads "Perfect Pairings. Because You Deserve Your Happily-Ever-After!"

Sweet Jesus. I've wandered into hell.

Dick shuts off the engine and turns to me, his face serious. "Mason, I won't allow you to self-destruct. As long as I'm your agent, *I won't allow it*. You hear me?"

"Let's do the math. One: my ears aren't broken. Plus two: you're shouting twelve inches away from my face. Equals three: I hear you."

"Good. Now if you will just let me do the talking when we get in there, everything will be fine."

I examine his craggy face. He looks nervous, which is strange. Dick is usually about as nervous as a plank of wood.

"What's got you so riled up about this meeting? The owner a nightmare or something?"

"The opposite of a nightmare. She's sweet, okay? One of those Southern belle types. A lady."

I picture an old biddie in pearls with phosphorescent white dentures wearing a straw hat with plastic flowers on the brim and feel a pang of longing for the Irish pub we passed on the way here.

Dick says, "She won't like it if you curse or"—he waves an aggravated hand at me—"act like your usual constipated self."

"Excuse me, but my bowel movements are very regular."

"You know what I'm saying! Behave!"

Because Dick is nervous, I start to get nervous, too. Empathy is one of the many things I hate about myself. If I could just block everyone else's feelings out, life would be so much easier. But I'm like an emotional sponge. All that shit sinks into me.

Which is one of the reasons I drink so much. Alcohol helps me stay numb.

A pair of big boobs in my hands doesn't hurt, either.

Dick throws open the driver's door and sends me one final glare of warning before getting out of the car. I watch him amble up the front steps of the portal to hell—cleverly disguised as a matchmaker's office—until he turns and motions impatiently for me to join him.

With a heavy sigh, I step out of the Benz into the beautiful morning.

Atlanta in May is one of the prettiest places I can imagine. Birds are chirping. Flowers are blooming. The sky is a dazzling shade of brilliant blue.

And here I am, a twenty-eight-year-old man who's so fucked up his agent thinks finding him the perfect wife will save him from himself.

I'm only going along with it because I don't have the heart to tell him that ship's already sailed.

That ship has fucking sunk.

We walk through the front door of the building into a waiting room, and I have to stop myself from running right back out.

Everything is pink. Everything. The walls, the carpet, the sofa and chairs. It's like being inside a bottle of Pepto-Bismol.

Looking around in horror, I say, "What. The actual. Fuck."

Dick hisses, "It's romantic! Now shut the hell up!" Plastering a fake smile on his face, he strolls over to the counter behind which a woman with a frizzy red perm dozes in a chair. Her eyes are closed. She's snoring gently.

And by "gently" I mean "like a chainsaw." I've heard riots quieter than this.

Dick has to clear his throat several times to be heard over the racket, until Sleeping Beauty wakes with a start.

Then she screams.

I say, "I know exactly how you feel, lady."

Then everything falls into slow motion.

A door on the other side of the room swings open. Through it steps a young woman. She's slim and petite, just over five feet tall, and dressed demurely, like a librarian.

A beige skirt hangs past her knees. A simple white blouse is buttoned all the way up to her neck. On her nose perches a pair of delicate gold-rimmed glasses. Her dark hair is gathered back into a tidy bun.

She doesn't have any jewelry on. The only makeup she's wearing is lipstick.

It's the same horrific shade of pink as the walls.

She looks at the woman who screamed. She looks at Dick. Then she turns her head and looks at me.

She smiles.

I feel that smile all the way down to the darkest corner of my soul, the place where light never shines and I keep all the monsters hidden under lock and key.

She smiles with her whole body. With her whole *being*, like she's a conductor of light itself and all that's good and pure in the universe is being channeled through her on its way to me, where it surrounds me and bathes me in golden rays of sunshine, so warm and sweet I could almost cry.

I stand there stunned, stupidly gaping at her, until she speaks.

In a voice like music, the librarian says, "Hello."

That's it. One word. A simple, common, everyday word I've heard a million times before, except never in that voice, from that mouth, from those lips in their hideous pink lipstick.

In response, I think a simple, common word.

FUCK.

Remember my point from earlier, the one I said I had? Here it is:

For the first time ever, in all its variations, as a noun, verb, or adjective, that word doesn't even begin to cover what I feel the first time I set eyes on Maddie McRae.

Unfortunately, I'm still me. Guess what happens next.

Spoiler alert: I fuck it up.

2

MADDIE

I've never had an out-of-body experience before, but today is a day of firsts.

First time meeting the infamous Mason Spark.

First time seeing size eighteen feet in real life.

First time wanting to commit murder.

So here I am, looking down at myself from my vantage point on the ceiling where my soul has fled in horror as the scene unfolds below, terrible but weirdly compelling, like one of those accidents you pass on the highway where you know it's wrong to but you still have to slow down to check for blood and mangled bodies.

At least my hair looks good from up here.

The same can't be said for my new client, who appears to have an angry goth porcupine nesting on top of his cranium. "Bed head" doesn't even begin to cover it. It looks like his preferred hair styling method is sticking his head into a blender and setting it to puree.

That would account for his beastly attitude, too. His brains are obviously scrambled. I've met bears nicer than him.

It started to fall apart the minute we laid eyes on each other.

Or, I should say, the minute *he* laid eyes on *me*. I opened my office door to Auntie Waldine's scream and found two men in the waiting room, one of whom was as tall as a skyscraper… and just as friendly.

He took one look at me, froze, then curled his lip into a sneer so acidic he could've bleached the walls with it.

At first I thought it was on account of Auntie Waldine and her startling scream, but even after I explained that she suffers from narcolepsy—a sleep disease that makes sufferers of the condition fall asleep suddenly and sometimes hallucinate frightening things when they just as suddenly wake—he still kept staring at me in disgust like I was the Creature from the Black Lagoon.

Honestly, I've never met a man with such a serious case of resting bitch face.

"I told you this was matchmaker thing was bullshit," snaps Prince Charmless to his sidekick, a short, sweating man with bug eyes who thought it was a good idea to wear an entire bottle of cologne and every piece of gold jewelry he owns to a morning business meeting.

And let's not talk about the plaid leisure suit. Or the white leather shoes. Or the toupee, which looks like a taxidermy experiment gone horribly wrong.

Somewhere out in the world, a dead badger is missing its scalp.

The sidekick—who goes by Dick, because apparently Richard is too dignified—waves a hand in the air. I'm nearly blinded by the light flashing off his rings.

"Now, listen here, Missy—"

"It's Maddie," I remind him, eyeing the porcupine on Mason's head.

"—my boy here signed a contract with your company, a very expensive contract, I might add, and we expect results." Leaning forward in his chair, Dick stabs a stubby index finger repeatedly onto the top of my desk. "Qualified. Guaranteed. Hand-selected matches. That's what we were promised."

I want to ask if he's performing later in Las Vegas at a Rodney Dangerfield tribute show, but I was raised better than that. "And that's exactly what you've been given."

Dick throws his hands in the air. "Not a single girl you've presented has been a match!"

My mistake was presenting lovely, intelligent, gracious single women who desired to meet equally lovely, intelligent, gracious single men.

What Mason Spark needs is a lady gorilla.

Since he sat down fifteen minutes ago, he's been nothing but combative. Hostile, even. He even had the nerve to roll his eyes at me when I offered him a sweet tea, as if it were an insult to his manhood.

The manhood that's—*ahem*—threatening to compromise the integrity of the zipper on his jeans.

Which I'm not noticing. Am. *Not.*

Number one, I'm not that type of girl. Number two, I'm not attracted to athletes. Especially arrogant, irritating athletes with supersized egos. Numbers three through ten, I don't date clients.

Especially when I'm about to fire them.

I fold my hands in my lap and smile, because Southern girls don't need a gun to shoot you dead. "Unfortunately, Dick, the Bride of Frankenstein was already taken."

From the corner of my eye, I see Mason's lips twitch.

Is he trying not to laugh? Doubtful. He's probably imagining all the ways he could hide my decomposing corpse. I'm barely five-foot-two in heels, so he's got lots of options.

When Dick opens his mouth to protest, I politely cut in.

"Every candidate I've presented in the two weeks since 'your boy' signed with my agency was carefully screened and selected against your list of qualifications"—the ridiculous list that included things like optimum breast size (36 DD in case you're wondering)—"with photos and detailed profiles that you approved."

"Sure, but one phone call with all those girls and he knew they were all wrong for him!"

Ah yes. The infamous phone calls.

A few of the ladies Mason had been matched with had contacted me in tears after their initial get-acquainted chat. One described it as being barked at by a drill sergeant with IBS. Another said she'd had more pleasant experiences at the gynecologist. None of them got past the phone interview, but they all agreed that Mason Spark is a first-class jerk.

I flick my gaze toward the jerk in question. "I can only lead a horse to water, sir. I can't make him drink."

Slouched in his chair with thunderclouds boiling over his head, Mason glares back at me from under lowered brows.

It's too bad the man has the personality of a chupacabra, because he's actually very good-looking. Six-five, full lips, chiseled jaw, the whole nine yards. Dressed in jeans, a black T-shirt, and cowboy boots, he looks like the quintessential Marlboro Man.

If the Marlboro Man had tattoos that decorated his arms, all the way from his bulging biceps down to his thick wrists.

Plus, he's got long-lashed eyes that would be gorgeous if they weren't narrowed and filled with disdain. They're an unusual shade of gray. At first I thought London fog, but that's too romantic. Maybe L.A. smog?

And, if the rumors are true, he's also a god in bed. He didn't earn the nickname Sexual Chocolate for nothing.

I can't align the nickname with the anti-social grouch sitting across from me, but who knows? Maybe he hates clothing and turns into a pussycat the moment he's naked.

Mason's gaze sharpens. I realize I've been thinking about his sexual prowess while staring right at him, and my cheeks grow hot.

I sit upright in my chair and straighten the stack of candidate folders on my desk for something to do with my hands. "I'm sorry you haven't been happy with the service. Per the contract, your money will be refunded—"

Mason says flatly, "I don't need my money back. I need a wife."

Sensing something's up, my intuition tingles. I look back and forth between Mason and Dick, who mops at his damp forehead with a wilted handkerchief.

"Need?"

When Dick freezes, eyes widening, I know I've hit a nerve. "Mason? Will you please explain what you mean by you *need* a wife?"

Dick harrumphs, waving his hankie around theatrically. "He doesn't mean anything!"

"For my career," says Mason, pinning me in a freezing glare. When Dick squawks, Mason grunts dismissively. "She signed an NDA. It doesn't matter."

Oh, but it does matter. Regardless of the non-disclosure agreement Dick made me sign, it definitely *does* matter that I went into this contract under false pretenses.

I do what I do because I believe in love. I *love* love. Matchmaking is my passion and my calling, and I'm proud to say I'm pretty dang good at it.

And, if I'm not mistaken, Mason Spark has turned me into a pimp.

A madam. Whatever. It's bad.

"Just so we're clear," I say slowly, "you're saying you don't really want to get married, but you have to…for…*football*?"

When Mason explains, I think poor Dick might faint.

"I've got strict morals clauses in my contract with the Pioneers, and also in all my endorsement deals. I'm on notice that any more…" Agitated, he drags a hand through his thatch of dark hair. "*Incidents*, and I'll get cut from the team. I could lose everything. So I need to settle down." He smirks at me. "Or at least look like I am."

I pick up the desk lamp and bludgeon him with it. Except only in my head. "I'm not in the business of fake relationships, Mr. Spark—"

"It's Mr. Spark now? Ten seconds ago we were on a first name basis."

"Ten seconds ago, I didn't know you were lying to me."

"What difference does my reason for wanting to get married make?"

"It makes every difference."

"The end result is the same."

"Not at all."

"How so?"

"Oh, just this little ol' thing called love. You know. The reason people usually get married?"

His gray eyes skewer me. "Half of all marriages end in divorce. Basing a relationship on love is about as solid as building castles in the sand."

Oh dear. Someone needs an enema.

Though I do agree that there are other important factors that make a successful match, a couple can't go the distance without the glue of love. It's what holds everything together when things get messy. But I decide the point is moot.

Smiling my best *bless your heart* smile, I say, "And what do you propose marriage be based on? Breast size?"

He deadpans, "The odds of it lasting are just as good."

I take a moment to marvel at that statement. I'm not sure I've ever met a person more cynical than this pretty football star staring at me like he'd like to pop my eyeballs out with his thumbs.

Whatever made him so anti-love, it must've been a doozy.

"I'm sure there are plenty of large breasted women out there who'd be happy to accommodate your enchanting views on marriage, Mr. Spark, but you won't find one of them through me. Unfortunately, *I* believe in love."

He snorts. "You believed in Santa Claus and the tooth fairy once, too. Grow up."

I stare at him, my smile fading. For the first time since he walked into the room, I feel something other than aggravation for him: I feel pity.

If this is truly how he feels…well, that's just an awful way to go through life.

Holding his gaze, I say, "I'm a simple girl, and I certainly don't claim to have any special insight on life. But there's one thing I know beyond a shadow of a doubt, and that is that love is the only thing you gain more of by giving it. Until you learn to open your heart, you'll always be as lonely as you are now."

Mason blinks, as if startled. He says too loudly, "I'm not *lonely*."

Okie dokie, then. So much for the inspirational speeches. I stifle a sigh and glance meaningfully toward the door, hoping he'll take the hint. "I see. My mistake. Now, if you'll excuse me, I have another meeting—"

Mason says suddenly, "I'll double your fee."

I'm not the only one that statement gives whiplash to. Dick nearly falls out of his chair.

He sputters, "Now, now, wait just a minute. We can try another company, Mace! Don't go wastin' your money on one that can't deliver the goods!"

The goods. As if women are sports equipment. Just so many footballs, indistinguishable from one another, useful only as a tool to score. *Things.*

Life would be so much easier if murder were legal.

To Dick, I say, "Don't worry about the money. Every penny will be refunded by the end of the day tom—"

"I'll triple it," Mason breaks in.

When I stay silent, biting my tongue because arrogance and

ignorance are two of my least favorite things, Mason takes it as a negotiation ploy.

"Fine," he says gruffly, sitting forward and resting his elbows on his knees. He pins me in that weirdly intense gray gaze of his again. "Name your price."

"I don't want your money, Mr. Spark." I enunciate every word, because I'm starting to think he might be a little thick in the head. Maybe one too many concussions.

The laugh he produces in response lacks any human warmth whatsoever. "That's a first."

By now, any shred of pity I might have felt for him has shriveled up and died.

Whoever this man's mama is, she did *not* teach him manners.

I say politely but firmly, "Perhaps I'm not making myself clear. I'm a businesswoman. Not a mercenary. And I'm certainly *not* running an escort service. Dick told me you were interested in finding a partner, someone to share your life with, who has compatible values and goals. I was led to believe your travel and game schedule interfered with meeting suitable women, and you hoped my service would assist you with that. That's what I signed on for, because that's what I do.

"What I do *not* do is knowingly mislead my clients. The ladies who come to me looking for healthy relationships are good people. Each of them deserves a good man."

I leave the obvious unsaid: I doubt he's one of them.

But Prince Charmless isn't done with me yet. His tone challenging, he says, "Is that what you have? A good man?" He glances at my bare ring finger.

There's another finger I'd like to show him, but I refuse to let him rattle me. I say coolly, "My private life is just that, Mr. Spark—private."

"So you're single."

He says it like an accusation. Like I've failed some sort of test.

Holy cheese and rice, I'd like to smack that smirk right off his face.

Instead, I rise and gesture toward the door. "Thank you for your time. I'm truly sorry I wasn't able to be of service. As I said, the money will be refunded—"

"Give us a minute."

Rising to his full, intimidating height, Mason speaks to Dick, but stares straight at me.

It could be my imagination, but I could swear I see a strange look cross Dick's face. A sly look, like a lightbulb has blinked on over his head as he glances between me and Mason.

But then he stands and heads toward the door and I forget about all that, because Mason Spark is about to reach across the desk and strangle me.

3

MADDIE

When we're alone, Mason and I engage in a long stare-off where the only sound is the clock ticking on the wall and the air conditioning whispering through the vents.

I hold his gaze, waiting for him to speak first. If he thinks I'll be intimidated by him, he'll be disappointed. I've got four older brothers. I can play the staring game for days.

A muscle in Mason's jaw starts to flex. A while after that, he says, "You're not blinking."

"Funny, I was just thinking the same about you."

"Really? I could've sworn you were thinking about stabbing me in the neck with that letter opener on your desk."

"Don't be ridiculous." I pause for a beat. "I just had the carpet cleaned."

His lips do that twitching thing again. "You're right. A neck wound would produce a lot of blood. You could push me out the window."

"I would, but we're on the ground floor."

"Good point. Rat poisoning?"

"Tempting. However, I have no interest in going to prison."

His smirk makes a reappearance. "Too busy doing single lady things, hmm? And who would take care of all the cats while you were away?"

I take a moment to consider how long I would go to jail for murdering a famous athlete, but decide he's not worth the trouble. "I don't own cats, but thanks for that zinger. You must be very proud of yourself. Was there something you wanted to say to me, Mr. Spark?"

His smirk fades. For a moment, he seems hesitant. A crease forms between his brows. He chews his lower lip. I can almost imagine how he looked as a boy, sweet and shy.

But then he folds his big arms over his chest and stares down his nose at me, and the illusion of sweetness vanishes.

He says accusingly, "Aren't you supposed to meet your clients before you start setting them up on dates?"

I blink. "Excuse me?"

"Today's the first time we've met."

Hello, Captain Obvious. I take a breath and square my shoulders. Dealing with this man requires the patience of a saint. "Normally, yes. However, Dick made it clear that you weren't available to come in for a personal—"

"You didn't even call me."

I look at him askance. *Where's he going with this*? "Dick informed me he'd be the liaison between us. But you filled out an extensive personal profile—"

"So you thought you knew me from some questions I answered?"

I open my mouth, close it, then take a moment to compose myself. "I'm sorry, I don't know what you're getting at."

He says deliberately, "You knew who Mason Spark was before today. Right?"

I'm not sure why he's pushing this particular point, but I decide to proceed with caution. He's got more money than God, and I can't afford to defend a lawsuit. Business is going well, but I don't have a spare hundred grand lying around.

And we all know how litigious people are these days. Even though my client contracts are thorough and I make no guarantees about outcomes, nothing is bulletproof. This man could ruin me if he really wanted to.

I say carefully, "Many of my clients are successful business people who don't have the time to meet me in person. Or they live out of state, and an office visit would be inconvenient. But we complete full background checks, verify identities, and confirm—"

"Answer the question."

Interrupt me one more time, and you'll never be able to father children. I count to ten, reminding myself of all the reasons slicing off his testicles with my new scissors would be a bad idea. "I was aware of the name Mason Spark, yes."

"You've read about me in the tabloids," he says flatly.

"I don't read the tabloids."

"Online gossip sites?"

I stifle an exasperated sigh and stare at him. "No, Mr. Spark. I'm far too busy looking after my two dozen cats to have time to troll gossip sites."

I can tell he wants to smile at that, but he doesn't. "How'd you hear about me, then?"

"Because I don't live in a cave?"

His expression sours.

Folding my arms across my chest to mirror his posture, I say, "I grew up in a home with five males. I'll let you guess what was on TV every week between September and January."

He pauses for a beat, staring at me skeptically. "You're a football fan?"

I chuckle. "That's much too generic. I'm a *Patriots* fan."

Mason looks as if he's physically ill and is about to barf all over my desk. "Lemme guess. Because Tom Brady's just so *dreamy*."

The amount of condescension in his tone could flatten entire city blocks.

If this meeting ends without the police being called, it will be a miracle.

"No, because Bill Belichick's philosophy of stressing team work, preparation, strong work ethic, and lack of individual ego has led to six Super Bowl victories, eighteen consecutive winning seasons since 2001, a record for most wins in a ten-year period, the longest winning streak of regular season and playoff games in NFL history, the most consecutive division titles won by a team in NFL history, *and* the most Super Bowl appearances by a team in NFL history."

When Mason only stands there gaping at me in disbelief, I smile. "Plus, Tom Brady's just so dreamy."

After he's recovered from what appears to be a brain aneurysm, Mason says accusingly, "I think you had preconceived notions about who I am and set me up with the wrong women."

Dear Lord, please grant me the patience to deal with this man without resorting to violence. "I went strictly by the information filled out in your paperwork, nothing else."

"What about chemistry?"

"That's why you have an initial phone call with the ladies you're matched with, and then a lunch date if the call goes well."

"As we both know, the calls didn't go well. So there weren't any lunch dates."

I take a moment to assess the situation. Then finally my patience comes to an end. "I believe you have a point. Feel free to make it before we both die of old age."

Now I *know* he's trying not to laugh, because a dimple flashes in his cheek, there then quickly vanished. I get the sense he's suppressing it with sheer force of will and feel sorry for that dimple. It's probably going to get a beating later on.

Sounding like a teacher reprimanding a misbehaving student, he says, "I'm very disappointed in your service."

When I open my mouth, he holds up a hand. "No—don't tell me again about refunding my money. We're past that. What you have to do now is make it up to me."

My eyebrows decide now would be a good time to climb up my forehead and disappear into my hairline.

Seeing my expression, Mason gifts me with his signature smirk. "We can work it around your busy cat grooming schedule."

It's a few moments before I can get my tongue to work. "And how exactly do you propose I make it up to you?"

He hesitates again. Eyes burning, he shifts his weight from one enormous foot to the other. He seems to be struggling to put something into words, but then he startles me by throwing his hands in the air and thundering, "How the hell am *I* supposed to know? You're the damn matchmaker!"

He turns around and storms out of my office, throwing the door open so hard it slams against the wall and rattles all the windows.

After a moment, Auntie Waldine pops her head around the threshold of my door. Her blue eyes are as big as saucers. The color in her plump cheeks is high.

"Land's end, Maddie, what did you say to the poor man? He ran outta here like his tail was on fire!"

"Pfft. I *should* have set him on fire, I'll tell you what. Never in all my life have I met a man so…"

"Good-looking," says Auntie Waldine, sauntering into my office with her hands propped on her ample hips. Nodding, she clucks her tongue. "I hear you, child. That man was—"

"Ornery as a goat."

"I was gonna say fine."

I huff out an aggravated laugh. "There's nothing fine about him. Not his manners or his temper or anything else. I think he's got to be the most unpleasant person I've ever met. He took one look at me and decided he hates my guts."

Auntie Waldine stares at me for a beat, her lips pursed. "Well, honey, that lipstick you're wearin' does make you look a trifle frightenin'. Maybe he was just scared."

This from the woman dressed in a yellow polyester muumuu with a floral print pattern so busy it could cause a seizure if you stare at it too long.

I demand, "What's wrong with my lipstick?"

She scrunches up her face. "It kinda looks like you lost a dare."

I mutter, "Oh, for goodness sake," and open my desk drawer. From it, I pull out a compact and check my lipstick in the little round mirror. "It's just pink!" I say, staring at my reflection. "Plain old pink!"

"More like Meth Addict Barbie pink."

I stare at her, nonplussed. "I don't even know what that means."

"That color pink is where all the other pinks go to die, honey. And it does nothin' for your complexion. You should be wearin' siren red."

"But pink is my favorite color!"

Auntie Waldine lets her gaze drift over the walls, to the cardigan draped over the back of my chair, and down to the carpet, then murmurs drily, "You don't say."

I never should've gotten out of bed this morning.

4

MASON

Dick is quiet as we drive back to the house. So quiet I start to worry he's mad at me. I hate it when he's mad at me, so I decide to throw out a fishing line to see if I'll get a bite.

Looking out the window, I mutter, "That was interesting."

If he explodes, I'll know to keep my mouth shut for the rest of the ride. Probably the rest of the week, too.

But he only says neutrally, "Sure was."

No explosion. I exhale a breath of relief. "I told her she had to make it up to me for failing so far. How do you think she'll do it?"

"Doesn't matter. We're not gonna use her, anyway. That broad's a nut."

Irked by his dismissive tone, I frown. "I mean, she's a little quirky, I guess."

Dick laughs. "Quirky? That's being generous."

Now I *really* don't like his tone. I sit up straighter in my seat. "What do you mean? On the way over, you kept going on and on about what a lady she was. How sweet. How she wouldn't like it if I cursed. You sounded like you like her more than you like me."

It's probably my imagination, but I think I see the ghost of a smile flit across his face before he answers. A satisfied smile, like he just won a bet with himself.

He says, "You're exaggerating. I didn't go on and on."

"Well, you definitely made it sound like you liked her. And now you're saying she's a nut?"

His sigh sounds aggravated. "Fine. She's not a nut. She's a mouthy shrimp with a Napoleon complex. And homely to boot."

My nostrils flare and my stomach tightens and I have to take a few slow breaths to manage the anger suddenly flowing like lava through my veins.

Which—what the fuck is *that* about?

Okay, I know exactly what it's about.

FUCK.

"I don't think she's any of that, especially homely. In fact, she's actually quite pretty."

Dick snorts. "Pretty? What've you been smokin'? That girl is as pretty as a dumpster fire! Dresses like a nun, too. *Zero* sex appeal." He shakes his head, chuckling. "It's no wonder she's single, poor thing. If she lived in a village in the fifteenth century, the townsfolk woulda burned her at the stake for bein' a witch."

His voice turns thoughtful. "That's probably why she went into the matchmaking business, bein' so unattractive and all. Couldn't get a man for herself, so she decided to help out other single ladies. Plus, it's not like her lady clients would have to worry about her stealin' their men. Who'd want to stick his dick in that dog?"

Heat starts to crawl up my neck. "That's fucking rude."

He ignores me. "She sounded nice on the phone, but hoo-*ey* was that a snow job. I'm insulted on your behalf for the way she talked to you. She's *way* too high and mighty for such a homely girl."

Through gritted teeth, I say, "Call her homely one more time."

Startled, Dick looks over at me. Then he gasps. "Oh my God. Don't tell me you *like* this broad?"

"No." *Yes.* "But considering she doesn't have a face tattoo or an ex-husband she's related to by blood, you should be thrilled if I did."

He shouts, "Are you kidding me? You think I want you runnin' off with some crazy virgin with a face only a mother could love who knows every trick in the book about how to manipulate a man into marriage? She's the last person I'd want to see you with!"

Dick is seriously in danger of getting his lights punched out.

I glare at him, seething.

Then I tell myself to get a grip. It's not like Maddie liked me, anyway. She made it clear she thought I was rude, crude, and socially unacceptable.

Besides, she's not my type. Any woman who wears her blouse buttoned all the way up over her A cups is *totally* not my type.

I mean, forget about those big brown eyes. And that smartass mouth. And that scathing sense of humor.

And that heartbreakingly beautiful smile. That sweet angel's smile. Forget all about *that.*

Yeah, forget it.

It was a Hail Mary pass, anyway, demanding she make it up to me for not finding me a match. She's just gonna refund my money and forget she ever had the misfortune of meeting Mason Spark.

I stare out the window at the passing morning, knowing deep down that's for the best.

Angels don't have any business hanging out with devils like me.

5

DICK

You've hearda reverse psychology, right?

Yeah, you know—that tactic you use when you want someone to do the opposite of what you're tellin' him to do, because you can't come right out and say the real thing you want, 'cause he's stubborn as a mule and won't do it. He's gotta think it's *his* idea.

Like God did when he told Adam and Eve not to eat the apple.

That was one epic reverse psychology move right there, ladies and gents. Think about it. We're that dumb as a species that any halfway intelligent supreme being couldn't come right out and say, "Do this. I'm your Creator, and it's what I want."

No. Humans would be all, "Hey, you're not the boss of me, asshole!"

So instead, God had to say, "*Don't* do this, or you'll forever be banned from this awesome garden," because what he really wanted was for us to stop bein' so lazy and naked and get outta that garden and start up human history.

So he gave us a little push.

Only slick like, so we didn't guess what he was doin'.

Because when it comes right down to it, we're only like four or five chromosomes away from bein' monkeys, am I right?

Or was it slugs? I can't remember.

Anyway, some of us monkeys and slugs are older and smarter than others.

Which is how I know I have to keep Mason directly in the bright pink path of Little Miss Sunshine, Maddie McRae.

You been around as long as I have, you know real chemistry when you see it. I mean, sometimes it looks a lot like burning hatred, but trust me, that's chemistry.

Only I can't come right out and *say* she's absolutely perfect for him because I know him too well.

You wouldn't know it by lookin' at him—or talkin' to him, either—but he's a huge softie. As soft as they come. A marshmallow is harder than Mason. Only he's been through some tough shit and sometimes when people've been through enough tough shit, they get all calloused and crabby and start actin' like dicks. Like a defense mechanism thing.

Because people are like thigh bones: remarkably strong, but hit 'em just the right way and they shatter.

And if you give 'em a bad enough break, they're broken for good.

I know he thinks I only care about him for the money, but he's not as smart as he supposes. The kid's got heart. And incredible talent. He signed one of the biggest deals in the history of football. He could be one of the greats of the game… or he could be a cautionary tale.

Like my son was.

Greatest regret of my life, that.

And I'll be damned if I'm gonna let Mason Spark go down the same road my son did, no matter how much reverse psychology or guerilla warfare tactics I have to resort to.

Love is war, ladies and gents. Sometimes you win, sometimes you lose, and sometimes you need your fairy godfather

Dick to swoop in and scream at your dumb, stubborn ass to NOT invade that nice little ladylike pink country because it will end in disaster.

When really what you want him to do is the opposite.

Because fairy godfathers know what's best for you, even if you don't.

6

MADDIE

I can't sleep that night. I just lie in my bed and stare at the ceiling, going over every word of my conversation with Mason. Going over everything that happened since he walked through my office door. Going over every single minute of that train wreck of a meeting we had.

The train wreck that was all my fault.

I'm not usually so triggered by people. In fact, I pride myself on my even temper. I wasn't voted Miss Congeniality four years in a row by my college sorority for nothing.

But from the minute we met, Mason Spark burrowed under my skin like a deer tick and started gnawing on my nerves.

If my mama could have seen how snarky I'd been with him, she would've been appalled.

There's never an excuse for bad manners, Madison McRae! she used to scold me when I was little and had disappointed her with some social failing. She was the epitome of Southern grace and expected me to be the same. As the only girl of her five children, I shouldered all her dreams of debutante balls and opera gloves, of garden parties and cotillions, of handsome callers and white weddings.

Especially the white weddings.

She died long before she got a chance to see me get married. She had her heart set on Bobby Cavendish, a boy I grew up with who'll probably be elected president by the time he's forty. To this day, all my girlfriends practically drop their drawers when he walks into a room with that Ivy League air and gleaming smile, but though I tried and tried to fall in love with him, I never could.

It's really too bad, because we're perfect on paper.

When my alarm goes off at six o'clock, I drag myself from bed and do my morning ritual, which consists of yoga and twenty minutes of meditation before drinking a tall glass of cold water and reading something inspirational. Then I shower and dress.

Then, as I do every day, I drink a triple espresso with exactly two teaspons of sugar and make myself bacon and eggs.

It's while I'm chewing on a delicious, crispy piece of bacon that the idea comes to me.

Before I have time to talk myself out of it, I fire up my laptop, log onto my office computer, and click on the file I'm searching for. Then I pick up the phone and start dialing.

The voice that answers when the call goes through is cold, gruff, and irritated, all at once.

"Yeah."

Good Lord, the man even sounds like a son of a bee sting over the phone. I say cheerfully, "Good morning, Mr. Spark. This is Maddie McRae."

The answering silence is so loud for a moment I think we've been cut off. But then Mason clears his throat and says, "Lemme guess. You're calling to tell me you refunded my money."

"No. Actually, I'm calling about making it up to you."

Another silence, this one louder and longer. Truly, it's cavernous. The Grand Canyon doesn't echo so much.

"Um, like you asked me to?"

"I remember," he says, his voice rough. Then he doesn't say anything else.

I can see I'll be doing all the heavy lifting in this conversation. The man has the social skills of a wild boar. "So, Mr. Spark, I had this idea—"

"Mason."

I'm startled by his forceful interruption and for a moment lose my train of thought. "Um…"

"I want you to call me Mason."

He sounds frighteningly intense, as if someone is holding a gun to his head and will blow out his brains unless I agree to call him by his first name.

When I say carefully, "All right, then…Mason," my reward is a grunt of satisfaction. Or he could be smashing something with a rock. It's hard to tell.

"As I was saying, I was sitting here eating my breakfast when the thought occurred to me that—"

"Are you always up this early on Saturdays?"

"Oh, I'm so sorry! Did I wake you? I assumed you'd be up since it's…" I check my watch, frowning when I see the time. "After nine."

"I didn't say I wasn't up. I asked if you were. Always. You know. Up. This early."

I look around my kitchen helplessly, hoping a translator who speaks Deranged Football Star will pop out of a cabinet and help me out. "Yes. I get up at six every morning."

He takes a moment to mull that over, probably thinking about how long it takes me to open all the cat food cans and clean out all the litter boxes. Then he demands, "What did you have for breakfast?"

I settle back into my chair, understanding that we're on his time table here, not mine. I suppose we'll get around to the reason I called eventually. "Bacon and eggs."

A pause. "Sunny side up?"

He sounds condescending. As if liking eggs prepared that way is a character flaw.

"No. Poached."

"*Poached*?" Now he sounds incredulous. "Who makes poached eggs for themselves at home?"

I can almost hear the answer he left out: *A cat hoarding spinster, that's who.*

When I feel the heat creeping up my neck, I hear my mother's scolding voice in my head. *Be nice, Maddie! There's no excuse for bad manners!*

Tell that to Godzilla.

I take a breath and try to put a smile in my voice. "What kind of eggs do you like?"

He says flatly, "I hate eggs."

Of course you do. I close my eyes and pinch the bridge of my nose between my fingers.

After a moment, he seems to realize the conversation has fallen off the edge of a cliff and offers a mumbled, "I love bacon, though."

It's a miracle: Mason Spark and I have something in common.

"Crispy or chewy?"

He hollers, "Chewy is disgusting!"

Gee, have an opinion, why don't you? I say calmly, "I prefer crispy, too."

He exhales. Even that sounds aggravated. I can't imagine what it must be like to go around like that, with so much pent up anger you can't even talk about breakfast foods without exploding.

After an uncomfortable pause wherein all I hear is the sounds of his footsteps thumping back and forth as he paces—or at least I imagine he's pacing, it seems like something he'd do, but for all I know he's on his way to the cellar with the dead body he needs to dispose of—I say, "Would you like me to tell you why I called now, or do you have more shouting to do? If so, I can wait. Just checking."

There's a noise—a chuckle?

No. Impossible.

He blurts, "What's with the pink?"

And we're off. "The pink what?"

"All the fucking pink at your office. It's really fucking weird."

Now I understand why pious Catholics are always crossing themselves. They're praying to God to come and take them to heaven, because they've got their own Mason Spark in their lives and they're *this close* to sharpening that hatchet in the garage and burying it in his skull.

I feel so, so sorry for all those girls I set up with him on the phone.

"Mr. Spark—"

"MASON!"

When my hearing returns and the dishes in the cupboards have stopped rattling, I say, "Mason, I would appreciate it if you wouldn't curse at me. It's a pet peeve of mine. If we're going to continue working together, I need you to show me a certain level of respect. Agreed?"

The footsteps on the other end of the phone stop abruptly. "I wasn't cursing *at* you. I was just cursing in general. There's a difference."

His voice sounds subdued. I think that's as close to an apology as I'll get, but it's good enough.

"I see. So the reason for the call—"

"Is your problem with all cursing, or just the F-word? Because honestly, the F-word is so useful for so many different situations, I don't think I'd be able to speak a full fucking sentence without it."

I lower my head and bang it gently against the kitchen table.

"Hello?"

"Still here."

"You sound weird."

"That's because my brain is leaking out my ears."

"Probably 'cause of all those poached eggs. The yolks are never cooked enough. You know what's in runny eggs? *Salmonella*. You're probably dying from a brain infection as we speak."

Already exhausted by this conversation, I exhale in a huge gust. "Salmonella affects the intestinal tract, not the brain."

"Really? Hmm. What bacteria do you get from handling kitty litter?"

I actually know the answer to that, but I realize he's baiting me and won't give him the satisfaction. I say sweetly, "Probably the same bacteria you get from sweaty jockstraps."

There's a moment of stunned silence before Mason starts to laugh.

It's a big, beautiful sound, open and honest, unselfconscious and deep. I lift my head and simply listen to him laugh until the guffaws taper down to chuckles and my shock has lessened to somewhere south of total organ failure.

He says, "For such a librarian, you're funny."

I sniff. "Librarians are smart and essential in helping kids develop critical thinking skills and guiding them through media literacy, so I'll take that as a compliment."

His voice gets low and gruff again, all the laughter gone. "It was. You're very..."

I lean forward, holding the phone tighter, my ears pricked and my pulse ticking up, until Mason blurts, "Prim."

Prim. Ah yes. How every woman longs to be described.

Romeo, O Romeo, where in the F-word art thou?

I enjoy a brief but vivid image of myself with a handful of darts and Mason strapped to a board several yards away with a target painted on his bare chest, hollering curses at the top of his lungs as I smile, take aim, and let the darts fly, one after the other, hitting a bull's-eye every time.

Really, who could blame me?

Before he can interrupt me again, I say, "I want to be your dating coach."

Silence.

I've never met another person who can make it seem so loud.

Then, sounding like I've called his manhood into question, he growls, "Believe me, I don't have a problem finding dates."

I roll my eyes. *Athletes and their egos.* "But you want a wife—"

"*Need.* Not want."

The vehemence in his voice stalls me for a second. "Mason?"

"Yeah?"

"You know a woman can't fix whatever's wrong with your life, right?"

"Dick thinks it will."

"What do *you* think?"

There's another of his signature silences, then a heavy sigh. In a low voice, he says, "I think there are some kinds of broken that can't be fixed. But Dick's the only thing close to family I've got. I don't wanna disappoint him."

I remove the phone from my ear and stare at it in disbelief. He'd make a lifelong commitment just so his agent wouldn't be disappointed in him?

That's either the stupidest thing I've ever heard or the saddest.

When I don't say anything for too long, Mason snaps back into wild boar mode. "I can hear you judging me!"

I say soothingly, "I'm not. I promise. But it does occur to me that you could find a woman all by yourself who'd be happy to go along with a sham marriage to you."

Like quicksilver, his mood changes again. His voice grows

quiet and intense. "Why? You think it would be good to be married to me?"

Dear God in heaven, I'd rather be sentenced to life in prison. "What I meant is that you're rich and famous. The world is full of women for whom that would be more than enough. Couldn't you just find one of them and make some sort of arrangement?"

He laughs, only this time it sounds unnerving. Dark, as if I've said something funny but also incredibly naïve.

"The kind of woman I'd pick would steal all my money, burn down my house, and fuck all the guys on my team. Er, sorry —screw."

I make a face at the phone. "Forgive me for saying this, but you don't need a matchmaker to work out that particular knot. You need a therapist."

"Got one."

You can't be paying him nearly enough. "And what does he have to say about this marriage scheme?" I know it's none of my business, but honestly, I'm fascinated.

"She. And she doesn't know about it. Nobody does, except Dick." Loaded pause. "And you."

"And the candidates I sent who you talked to on the phone."

His voice hardens. "Who all signed NDAs. Right?"

I get up from the table and start to rove around my house, because I'm feeling antsy. "Yes, of course. Dick insisted on it. Though technically, they all thought you were sincere about finding a wife."

"I am sincere."

"You are totally *not* sincere."

"Just because I don't want a wife doesn't mean I'm not sincere about finding one."

I stop wandering and stare out my living room windows into the gorgeous morning beyond. "Are you aware how insane that sounds?"

"Look, I just need you to find me a nice girl I can settle down with, okay?"

"No."

After a blistering pause, he says, "Oh. Right. You believe in *love*."

He says the word with so much disdain it almost drips from the phone.

This man is bad for my blood pressure.

"Yes, I do, but even more than that, I believe in honesty. You can't build a foundation for a relationship on a lie."

"Sure you can," he shoots back. "People do it all the time."

"Just out of curiosity, are you deliberately trying to make my head explode?"

Ignoring that, he says impatiently, "What if we tell the next round of girls that I'm looking for a pretend wife? We'll be honest with them. Would that make you feel better?"

"No! I'm not matching you with any more women! And by the way, if you're only looking for a 'pretend' wife, what difference does it make whether or not you have chemistry with her?"

"I don't know about you, Pink, but *I* can't have sex with someone I'm not attracted to."

It sounds like he's accusing me of prostitution. "I don't have sex with people I'm not attracted to!"

"Oh, so you're all about the lust factor, huh?"

"Wait, you just said—"

"Seems kinda superficial for someone who goes on and on about love."

"I *never* mentioned *anything* about lust—"

"Hey, you don't have to get huffy," he says nonchalantly. "I'm just pointing out the double standard here. You're getting all down on my choices, but it sounds to me like you're the one having a bunch of meaningless sex—"

I shout, "*I'm not having sex with anyone!*"

After a beat, Mason says, "You're celibate? Huh. Is that for religious reasons?"

I look around for something heavy to throw at the wall. Instead, I hurl myself down on the sofa and throw an arm over my eyes. "Actually, it's because I can't find a man who isn't allergic to all the cats."

I expected a laugh. Hoped for it, honestly. His laugh has been the only pleasurable thing about this entire conversation.

But all thoughts of laughter flee my head with Mason's next words, spoken in the husky tone of a sex line operator.

"I'm not allergic to cats."

When I don't respond because I'm too shocked, he says with a casual laugh, "Just kidding. I hate cats. What was it you called for again?"

If I could get my head to stop spinning, I'd tell him. But I'm flushed and breathless, and pretty sure I've fallen into another dimension.

Did Mason Spark just flirt with me?

7

MASON

Kill me. Just kill me now.

I could literally *hear* Maddie's disgust in the pause after I blurted out that dumbass line about not being allergic to cats. I mean, it's true. I'm not allergic to anything except the sight of Tom Brady. But I didn't mean for it to come out so pervy.

I sounded like a total molester. *Hey, little girl, want some candy?*

Which is probably on account of the dream I had about her last night, but I'm not thinking about that.

I can't think about it. My dick might explode.

I had to get up and take a cold shower, if you can believe that. Fucking ridiculous. Like I'm some horny teenager.

And then she called! She fucking called me! I'm standing in my bathroom with a towel around my waist when the phone rang. And who does it turn out to be?

Her.

Maddie McRae.

The smart-mouthed librarian with an unnatural obsession with the color pink.

Who, because the universe has a really fucking dark sense of humor, is apparently celibate.

"I'm not having sex with anyone!" she hollered, like something as basic as sex is beneath her. Like she tried it once and found it super gross. Too sticky, probably. Too messy. But my dick took it as a personal challenge and stood up at attention.

Again.

So now I've got a boner that could cut steel and a raging desire to see Maddie naked underneath me, unraveling at the seams.

Which will never happen, because I believe in one night stands and she believes in happily-ever-afters, and even if somehow the stars aligned and I had the opportunity to fuck her, I wouldn't.

I've already ruined too much in my life. I don't have to ruin her, too.

On the other end of the phone, she clears her throat. When she speaks, her voice is unsteady. "Um…I…part of our service is relationship coaching."

I repeat doubtfully, "Relationship coaching."

"Yes. Either pre-commitment with a couple who are considering marriage or with singles who've had trouble with past relationships and want to develop strategies to build better relationships in the future."

If I hear the word "relationship" one more time, I might die.

When I don't say anything, she continues. "People who are serious about having a successful life partnership can work with a coach to move faster toward that goal. I can help you identify your strengths and weakness in dealing with women."

I laugh, because seriously. This is getting silly now. "Oh, trust me, Pink, I know *exactly* what my strength with women is."

After a short pause, she says something that throws me for a complete fucking loop.

"You're much more than what's between your legs, Mason. You have a lot to offer."

I open my mouth, then shut it. Then I turn my back on the bathroom mirror because I can't stand that look on my face. That stunned, baby deer look.

I had that look on my face a lot when I was a kid.

It only ever meant one thing: weakness.

"You don't have to give me fake flattery," I snap, pacing into my closet. I whip off the towel and throw it onto the floor. "You've already got my fucking money."

"Yes, I do," she snaps back. "And if you curse at me one more time, I'll shred it and send it all back to you in a big black garbage bag so you know exactly how impressed I am by it."

She huffs.

I hate myself that I think it sounds adorable.

I spend a minute glaring at my clothes hanging in row after row in this stupid closet that's so big it could double as a spare bedroom, until I realize she's waiting for me to say something.

I shock myself by making that something an apology.

"You're right. I'm sorry. It won't happen again." My voice is low and gruff, but sincere. Holding my breath, I wait for her to reply.

"Thank you," she says, her voice soft. Then, after a pause: "As your coach, I have to tell you that that was excellent. Taking responsibility and apologizing when you've done something to upset your partner is a really healthy way to communicate."

I'm so mind fucked by the quiet appreciation in her voice that I don't know how to respond. So, unfortunately, I revert to baseline—asshole mode.

"I haven't agreed to this coaching thing. And you're *not* my partner."

The minute it's out, I know it's all wrong. Too loud, too mean, too insulting. Her silence is frosty. But I can't take it back, and it's probably for the best anyway.

She should know who she's dealing with.

But she surprises me again. In an untroubled tone, she says, "No, you haven't agreed, but you will. And then I *will* be your partner, though strictly in a business sense. So I'll tell you up front what my expectations are. First and foremost, you must always be honest with me. Good or bad, just let me have it. I can't help you if I don't know how you really feel."

"Let me stop you right there. I don't do *feelings*, okay? As far as I'm concerned, that's a four-letter word."

She totally ignores me. "Secondly, I expect you to listen to my suggestions. You don't have to agree with them, but I want you to at least give them serious consideration."

"Like what?" I challenge.

"Like if I suggest you think about how the outdated and ridiculous myth that men don't have feelings is harming you."

I close my eyes, drag in a few breaths, and debate whether or not to hang up. But my thumb refuses to hit *End*, so I just stand there and breathe heavily at her for a while.

When I've collected all my broken pieces off the floor, I say sourly, "You sound just like my therapist."

"She's obviously a brilliant woman," comes the crisp response. "My third expectation for this business arrangement going forward is that after every date you go on, you call me and we can discuss it together. The good, the bad, and the ugly."

"Yeah, that's a hard no, Pink."

"It's the only way you can gain insight into what behaviors—"

"I'm not calling you to give you a blow-by-blow of every time I get laid, all right?"

She sounds confused. "No, I'm not talking about your sex life. What I mean is, after every date you go on. Like to the movies, out to dinner, like that."

When I just stand there smirking at the phone, she groans. "Oh no."

"Oh yes."

"That can't be true."

"Hey, you're the one who's insisting on total honesty."

"*Every* time?"

I shrug, pulling a pair of briefs out of one of the drawers in the dresser in the middle of the closet. "I guess your definition of a date and mine are a little different."

"Mason, that's just sad."

I laugh at that, long and loudly. "Uh, no, Pink. I can assure you, it's totally not."

She switches into librarian mode, saying prissily, "Well, I certainly hope you use protection."

"Would you like to know the brand of rubbers I use?"

She mutters, "Lord, have mercy."

"Hold on, I'm gonna put you on speaker so we can keep talking while I get dressed."

I hit the speaker button then set my cell on the dresser. Pulling out a pair of jeans and a T-shirt from another drawer, I realize she's not talking. "Did I lose you?"

"I'm still here."

"Why do you sound funny?"

"I don't."

Yeah, I'm calling bullshit on that. "Oh, okay. So we're not doing the honesty thing anymore? Cool."

After a delicate throat clearing, she says, "Well, if you must know, it's just that I didn't realize you were, um…"

"Naked? Yeah, that happens a lot around here. It shouldn't bother you, it's not like you can see me or anything."

"I didn't say it bothered me."

I stop short at the tone of her voice. It's high and tight, almost as if she's embarrassed. Like she got caught doing something wrong.

Holy shit. Is she thinking about me naked?

Is thinking about me naked turning her on?

I say slowly, "You sure?"

She laughs, but I can't tell if it's a real laugh or not. I don't know her well enough.

"Yes, I'm sure, Egozilla."

"*Egozilla*? That's a terrible nickname."

"I'm not a professional nickname maker."

I smile at that. "No, you're a professional matchmaker. By the way, how the fu—" I stop myself just in time. "How the heck did that happen?"

She replies airily, "Oh, it's a long story. Anyway, I'll let you go. I'm sure you've got all sorts of important things to do today. Conquests to be made, bedposts to be notched. Let's touch base on Monday and we can go over the coaching in more detail—"

"Tomorrow," I interrupt, so loudly I even startle myself.

When I don't get a response, I try to play it cool. Like I'm not eager to see her. Like I could care less about those big brown eyes. Like I don't already know a girl like her could blow up my whole world and this is a total fucking nuclear disaster in the making.

Like I'm unfamiliar with the fact that anything good I touch I turn to shit.

She says tentatively, "Tomorrow's Sunday."

"Yep."

After a moment in which I can hear my heartbeat roaring in my ears, she says, "Okay, you're on. I'll text you my address. Pick me up at eight-thirty sharp."

My brows knit. "Eight-thirty? In the *morning*?"

"Yeah, superstar. I don't want to be late."

"Late for what?"

There's a hint of laughter in her voice. "I want to introduce you to *my* relationship coach. You're going to love him."

Him?

She hangs up on me before I can ask any more questions.

8

MADDIE

When Mason picks me up in the morning, he's not alone. Dick sits in the driver's seat of a big black car parked in my driveway, looking at me through the windshield with a satisfied smirk.

Mason, meanwhile, stands on my porch wearing a glower that would strike a lesser woman dead from sheer fright.

But he doesn't scare me. I'm familiar with his thunderclouds and have already girded my mental loins. Plus, I'm probably getting points from the Man upstairs for this, so it's a win-win.

Standing in my doorway, I smile at Mason and say brightly, "Good morning!"

"Hey." He glares at my dress, looking as if his breakfast is about to come back up.

I say, "If I'd known the color pink makes you want to vomit, I would've worn something black instead."

His gaze snaps up to my face and settles there, burning. "I'll bet you a million bucks you don't own anything black."

I have to think about it for a moment. "I'm pretty sure I've got a black skirt I keep around for funerals."

I step onto the porch and turn to lock my front door. When I turn back, Mason is staring at my hair like there's a big stink bug crawling around in it. I drop my keys into my handbag and self-consciously pat my bun. "What?"

"Nothing."

I examine his expression. "Really? Because that's a whole lot of nothing."

He shifts his weight from foot to foot, flexing his hands open and closed like he doesn't know what to do with them. I get the sense he's refraining from saying something with a gargantuan effort of will.

"Oh." I laugh. "Let me guess: you like buns as much as you like the color pink. Fortunately for me, you don't get a say in the matter. We ready to go?"

When he doesn't say anything and only stands there staring at me, I look past him to the car. When Mason turns his head to follow my gaze, Dick's smirk vanishes, replaced by a frown.

"Is everything okay?"

Mason turns back to me, scowling. "Yep."

I sigh, folding my arms over my chest. "Remember that thing I said about honesty?"

He blows out an aggravated breath and drags a hand through his hair.

Apparently he found a comb, because today his unruly tresses are tamed, pushed back from his temples in glossy dark waves. He shaved, too, and is wearing a crisp button-down white dress shirt with his jeans. It's even tucked in.

The beast almost looks human.

"We kinda got into an argument on the way over. It's no biggie. Forget about it."

He turns around and stalks away, stomping down the porch steps and out to the driveway. He throws open the back door of the car, climbs in, and slams the door shut.

I stand on the porch with my arms folded across my chest until he throws the door open again and climbs back out. Standing there, he hollers across the yard, "You coming?"

I shake my head.

He hollers, "What's the problem?"

I don't move, except to crook my finger.

He heaves an exasperated breath and stalks back toward me, until he's on the porch in front of me again, six-and-a-half feet of bristling, ill-mannered male, waiting for me to speak with the impatience of a child.

In a calm tone, I say, "A gentleman escorts a lady to the car and helps her in before he gets in himself."

When he opens his mouth, I cut him off before he can shout some kind of obscenity at me. "I realize this isn't a date. However, as your dating coach, it behooves me to point out that any woman of quality won't be charmed by your expectation that she tag along behind you like a dog. Let's start over, shall we?"

He spends a while grinding his teeth, until it becomes apparent the urge to murder me has passed and he can speak again.

"Sorry. I'm not used to… I don't normally have to…" He takes a breath, then blurts, "I'm not a gentleman, all right? I'm more like a friggin' wolf!"

No truer words were ever spoken.

"A gentleman is a wolf, just a patient one. Having manners doesn't mean you're neutered, it simply means you've mastered your inner animal. It means *you* choose when to let him off the leash. And thank you for the apology and for not cursing. I appreciate it."

Mason blinks at me. Once. Slowly. Then he says, "If gentlemen are wolves, does that mean ladies are bunny rabbits?"

I burst out laughing. "Don't be silly! A true lady is the most ferocious creature you'll ever meet."

He stares at me, his expression indecipherable. "I'm beginning to get that."

~

After I give Dick the address, the ride to our destination is spent in silence. One of those unnerving silences that isn't really quiet at all, but crowded with unspoken words and violent emotions all flapping wildly like Hitchcock movie birds in the air around your head.

Dick glances at me in the rearview mirror so many times that I finally raise my brows and send him a questioning gaze. His response is a wink. Then he turns his attention back to the road and arranges his face into a scowl.

For his part, Mason stares out the window like the passing view is personally offensive to him and he wants to leap from the car and strangle every chirping bird and blooming tree.

By the time we pull to a stop in the parking lot, I'm craving something strong to drink.

Looking out the windshield, Mason does a double take. "Wait." He looks at me in horror. "We're not going in *there* are we?"

"Why, will you burst into flames if the shadow of the cross falls on you?"

"You never said anything about going to church! I don't do church!"

In the driver's seat, Dick coughs. It sounds suspiciously like a stifled laugh.

I stay calm in the face of Mason's impending meltdown. "One doesn't *do* church. It's not a sporting event. One attends mass to cultivate a healthy spirituality, give thanks for the many blessings of life, commune with neighbors, and worship God."

He says flatly, "I don't believe in God."

"I hate to break it to you, Egozilla, but God isn't like Tinkerbell. He doesn't need you to believe in him to exist. Now get your cantankerous behind out of this car and follow me."

I open the door and step out, then lean back in and look at

Mason, who's glaring at me in icy outrage. I smile. "If it will make you feel better, we'll go get brunch after the service and you can shout at me over your crispy bacon about how much you hated it."

He grimaces. "What if someone sees me?"

I say drily, "Yes, it would be truly awful to be seen attending a church service. I'm sure your reputation would never recover."

Though it was sarcastic, the mention of his reputation does the trick. Shaking his head, he mutters something under his breath. Then he bursts from of the car as if it spit him out and starts striding toward the entrance, not looking back.

Here we go again.

I call out, "Oh, Mason?"

He stops dead in his tracks, scrubs his hands over his face, then swings around to stalk back toward me. "Sorry," he says gruffly when he reaches my side. "Habit."

"That's all right. I've got my share of bad habits, too."

Surprised, he lifts his brows. "Oh yeah? Name one."

I know I can't tell him about my hopeless addiction to collecting Harry Potter memorabilia, or that I can't eat a bag of M&Ms without first sorting them into separate colors and counting them, or that all the food items in my pantry have to be aligned in perfect rows by size and color with all their labels facing out or I can't sleep, because he'll tease me ruthlessly.

So I decide on something a little less out there.

"Netflix. I'm a serious binge watcher."

Something that could be a distant relative to a smile crosses his face. Looking down at me with his lids half lowered, he says, "But how else would you fill all those lonely, celibate nights spent with your cats?"

Ouch.

I lift my chin and sniff. "You're not half as funny as you think you are. And by the way, I never said I was celibate." I sail past him, heading toward the front steps of the church, where a small crowd is milling, waiting for the service to begin.

Auntie Waldine is among them, wearing her Sunday finest. She spots me and waves, making the ostrich feathers on her wide-brimmed Derby hat quiver.

In a few long strides, Mason has caught up with me. "How come you get to walk away from me, but I don't get to walk away from you?"

"I'm surprised that in your vast experience with women, you haven't yet discovered that insulting us makes us testy. And if you're being rude, we're not obligated to stick around for seconds."

"Hey, you're the one who said you said you weren't having sex with anyone. I hate to break it to you, but that's the definition of celibacy."

Grr. The smug SOB. His smirk tells me exactly how much he enjoys throwing my words back at me. "Thank you for that fascinating input. Now let's drop the subject, please."

"No, I don't think I will. In fact, if you're going to be my dating coach, I think this honesty and openness thing needs to go both ways."

I stop short and look at him. "Remember when you came to my office and I told you that my private life was private?"

"Yeah?"

"That still stands."

"How am I supposed to feel comfortable sharing everything about myself if you won't do the same?"

I realize we're doing that unblinking stare-off thing again and take a moment to compose myself. It would be unforgiveable if I smacked him upside his skull with my handbag. Plus, I like this handbag, and his thick skull would win that matchup.

Maybe logic will work better than violence.

"Your therapist doesn't share everything with you, correct?"

His voice drops. "I don't share everything with her, either."

I frown at him. "Why on earth not? Isn't that the whole point of therapy?"

"Because I don't trust her," comes the instant response.

"Perhaps you should find a new therapist, then."

"I don't need a new therapist. I have you."

That statement leaves me feeling like something large has collided with my solar plexus. "A matchmaker can't substitute for a licensed therapist. That's not what I do."

His voice contains a challenge. "You've got a degree in marriage and family counseling."

"How do you know that?"

"I checked out Perfect Pairing's website. That bio of yours was pretty detailed."

He looked me up? I'm not sure what to make of that. "Surely you don't expect me to psychoanalyze you, Mason."

His gaze drops to my mouth. He chides, "Oh, come on. It's not like you haven't already."

Flustered by the way he's looking at my mouth, I answer too sharply. "What's that supposed to mean?"

When he lifts his lashes and his burning gray gaze meets mine, our eyes lock together with a force that's startling. He says, "Tell me you don't think I'm a self-centered jerk with no manners and more dick than brains."

My mouth falls open, but no sound comes out.

He goes on, still in that soft, chiding tone, his gaze never leaving mine. "Tell me you don't think I'm superficial. Angry. Lonely. Tell me you *don't* think you've already got me all figured out."

Why are we suddenly standing so close together? And why is my stomach in knots?

I shouldn't have had that third piece of bacon.

"Of course I don't think I have you all figured out. We barely know each other. But yes, I've formed opinions based on how you've conducted yourself around me."

When his nostrils flare, I say, "Just like you've done with me. The pathetic single cat lady? That ringing any bells?"

He glares at me in silence, his jaw working.

Holding his gaze, I say with heat, "And if you want total honesty, I do think you're angry. I won't pretend to know why, and I won't ask either, because that's none of my business. As for your being self-centered, I can't really speak to that, but since we're not holding back here, I will admit I think that any man who has sex on every date he goes on and only wants a wife to help save his career and doesn't believe in love is either extremely superficial or extremely—"

When I stop abruptly, Mason steps closer. "What?" he prompts, his voice hard and his eyes flashing.

But I'm too busy having an epiphany to answer.

"What, Maddie?" says Mason angrily. "What's the word you were gonna say?"

I whisper, "Hurt."

Mason's face drains of blood. As if on cue, the church bells begin to ring.

Through gritted teeth, he says, "It's a good thing you didn't become a therapist. You would've sucked at it."

I swallow, because that stung. But I won't snap back at him just because he dented my pride.

"If you were trying to make me feel bad by saying that, it worked. I'm sorry that I offended you. Also, just for the record, I don't think you have more dick than brains. You actually seem to me like the type of person who's a lot smarter than he likes to let on because it doesn't fit with his image. I do think you're a little F-worded up, but so is everyone else. We're all just doing the best we can.

"Now, if you'll excuse me, I have to walk away again because I'm feeling a little emotional and I don't want to make a fool of myself by bursting into tears in front of you. My client. If you still are my client after today, that is."

I turn and walk a few feet away, but stop and turn back.

Mason stands stock still where I left him, staring at me as if he's been electrocuted.

I say, "Also for the record, I hope you *will* still be my client. And if you are, I promise not to make any more comments about your personality. I don't want you to feel like I'm judging you. I know I seem… stuffy—prim was your word—but I'm not heartless. I would never want you to feel like I think I'm better than you, because I don't."

I hate myself that my voice cracked on that last word.

I whirl around and walk away from him, quickly making my way toward the side door of the church to avoid the crowd at the main steps and Auntie Waldine, who'd make a scene if she knew I was upset.

And she would know, even if my eyes weren't watering. The woman's powers of observation are supernatural.

Literally. She sees auras.

She claims it runs in the family—the female side of the family, anyway—and that my mother, her baby sister, had the power, too. But she also claims I have the ability, only I'm too "repressed" for it to present, so her whole argument is moot.

The only energy field I've ever seen was around Tom Brady when I watched him win the Super Bowl the sixth time, and I'm pretty sure what I was seeing was just my own haze of lust.

I slip inside the sanctuary and take a seat near the end of the pew in the last row, then slouch down and dig a tissue from my handbag.

I don't know why I'm so upset about our conversation, but Mason Spark has a way of getting under my skin.

It's several minutes later, when I'm dabbing at my eyes, that a large, masculine form appears beside me.

I don't have to look up to know who it is. The man has the presence of an erupting volcano.

Without a word, he slides into the pew next to me, stretching one long leg out into the aisle. Staring straight ahead, he folds his arms over his chest.

Just when I think my breathing has gone back to normal, Mason nudges me with his elbow. When I ignore him, he leans over and whispers, "You said 'dick.'"

His voice is teasing. When I glance at him, his eyes are warm. Biggest shock of all: he's smiling.

That smile transforms his face. For one heart-stopping moment, he's the most handsome man I've ever seen.

But then he ruins it by going stiff and thundering, "*Are you crying?*"

"I have allergies," I hiss, looking around in horror. I notice several people looking in our direction and slide lower in the pew. "And please keep your voice down!"

"You *are* crying," he accuses, his voice not a single decibel lower. It echoes off the rafters. "I thought you were joking when you said that thing about bursting into tears!"

I drop my face into my palms and beg God to send a heavenly thunderbolt to kill me.

Instead, He demonstrates his black sense of humor and sends Auntie Waldine.

9

WALDINE

I took one look at my niece walkin' across the parking lot and I *knew* somethin' was wrong.

It wasn't the stiff set of her shoulders or the way she was hurryin' toward church like she was bein' chased by a horde of demons sent by Lucifer himself. No, it's not unusual for Maddie to look like there's a stick wedged up her patootie. I swear, that child is her father's daughter through and through: Up. Tight.

How I knew something was wrong was that her aura was all off.

Now, normally her psychic energy field is a clear sunny yellow, which matches her personality. Yellow auras reflect confidence, a strong sense of self, and perfectionism, and people who emit an aura in that color are natural born leaders.

The downside is a tendency toward bein' anal retentive, which Maddie suffers from in spades. I love her to bits, but in comparison the child makes people with obsessive-compulsive disorders look like underachievers.

But today, her aura is a brilliant bloody red, hotly pulsing, all ragged around the edges like a fresh wound.

What does that mean, you ask? Well, darlin', I'll tell you:

Sexual energy. *Loads* of it.

My proper, buttoned-down niece's lady bits were lit up like a Christmas tree and her hormones were goin' off like a fireworks show on the 4th of July.

Now, that by itself would've been odd enough. Maddie's about as sexual as a Hallmark card. But then I saw who was followin' her as she made her way toward the side church doors, and my best Sunday hat almost flew right off my head.

And when I say *who*, I mean *what*. In all my life, I've only once before seen an aura like his… and it gave me such a start, I screamed.

Yessiree, Mason Spark's energy field is so powerful it could probably be seen from outer space.

You know, the same way a category 5 hurricane can.

Or a nuclear explosion.

"Why, hello, Mr. Spark! How nice to see you again!"

I wriggle my fingers and beam at him as I pretend not to notice Maddie havin' a nervous breakdown right next to him on the pew.

I know she's mortified enough as it is, bein' emotional in public. But bein' *turned on* in public—now that's really tossing her salad.

She's probably mistakin' it for indigestion.

It's fantastic, if I do say so myself.

I've been waitin' for ages for somethin' to come along that was strong enough to disrupt her rigid routine, and by golly if this good-lookin' tatted up hunk of man isn't it.

Yes, I'm oglin' his forearm tattoos. If Jesus won't judge me, you don't get to, either!

"Hey," says Mason, looking dumbfounded as he stares at Maddie. Then he gazes at me for help. "Uh, I'm not sure how, but I think I'm responsible for this."

He points at her. All red-faced and squinty-eyed and lips puckered up so tight they look like a cluster of hemorrhoids.

Poor baby. The only other time I've seen her get emotional is at her parents' funeral when she was sixteen. Right after that is when she started dressin' like she was Amish and smilin' so hard I thought her face would crack from the strain.

Everybody deals with grief in their own way.

Me? I drank my way through a few barrels of wine and took a lover half my age until the worst of it had passed and I could look at my sister's picture without wishin' out loud that it had been me instead of her in the car that rainy night.

Maddie went the other way. She didn't act out. She held it all in.

In my personal opinion, that's far more dangerous.

"I told him it was my allergies." She begs me with her eyes to play along.

If she slides any lower in the pew, she'll be on the floor.

"Ah, the allergies," I say with a straight face. "Terrible this time of year."

When she closes her eyes in relief, I send a conspiratorial wink to Mason. He misses my meaning and raises his brows like he thinks I'm makin' a pass at him, right here in church, for the love of the holy ghost.

So the boy's not the brightest bulb.

Still pretty, though. And I can tell he likes Maddie, because his crazy hurricane aura is all dreamy purple on the side next to her, so I can deal with him bein' a trifle dim.

There are much worse things in life than bein' a few cards short of a full deck, if you know what I mean.

Looking slightly relieved by all the allergy talk but still hesitant, Mason glances at Maddie. He bites his lower lip.

Bites his lip. Land's end, I've never seen anything so sexy.

Resisting the urge to fan myself, I sit down next to Maddie and pretend not to notice her absolute horror when I reach across her, take one of Mason's big man paws in my hands, and open my mouth.

"Now, tell me, Mr. Spark, how's the wife search goin'? Because there are several fine young ladies I'd be happy to introduce you to this morning."

Maddie bolts upright. "No more matches! We're doing dating coaching now, that's all!"

"Oh, I see." Instead of smirking, I bat my lashes innocently.

Maddie givin' dating advice to this stud makes about as much sense as a bird teachin' a fish how to swim, but her juicy red aura is tellin' me everything I need to know about why she's not settin' him up with any more women.

Even if she's tellin' herself otherwise.

Which she most certainly is. The girl wouldn't recognize desire if it walked right up to her and smacked her in the face.

Then, with suspicious nonchalance, Mason drawls, "Actually, I'd be grateful if you could introduce me around. Church seems like the perfect place to find a good wife."

When Maddie shoots him a frosty glare and he ignores it and sends me a lazy smile, I think I might have underestimated him.

Maybe this boy isn't as dim as he seems.

I wrack my brain for the name that will most appall Maddie. Because if I'm gonna do this, I'm gonna do it *right.*

When I find it, I nearly giggle.

I give Mason's hand a squeeze and sit back so I can better take in Maddie's expression when I lob this grenade into her lap.

"I wholeheartedly agree! And I know just the girl for you, if I do say so myself. Bettina Walters will be *so* excited to meet you."

Two bright spots of red appear on Maddie's cheeks. Through stiff lips, she repeats slowly, "*Bettina Walters*? Are you crazy?"

She's furious.

Lord forgive me, but this is gonna be so. Much. Fun.

Bettina Walters makes Jessica Rabbit look like a nun. The word "bombshell" was invented for women like her. When you look at her, it's hard to decide what to focus on first: the hair, the boobs, or the caboose at the back end of it all, swayin' like a metronome and mesmerizin' all the males within a five mile distance.

"I think it's a fine idea, dear niece," I say airily, smiling at Mason. "This here's a red-blooded American man—"

Maddie cuts in, "As opposed to a blue-blooded Amazonian reptile?"

"—who will surely appreciate the many God-given assets Bettina possesses—"

"Ha! If you count gold digging and ex-husband collecting as assets."

"—along with the fact that she's tryin' to better herself by gettin' closer to the Lord—"

"Or using church as a smokescreen for her reputation."

"—and how she won't be after him for his money 'cause she's got a boatload of her own."

Her eyes murderous, Maddie grinds her jaw. She doesn't have a smart response to that, because it's true. Divorced four times from an ever-wealthier succession of older men, Bettina Walters is richer than Midas.

She's trash, but she's rich trash, and always on the lookout for her next ex.

And if I'm readin' this situation right, no amount of money or boobage is gonna sway Mason Spark toward the dark side, because his eye's already been caught by someone else.

That someone else just needs a little helpin' hand to see what's right in front of her.

Leaning back against the pew and grinning, Mason says, "Well. This Bettina sounds like just my type."

Maddie lifts her chin and sends Mason a look so freezing I'm surprised the boy doesn't instantly turn to stone. She says darkly, "She is."

Then she folds her arms over her chest and directs her frosty gaze toward the front of the church and the cross hanging above the altar. She appears to be prayin' for the strength not to murder me and Mason both.

My job done, I slump abruptly against the pew and have myself a nice little nap just as the pastor begins his sermon.

I know it's probably a sin, but faking a case of chronic narcolepsy seems so mild compared to all the other sins I've committed in my life, and is honestly so useful in so many situations, that I'm takin' my chances the good Lord will overlook it.

I mean, look at giraffes. And porcupines. And politicians!

If anyone's got a sense of humor, it's God.

10

MADDIE

I'm going to kill them both with my bare hands.

No—that's just the indigestion talking. Why should I care if Mason wants to meet that man-eater Bettina?

I don't. I don't care one bit.

I'm disappointed, but only in a professional sense. Here I am trying to match him with women of quality and Auntie Waldine throws the East Coast's most scandalous floozy right in his lap.

Was *trying to match him with women of quality. Past tense. Now I'll have to listen to him talk all about his "date" with Bettina after it happens,* and *give him advice about what to do next.*

Because me and my big fat mouth insisted on being his dating coach instead of refunding him his money, which I would've been well within my contractual rights to do.

Honestly, I don't know what I was thinking.

Maybe I'm coming down with the flu?

I touch my hand to my forehead, but it's cool and dry. No signs of illness. Ignoring Auntie Waldine snoring on my right side and Mason vacuuming up all the oxygen in church with his massive gravitational-pull presence on my left, I try to focus on the sermon.

It's useless. My brain keeps poking me and nodding in Mason's direction.

I close my eyes and practice deep breathing until Mason leans over and whispers, "You okay?"

"Hunky dory."

"Then why are you breathing like that?"

"Like what?"

"Like a beached whale."

I heave a sigh and open my eyes to look at him. "If I throw a stick, will you run away?"

He crinkles his nose. It's boyishly adorable, and I hate him for it.

"So I'm a dog now?"

"Would you rather switch with me and be a whale?"

He sucks in his cheeks, and I get the feeling he's trying not to burst into laughter.

When I turn my attention back to the pastor droning on at the altar, I know Mason's still looking at my profile. I know because the left side of my face feels as if it's on fire.

He leans in and whispers, "I'm sorry I said that thing about you sucking at being a therapist. I didn't mean it. You would've been great."

When I don't respond or glance in his direction, Mason adds, "I'm sorry about the cat lady thing, too."

Now I can't help but glance over at him. "So you don't really think I'm prim?"

"Oh, no," he says instantly, shaking his head. "That was just a bad choice of words. I should've said…"

Intrigued, I lift my brows and wait with anticipation as he thinks.

When he pronounces, "Puritanical," I have to physically

restrain myself from ripping the Bible out of the little pocket on the back of the pew in front of me and smashing it over his head.

Looking at my expression, he breaks into a grin.

It's so dazzling that for a moment I'm rendered speechless and simply stare at him in all his glory. Then I realize that he's teasing me. He's being playful.

Playful Mason is devastatingly attractive.

Originating somewhere just south of my belly button, an intense wave of heat spreads throughout my body, crackling over my skin and lighting every nerve on fire.

Auntie Waldine awakens with a snort.

"Hoo!" she declares, sending me a pointed look. "It's hotter'n Hades in here all of a sudden!"

My voice comes out strangled. "Must be that flu going around."

"The flu?" She cackles. "Oh, child."

At that exact moment, Bettina Walters saunters past, booty swaying. She never fails to arrive late so she can make a grand entrance, because why bother with church if you're not going to be seen?

And seen she is. An entire congregation of eyeballs swings in her direction and follows her as she makes her way slowly up the main aisle to her favorite spot in the front pew.

Her dress is electric purple, low cut, and so clingy she might as well be wearing plastic wrap for all it leaves to the imagination.

At the end of the aisle, smack dab in front of the altar, she drops her glittery little handbag.

"Oh!" she cries, then leans forward to pick it up—*without bending her knees*. Which means her big purple bottom is thrust out lewdly like a pair of overripe plums for all the males in the sanctuary to gape at.

I have to stop myself from shouting, "Come on!"

Beside me, Mason watches Bettina's rump with eagle eyes, sharp and unblinking.

I don't care. I don't care. I WILL NOT care.

Only I do care, though I'm loath to admit it, and I know exactly why.

Bettina Walters is the kind of woman men can't resist. She's sexy. Flirty. Luscious, and knows it. She's everything I'm not, from the top of her highlighted head to the tips of her expensive stilettos. She's a cherry red Ferrari and I'm a pre-owned Subaru: reliable and economical, practical and dull.

Boring.

Auntie Waldine leans over me and whispers to Mason, "That there's the lady I was tellin' you about, Mason."

I mutter, "Lady. Pfft."

Ignoring me, Auntie Waldine goes on. "Bettina's mighty pretty, don't you agree?"

Mason replies with a noncommittal, "Hmm."

Hmm my butt! He thinks she's the hottest tamale he's ever seen.

I snatch the bible from the pocket on the back of the pew and flip through it like I'm searching for the psalm the pastor's reading so I can follow along, instead of looking for a distraction from my growing aggravation with my meddling aunt.

We're going to have a nice, long talk later on about her role as my office assistant and how it doesn't include her taking matchmaking matters into her own hands.

I glance down at the page the Bible fell open to and have to suppress a dark laugh when I see the commandments. *Thou shalt not kill* jumps out at me like a personal warning.

God must realize I've begun compiling a list.

The rest of the sermon is a blur. I stand when I'm supposed to, sing along when I'm supposed to, and bow my head at the right times. Only I do it all on autopilot, my brain preoccupied with thoughts of Mason falling prey to the evil clutches of Bettina.

Even if he doesn't believe in love and only wants a wife to help his career, he doesn't deserve a woman like that. Nobody does.

But I can't stop the meeting, and I can't stop Bettina from being catnip for men, so the only thing I'm going to be able to do is stand by and watch as Mason sticks his foot right into her bear trap.

His foot and other body parts.

By the time mass is over, I'm completely depressed.

"Yoo-hoo! Oh, Bettina! Come on over here, hun!"

As the congregation files past us out the doors, Auntie Waldine stands on her tippy toes and waves her handkerchief frantically, grinning like an idiot as she tries to flag her target down. Mason and I stand silently beside her at the end of the pew and watch as Bettina catches sight of us.

When she notices Mason, she does a double-take so sharp I'm surprised her head doesn't snap right off her shoulders.

"Here we go," I say under my breath as Bettina starts to shove her way through the crowd, her eager gaze pinned on Mason, her smile shark-like.

Mason says cheerfully, "She sure looks friendly."

"Oh, she's friendly all right. Make sure you double wrap your carrot before you stick it in that dip."

He doesn't respond, but his smile looks mysteriously smug. Probably because he's remembering he just bought a brand new package of condoms and stashed half of them in his wallet. The beast.

Cool it, Maddie. If the man wants to ruin his life, that's his business.

"Well, hellooo," purrs Bettina, sidling up to Auntie Waldine but making googly eyes at Mason. "So good to see you again, Waldine. Who's your handsome friend?"

Completely ignoring me, Bettina bats her lashes at Mason. So hard she'd probably take off, if it weren't for her substantial cleavage weighing her down.

"This here's Mason Spark. He's a friend of Maddie's."

Bettina's glossy red lips part. Her baby blue eyes widen. She puts a hand to her throat and says in a thrilled whisper, "*The* Mason Spark? Of the Pioneers?"

Her astonished, starry-eyed expression has its intended effect: Mason looks like a cat stroked down its back.

"The very same," he drawls. "Are you a football fan, Bettina?"

"Oh, my goodness, no!" she declares with a girlish laugh. "I'm a *Pioneers* fan, Mr. Spark! Our boys are the best in the league!" More furious lash batting. "But, of course, the team wouldn't be anything without *you.* And may I say, you're even more handsome in person than on TV. Why, you could be a movie star!"

"Oh, stop," he says, clearly not wanting her to stop. "You'll make me blush."

"I'm serious! You make Tom Brady look like a chimpanzee!"

They beam at each other. Meanwhile, I'm repeating *Thou shalt not kill* silently inside my head.

Auntie Waldine, for some bizarre reason, looks like she's trying hard not to burst into laughter.

"Wait," says Bettina, appearing confused. For the first time, she notices I'm there and looks at me. Her perfectly arched brows draw together. "He's *your* friend?"

"Shocking, I know."

Bettina is too busy being perplexed to notice my sarcastic tone. She looks me up and down, the tiny hamster in her brain spinning furiously on its wheel. "How on earth did the two of you meet?"

"The local library," says Mason, smiling blandly. "There was a charity event a while back that I attended. Maddie happened to be there at the time. She told me the Sunday service here was great, so here I am."

That story is as holey as Swiss cheese, but I know he's only trying to avoid admitting he hired me to find him a wife. Unfortunately, his answer provides Bettina the perfect opportunity to take a dig at me. And dig she does, the witch.

Her lovely face projecting innocence, she says, "Yes, we all thought she'd become a librarian, being so bookish and all." Her gaze drifts over my hair, my glasses, my dress, then a faint smile lifts the corners of her lips. "She certainly does have the look."

Mason's voice gains an edge. "What's wrong with that? Librarians are smart and essential in helping kids develop critical thinking skills and guiding them through media literacy."

That stuns me as much as it does Bettina.

Her because she's probably never had a man speak to her in anything but an adoring tone, and me for that reason, too, but also because he repeated verbatim what I said to him when he teased me on the phone.

I can't decide if I'm more surprised he defended me to his next conquest or that he has such perfect recall of our conversation.

Sensing she's on thin ice, Bettina says haltingly, "Oh, yes… of course. Librarians are wonderful!"

She pats my arm. It might as well be the top of my head.

Then, because my life is a romantic comedy only there's no romance and nobody's laughing, the last man I had sex with strolls right up and joins the conversation.

11

MASON

"Hello, Madison," says a dude who looks like he has to spend four hours in front of a mirror every day practicing how to smile so he can pass as human.

Wearing a blue three-piece suit with a gray tie cinched so tight around his neck it has to be cutting off his circulation, he's tall, slim, and immaculate. His shoes and fingernails gleam.

I'd bet my Maybach that he gets weekly facials and eats lots of kale.

Staring at Maddie, he bares his teeth like he's expecting her to check to see if he's been flossing. Then they launch into this weirdly formal conversation, expressions blank, voices flat. Two robots practicing their speaking skills would be more animated.

He says, "You look wonderful. How have you been?"

"I'm well, thank you, Bobby. You?"

"Excellent. Thank you."

"I didn't know you were back in town."

"My mother's ill. I flew in a few days ago to look in on her."

"I'm so sorry to hear that. Is it serious?"

"It is, I'm afraid. She's in the hospital."

"Her heart again?"

"Yes."

"Please send her my best regards."

"I certainly will, thank you."

Bettina yawns, miffed that she hasn't been acknowledged. Waldine is looking at the empty space over the new arrival's head with a faint air of disappointment. And I'm wondering how this guy knows Maddie.

Is he her accountant?

"Hi." I stick out my hand. "Mason Spark."

He turns his attention to me. I see him register who I am, then he shows me his incisors, and we shake hands.

"Mason Spark, our very own hometown hero. I'm Robert Cavendish. Pleased to make your acquaintance."

I don't miss that Maddie called him Bobby, but he introduced himself as Robert.

Not her accountant, then. Family friend?

"You, too. Hope your mom will be okay."

He blinks like I said something surprising. "Thank you. That's very kind."

Then he seems to realize I was standing here before he walked up. He looks around, as if for an explanation. When his gaze settles on Bettina, examining her nails, his expression sours.

He turns away from her like you'd pull away from a spider about to crawl onto your hand. Which I find very, very fucking interesting, considering every other guy in here besides me wanted to bend her over the altar and make her see God.

"Hello, Waldine."

"Bobby," replies Waldine, still squinting at the air a few inches over his head.

He seems to know what she's doing, because he politely inquires, "Still the same?"

Waldine sighs, then pats his shoulder. "Gray as a granny's cardigan, darlin'. Send your mama my love, will you? I'd go visit her myself, but you know how hospitals clog up my third eye."

Robert the robot gazes at Waldine with something that looks suspiciously like affection. "I'll be sure to let her know." Then he turns his attention back to Maddie, and the warmth in his eyes flares hotter.

Wait.

No.

Holy fuck.

Were the robot and Maddie a thing?

"So how do you two know each other?" I ask, trying to sound casual.

Maddie says, "We've known each other since we were kids."

But at the same time, Robert is providing more interesting detail. "We dated on and off for ten years."

I stare at Maddie in horror.

Ten years? She dated this animatron for a decade?

Which means—oh fuck—*she slept with him.*

No wonder she's celibate! That block of ice could freeze the libido of a porn star!

Maddie's smile is tight. Without looking at me, she says, "Well, it's been a treat catching up, Bobby, but I must be going. Mason, why don't you and Bettina get better acquainted? I'll get a ride home with Auntie Waldine."

"Nooo." I catch her by her arm as she starts to bolt. Smiling, I draw her back against my side. "Brunch, remember?" I make up a hasty lie. "We were gonna talk about my friend who might need your service." *And I need to know all there is to know about you and Mr. Spock.*

Bettina perks up and inserts her tits into the conversation. "I can't imagine any friend of yours would need a matchmaker, Mason," she says sweetly, pushing out her chest in my direction.

Normally, I'd be all over this woman like stink on shit. Maddie was right. She's exactly my type.

Except my dick has zero interest. Less than zero. In fact, I think shrinkage is occurring as we speak.

I'd chalk it up to being in church, but I know my dick better than that. I could get it on in the Vatican in the middle of Christmas mass if I needed to.

Now I might not be a genius, but I know that if my dick is on strike, there's only one reason.

And that reason is looking up at me and blinking her big brown eyes in shock.

She says, "But…" and glances at Bettina, who pounces on the opportunity.

"What a wonderful idea! Yes, let's all do brunch together!"

That makes Waldine throw her head back and cackle like a witch.

The woman's nuts.

Maddie's expression darkens. She hesitates a moment, then lifts her chin in that stubborn way she does. Her lips thin, the hideous pink lipstick she favors doing nothing to reduce their full, feminine appeal.

Fuck, I'd like to bite those lips. I'd like to make them part on a moan.

A rush of heat to my head makes me dizzy.

"Ow!" Maddie pulls her arm from my grip, scowling at me.

"Shit, sorry," I say breathlessly, trying to steady myself as I stare down at Maddie. She has little indents in her upper arm where my fingers dug into her flesh.

What the hell is wrong with me? I'm acting like a caveman!

Waldine cackles louder.

Robert clears his throat and says politely, "I'd love to call on you soon, Maddie, if you don't mind? Maybe we could have lunch this week and catch up?"

Looking distracted as she rubs her arm, Maddie mutters, "Sure."

He's so pleased by that he almost levitates. When he shoots

me a victorious glance, I smother the urge to punch him in his nose.

"Should we all take one car to brunch?" Bettina's so happy she's almost chirping.

Waldine says, "Oh, no, I can't go. I've got the…" She hesitates, glancing at Maddie, who's looking at her with big, pleading eyes. All Maddie gets is a grin before Waldine goes on. "The thing. That thing I always do on Sundays after church."

"Thing?" says Maddie pointedly.

Waldine makes a queenly, dismissive gesture with her hand. I get the impression she has no idea what she does on Sundays after church but won't admit it.

So it's dementia. That explains a lot.

For some reason, Waldine's dementia makes Maddie angry. Her eyes flash, her chin juts out farther, and she squares her shoulders like she's about to ride off into war.

Angry Maddie is incredibly sexy.

I imagine her telling me off wearing nothing but a flimsy nightie, those brown eyes flashing at me instead of her crazy aunt.

When another wave of heat settles over me, Waldine snorts. She walks off without saying goodbye, chortling to herself, the big ostrich feathers on her hat bobbing as she goes.

"Is it safe to let her drive by herself?" I ask.

Maddie watches her aunt leave with an expression that's half love and half murder. "Yes. She never falls asleep behind the wheel."

"I meant will she be able to find her way home?"

Maddie looks at me like I've been smoking something funny.

"Oh, don't worry, Mason," says Bettina, sidling up to me and taking my arm. "Waldine's perfectly capable of driving home. Now, is that rumor true I heard about the Pioneers getting new uniforms? Because I, for one, happen to favor the silver and black."

I'm engulfed in a cloud of cinnamon and vanilla perfume. She smells like a cookie. I'm sure that's as calculated as everything else about her.

She leads me away from Maddie and Robert, who's smiling at Maddie like he knows what color panties she's wearing.

Which he probably does.

Never in a million years would I have thought I'd be jealous of a robot, but here we fucking are.

12

MADDIE

Men are imbeciles.

After stopping to sign a few autographs outside church, Mason swaggers over to his car with Bettina hanging from his arm like a leech. Honestly, I'd like to give him a smack for being such a cliché. But the man is only my client, not my friend, so I need to keep it professional. I'll just observe the two of them at brunch and give him my coaching feedback later.

If I don't stab Bettina in the eyeball with a fork first.

When the three of us approach the car, I hop into the front passenger seat without being asked. Dick turns to me, startled.

"What—"

He spots Bettina slithering into the back seat next to Mason, and blinks.

"Mason made a new friend," I say brightly. "We're all going to brunch."

Dick takes a long time examining my expression before breaking into a grin. "Well, ain't that cozy." He starts the car, smirking. "Where to?"

"Garwood's," says Mason.

At the same time, Bettina says, "The Four Seasons."

Then she pauses, leaning toward Mason boobs first while toying with a strand of her hair. Another round of furious lash batting commences. "I mean, of course, whatever you prefer, Mason. That other place just seems a little pedestrian for you."

Ooh, look who's breaking out the big words. I'd guess she'd been dating a professor, but they don't make enough money.

Mason glances at me, his expression impassive. After a moment, he says, "The Four Seasons it is."

By the time we get there, Bettina's endless chatter has given me a headache. All Mason has to do to keep the conversation going is insert a grunt here and there.

Then again, it's not her conversation he's interested in.

Dick pulls to a stop in front of the valet stand at the hotel. We all exit the car and head inside.

Then the real torture begins.

I try to stay discreetly behind them, but Mason turns and frowns at me, jerking his head for me to keep up as the hostess leads us to our table. I suppose he's accustomed to having a pair of female bookends, but I'm uncomfortable as the third wheel.

Especially because of all the attention he's getting.

Heads swivel as we walk by. Whispers rise in our wake. Eyes are drawn to him like moths to flame, then to Bettina in all her blonde, busty glory. Then to me, for a brief, dismissive look—*is that his assistant?*—then back to the two of them.

I'm the ugly step-sister in this pretty little tableau.

I'd like to say I don't care, but by the time we sit down, my cheeks are burning.

Just once in my life, I want a man to look at me the way they all look at Bettina.

As soon as the waiter leaves with our drink orders, Mason asks me, "You okay?"

"Oh, she's just fine and dandy, aren't you Maddie?" Bettina

sends a lethal smile in my direction that says *Just shut up and sit there while I work my magic.*

Reaching for the bread basket in the center of the table, I say, "Yes, thank you. Muffin?"

When I hold out the basket, she recoils from it like it's filled with snakes.

"Carbs? God, no."

Some people are so predictable.

I select the thickest, fluffiest candidate from the various scones and muffins in the basket, then slather butter over every inch of it while Bettina watches, scandalized. When I tear off a bite and pop it into my mouth, she nearly faints in horror.

"Have you girls known each other long?" asks Mason, watching me chew with hooded eyes.

Already bored with the subject, Bettina flicks her hair over her shoulder. "We went to the same high school. What was it you were voted senior year, Maddie? Most Likely to Remain a Virgin Until Marriage?"

And the claws are out. "You're thinking of Darcy Johnson. I was Most Likely to Succeed. And you were Most Likely to Walk Into a Glass Door, if I recall correctly?"

Bettina's smile doesn't waver. She won't be thrown off by the likes of me.

"Most Beautiful," she purrs. "And homecoming queen, of course."

"That's right," I say, chewing thoughtfully. "And a week after graduation is when you married that plastic surgeon, Mervyn—"

"Marvin," she cuts in, her voice more brittle.

"—Dingleberry?"

"Dinkelman."

"Yes, now I remember. I was so sorry to hear he passed away only six months after the wedding."

"Eight," she says flatly, now regarding me with open hostility.

Marvin Dinkelman dropped dead of a massive stroke, but not before gifting his bride with a ginormous pair of new boobs and a trust fund.

Bettina was eighteen. He was seventy-four.

Suffice it to say, she didn't spend much time in mourning.

"That must've been tough for you," says Mason with a straight face.

God bless him, there's hope for the man yet.

But Bettina, being Bettina, fails to detect the bone dry sarcasm in Mason's voice. She takes his statement and runs with it, launching into a long and detailed account of her grief. It leaves me cross-eyed and Mason looking like he'd give his kingdom for the sudden arrival of a comet to demolish the restaurant and everything in it.

The waiter returns with our drinks. Bettina only stops talking about herself long enough to give him her food order, then goes right back to it.

By the time my Eggs Benedict arrives ten minutes later, I need a break or my brain will implode. I take a few half-hearted bites, then excuse myself and head to the ladies' room.

Once there, I take my sweet time enjoying the quiet. I use the toilet and wash my hands, drying them on the soft towels stacked in a pyramid between the sinks. I check my bun for any flyaways, clean my glasses, and freshen my lipstick.

Just as I'm taking a deep breath and reminding my reflection not to make gagging noises when Mason asks Bettina back to his house, Mason bursts in, glowering.

He skids to a stop at the end of the sinks and stares at me accusingly.

I say, "Wrong room, superstar. Note the lack of urinals."

"I came to check to make sure you weren't climbing out a window. You've been gone forever!"

I glance at my watch. "I've been gone six minutes."

He looks around in panic like a cornered wolf. "It's gotta be more than that."

I snort. "Oh, are we not enjoying Bettina's sparkling personality?"

"She hasn't even stopped to take a breath. Not once. I didn't know that was physically possible."

"I could've told you she's Satan, but you were too dazzled by her cleavage to notice the forked tongue and the horns."

His brows drawn down over his eyes. "You have to come back to the table and save me."

"*Save* you?" I laugh. "No way, Romeo. You got yourself into this one, you get yourself out."

"C'mon. I'll owe you one."

I consider him, interested. He looks really desperate. It's oddly appealing.

A woman walks in the door, sees the two of us standing there, then turns around and walks back out.

I say, "This is unexpected," then stop, unsure if I should go on.

Mason folds his arms over his chest and looks at me down his nose. "I can see the wheels spinning, Pink. Spit it out."

"It's just that on paper, she's perfect for you."

When I don't continue, he prompts, "On paper."

"The questionnaire you filled out. Your preferences in women? Remember those?"

He's starting to look aggravated, so I hurry on before he can tear off one of the faucets and clobber me with it.

"Blonde, twenty-one to twenty-six, five-foot-seven or taller, athletic but curvy build—whatever the heck that is—and at least a 36 double D bust. Bubbly and outgoing. Enjoys sports. Non-smoking, non-religious, a social drinker who doesn't do drugs, doesn't care for politics, and doesn't want children, but enjoys travel and action movies and is sophisticated enough to hold her own around people of high net worth."

I stop for a moment. "Actually, it's a miracle I matched you with anyone at all. That list is ridiculous."

I don't mention that Bettina's out of his age range, but I'm sure her boobs make up for it.

He drawls, "I believe you have a point. Feel free to make it before we both die of old age."

He's quoting me again. I'm not sure what to make of it.

Then a sudden moment of clarity leaves me laughing at my own stupidity.

"What?" Mason demands, unfolding his arms and taking a step toward me.

"I just realized the problem."

He takes another step toward me. Now we're only an arm's length apart.

"Which is?"

"You forgot to include mute."

A muscle working in his jaw, his gaze drops to my lips. His voice comes out an octave lower. "You're right. Mouthy women are a pain in the ass."

I smile sweetly at him. "At least I don't make you want to chew off your arm in a restaurant booth to escape."

He says gruffly, "No, you make me want to—"

The woman who came in before interrupts us again, bursting through the restroom door. "Sorry, I can't hold it any longer." She rushes into a stall and slams the door.

Mason takes my arm and guides me out of the restroom.

He stops in the small vestibule leading to the hallway, but doesn't let go of my arm. We stand there looking at each other for a moment, until I say, "Just make up some excuse to leave. Maybe you're not feeling well."

What was he going to say? I make him want to… what?

Jump off a tall building, most likely.

"No, *you're* the one not feeling well."

"Why not you?" When his lips twist in derision, I say, "Right. Because you're way too manly to ever feel sick."

"Exactly."

I sigh. "Does it get tiring, dragging that huge ego around with you all the time?"

"No," he says with a straight face. "My biceps can handle it."

His hand is still on my arm. It's big and warm and gently squeezing, and we're both pretending to ignore it.

This is very confusing.

"Even if I did say I was sick, Satan would just tell you to have Dick drive me home."

"What kind of a guy would I be if I let my sick matchmaker be taken home by my agent just so I could finish brunch with Bettina?"

I crinkle my brow. "A normal one?"

He shakes his head. "You were right. She's a nightmare. Not even her thirty-eight double E's can make up for it."

"How do you know what her bra size is?"

He smirks, and I look heavenward. "God, in my next life, I want to come back as a pretty jock."

"*Pretty*?" Mason says, curling his lip in disgust. "I'm not pretty. I'm—"

"Please don't subject me to a list of adjectives describing your masculine beauty. I could go my entire life without hearing that."

His expression changes to one of keen interest. "Masculine beauty? You think I'm beautiful?"

"No, *you* said—oh, forget it."

"No, this is an interesting topic. I think we should discuss this in more detail."

His gray eyes are burning the way they do before he starts cursing, but he doesn't scare me. I scoff. "I know for a fact you have plenty of other sources for ego strokes, my friend. You don't need me for that."

His smile comes on slow and heated. He teases, "But librarians have such good vocabularies."

I say flatly, "I will kill you where you stand."

Why he likes it when I threaten him, I have no earthly idea, but his smile deepens and his eyes crinkle at the corners.

"For such a tiny thing, you've got a lot of anger inside."

"Believe me, it's a recent development."

He presses his lips together, trying not to laugh. Then his gaze drops to my mouth, and his amusement fades. He stares at my lips in intense concentration.

"Mason."

His gaze flashes up to mine.

"I know you hate pink, but when you look at my lipstick like you're trying hard not to puke, it hurts my feelings."

There's a long, crackling pause. Then he says, "Is that robot we saw at church the only man you've ever slept with?"

Shocked, I pull my arm from his grip and say icily, "That's none of your business."

"He is, isn't he?"

"See my previous answer."

"Because I'm thinking the only explanation for your total lack of awareness is that you don't have much experience with men."

Heat crawls up my neck, flooding my cheeks and making them burn. "I'm perfectly aware of how I look."

He steps closer, leans down into my face, and growls, "I didn't say anything about your *looks*."

I swallow. He's so close I can feel the warmth of him. I can smell his skin. I can see the little flecks of green in the depths of his burning gray eyes.

For one long, breathless moment, we stare deep into each other's eyes.

Then he pulls away abruptly, and I'm left reeling.

He snaps, "Now go find me that mute girl so I don't have to deal with this crap anymore."

He whirls around and stalks away, shoulders stiff.

I sag against the wall, pressing a hand to my thundering heart and trying to catch my breath.

It takes a few minutes before I'm calm enough to return to the table, but when I do, Mason's gone.

13

MADDIE

Naturally, Bettina is in a snit over Mason's disappearance.

"What did you say to him?" she hisses as I sit down.

I fold my napkin over my lap and dig into the Eggs Benedict, which are now cold. "What do you mean?"

"Mason excused himself to go to the restroom a few minutes after you did, and when he came back, he was totally pissed off! He didn't say a word, just threw some money down on the table and left! I *know* you must've said something to him."

I say calmly, "I didn't see him, Bettina. Maybe he got a phone call and had to step out for a minute to deal with something. I'm sure he'll be right back."

I'm not sure of anything of the sort, but I'm dang sure I'm not going to relay our conversation to Satan.

But why would he have left?

And why did he say I have a total lack of awareness?

And why did he keep his hand on my arm all that time?

And if it wasn't because of my pink lipstick, why was he really looking at my mouth like that?

Maybe he wanted to kiss me.

I freeze with a forkful of Canadian bacon halfway to my mouth. My heart stops dead in my chest, then takes off like a rocket.

No. That's ridiculous.

But… is it?

I think back to our first meeting. To how aggravated he was from the minute he laid eyes on me. To the way he flirted with me on the phone, and the way his gaze always seems drawn to my mouth.

Puh-lease! The man probably flirts with every woman he meets!

He didn't flirt with Bettina.

Perfect-for-him-on-paper Bettina, who, if you're interested, is about to rip out your hair by the roots.

"What?" I come back to reality with a jerk. "What were you saying?"

Bettina is a seething pool of rage. "I *said*," she spits, leaning toward me, "if I find out you talked trash about me to Mason, you weird little virgin, I'll ruin your life."

I roll my eyes. "Terrifying. Speaking of virgins, if you try anything with me, I'll have Bobby tell your next fiancé about the time he walked in on you taking it in every hole from the basketball team at that frat party his freshman year in college."

I smile at her. "I'm sure the video's still floating around somewhere. That pool table must've been really hard on your knees."

She sucks in a hard breath and goes sheet white.

Then she throws down her napkin and storms away from the table, trailing steam. I get back to my bacon.

After fifteen minutes, I'm certain Mason won't be returning. So I give the waitress the money he left and head out to the car.

I was expecting to see Satan sitting in the back seat, but when I climb into the front seat, Dick is alone, reading the paper.

He takes one look at my face and grimaces. "That bad, huh?"

"I can honestly say that was the strangest brunch I've ever attended. Where's Mason?"

"Your guess is as good as mine."

"You know him better than I do. Where does he go when he's mad?"

Dick starts to look worried. "*Mad* mad, or just cranky?"

"I'm thinking mad mad. There was a good bit of growling going on."

Dick's jaw tightens. He tosses the newspaper into the back seat, guns the engine, and peels out of the church parking lot.

"That's not exactly the reaction I was expecting." I grip the door handle as we careen around a corner, tires squealing. "Is he dangerous when he's upset?"

"Only to himself," mutters Dick, hunched over the steering wheel. "How long has he been gone?"

"Maybe twenty minutes."

When he curses, I start to get worried, too. "He can't possibly do too much damage in twenty minutes."

He says darkly, "You don't know Mason." Then he turns his attention back to the road and doesn't talk again, even when I suggest we call him.

I guess Dick knows Mason won't pick up.

We screech to a stop outside an Irish pub. Dick doesn't bother to turn off the engine, he simply flings open his door, jumps out, and runs inside faster than I would have imagined a paunchy middle-aged man in a tight polyester leisure suit could possibly run.

Within seconds, he reappears. Without Mason.

He jumps back into the car and we're off again.

"You gotta phone on you?"

"Yes, in my purse. Why?"

He takes a corner at top speed, throwing me against the passenger door. "Google every bar within a one mile radius."

"Oh dear."

"You have no idea. Hurry up." Then, under his breath: "Thank God he doesn't have practice today."

I dig around in my purse for my phone. "Maybe I oversold his level of anger. It wasn't like he shouted or got into a fight or anything."

"Were his nostrils flaring?"

I pause, remembering. "Yes."

"Did he have crazy eyes?"

I think of the unblinking intensity with which he regarded my mouth. "As a matter of fact, he did."

"Plus the growling," says Dick, shaking his head. "Yeah. We got a situation."

I find the phone, open the web browser, and type in *Bars near me*, then wait impatiently for the results to load. "Do these situations happen a lot?"

His chuckle is dark. "You don't read the sports section much, do you?"

"Too busy feeding all my cats," I mutter, peeved. "Isn't he in therapy?"

"Yup."

"And that's not helping with his anger issues?"

Dick looks over at me. "Just cause you let some steam escape from a nuclear reactor doesn't mean it still isn't about to blow."

"I'm pretty sure the only time steam escapes from a nuclear reactor is when there's been a meltdown."

"Exactly," says Dick, nodding. "And what you got then is some radioactive shit that's gonna get up into the atmosphere and poison all the air and cause mass destruction. Are you understanding me yet?"

He paints a very depressing picture. "Make a right at the next light. There's a bar halfway down the block on the left side. I'll bet he's there."

"What makes you say that?"

I say drily, "It's called 'The Quiet Woman'."

Dick looks at me strangely, but doesn't comment. When we pull into the parking lot, he says, "Why don't you go in and check if he's in there. If he sees me, it'll just be a fight."

"You're assuming it won't be a fight when he sees me."

"Not the same kind." He parks and turns to look at me. "If he's not in there, I'll take you home. You don't need to spend the rest of your Sunday chasin' after Mason."

"No, we'll go together. I won't be able to relax until I know he's okay."

He says nothing, only shrugging at my response, but his smile is full of secrets.

I swear, these two men are downright strange.

When I push through the door of the bar, I have to stand there blinking for a moment, letting my eyes adjust to the dim.

The place is so dark it might as well be underground, and it's unrelentingly shabby. Everything is faded, peeling, or cracked. An old jukebox plays 'Love Me Tender.' A guy with a bushy black beard in a Led Zeppelin T-shirt polishes glasses behind the bar.

It smells like cigarettes, stale beer, and lost dreams, and is quite possibly the most depressing place on earth.

And there, in the end booth in the corner, sits Mason, staring down at the empty glass in his hand.

My heart does a funny little flip under my ribcage. He looks so forlorn, like his dog just died and his car broke down and he's never had a friend in the world.

Then he glances up and catches sight of me, and his melancholy look changes to one of irritation.

I foresee more growling in my future.

Squaring my shoulders, I cross the sticky floor to his booth. I slide onto the seat opposite him, wishing I had a bottle of antibacterial gel in my purse.

"If your immune system is compromised, don't touch anything."

His voice is even. His expression has gone from irritated to guarded. But he's not yelling, so it's a start.

"I like it more than The Four Seasons."

When Mason lifts his brows in disbelief, I smile. "It doesn't smell like brimstone in here."

He chuckles. It feels like a victory.

"Is Bettina with you?"

I crinkle my nose. "Lord, no. She stormed out of the restaurant right after you did. Probably had to go polish her pitchfork. Dick's outside, though."

"He sent you in to get me?"

"He seemed to think our fight would somehow be better than yours."

Mason considers that, then says, "Huh."

An open bottle of Jack Daniels sits on the table next his elbow. Seeing me notice it, he picks it up and pours himself another glass, right up to the brim. With defiance in his eyes, he sets the bottle down and picks up the glass.

I say calmly, "You're not going to offer me one?"

Surprised, he sets the glass back down.

"If you want to get blind drunk on a Sunday morning, that's your prerogative. However, if a lady is present, it's only good manners that you offer her a drink as well."

He says sourly, "You're lecturing me."

"Incorrect. I'm coaching you. Unless you fired me between here and The Four Seasons and haven't gotten around to telling me yet."

"I'm surprised you wanna keep coaching me, seeing what a lost cause I am."

"You're not lost. You're just taking a detour."

He gazes at me for a beat, his gray eyes penetrating. "Do you even drink whiskey?"

I say archly, "Just because I wear a lot of pink doesn't make me a P-word."

Another chuckle, this one very dry. "That would've been so much more impressive if you'd actually said the P-word."

"If I'd actually said the P-word, my mother would've rolled over in her grave."

I can tell he's surprised by the mention of my mother, and intrigued, but he doesn't ask a question, so I offer up the information on my own.

"She and my dad died in a car accident when I was sixteen. I was in the back seat, but except for a few scratches and bruises, I wasn't hurt." I take the glass from his hand and swallow a big gulp of whiskey, grimacing at the burn.

"Fuck," he says softly. Then: "Shit, sorry." He winces. "Oh, crap."

I wave it off. "Don't worry about it. Sundays are cheat days, anyway."

"*Cheat* days?"

"Yeah, like when you're on a diet and you give yourself one day a week to go crazy and eat all the junk food and sweets you want."

He squints at me. "I'm having a hard time imagining you going crazy."

"It was a figure of speech." I take another swig of whiskey, then push the glass toward him. "You ever tried Glenlivet? That's my favorite."

Mason looks like he's going to fall out of the booth. "You really *do* drink whiskey."

I smile at him. "Let me guess. You thought I'd like… piña coladas?"

"I was thinking more along the lines of Shirley Temples."

That stings. "Right. I enjoy a few non-alcoholic cocktails while I'm grooming all my cats."

I look down at my hands, vowing to ditch my nude nail polish and start wearing something edgier. Maybe I'll get some of those pointy stiletto nails, too, and use them as weapons. I could claw Bettina's eyes out.

The thought makes me feel substantially better.

When I glance up at Mason, he's studying me with such focus my face flushes. "What?"

"Tell me about Robert."

I'm taken aback by his intensity. It's the kind usually reserved for stalkers. "Why?"

"I'm curious."

When I heave a sigh, he says, "You know everything about the type of woman I like, right down to bra size."

I say sourly, "Yes, and I really could've gone my whole life without that particular tidbit of information, thank you very much."

"Meanwhile, I'm in the dark about your type."

When I send him a questioning look, he says casually, "Maybe I know someone."

"You're assuming I'm looking."

"Aren't you?"

"No."

That surprises him. He leans back in the booth and simply stares at me.

"I'm too busy with work."

One corner of his mouth quirks. "Matchmaking."

"Don't say it like that. I'm helping people. I'm helping *you*, bozo."

Holding my gaze, he says softly, "Yeah, but we both know what I really need isn't a wife."

The flush spreads down my face to my neck. "If you're putting yourself down right now, stop it. I don't like it when you do that." When he doesn't respond, I start to get nervous. "Unless you were talking about, um, sex or something."

He arches his brows.

I ask timidly, "Were you talking about sex?"

"Let's get back to Robert."

"Let's not."

"Come on. I haven't fired you yet. You have to do what I say."

That makes me laugh. "Uh, *no*, superstar, that's not how this works."

Leaning forward on his elbows, Mason pins me in a gaze so hot and intense I feel for a moment like I'm sitting in a sauna dressed in every piece of clothing I own. Sweat breaks out along my hairline.

He says, "Did he satisfy you sexually?"

"*Wow*, go straight for the jugular, why don't you?"

Bypassing my shock, he continues. "Because I can't imagine a guy like that having any idea what he's doing in bed."

I feel insulted on Bobby's behalf. Our sex life wasn't great, but it wasn't terrible, either.

Okay, it was terrible, but hell if I'm going to admit it to the man who beds every woman he sees. "He was perfectly adequate."

I hate myself that it came out so—*gah*!—prim.

Mason pushes the glass back toward me. Thankful for the distraction, I take another swig.

"Is that why you broke up with him? Because he was 'adequate'?"

"Who said I broke up with him? Maybe he dumped me."

"He looks at you like you're crack and he's an addict. He didn't dump you."

"You're exaggerating."

"I'm not. Answer the question."

The song on the jukebox changes to "Let's Get It On", by Marvin Gaye, and now I think God's just screwing with me. "Why is this topic so important to you?"

"It just is. *Answer the question.*"

Exasperated, I slump against the hard leather back of the

booth and give up. "Fine. I broke up with him because I knew I'd never feel about him the way he felt about me. And he's a good guy. A really good guy, despite what you might think. He's smart, kind, and loyal. He should be with someone who loves him like mad."

After studying me intently for a long time, Mason says, "It took you ten years to realize you didn't love him?"

"I tried," I say morosely, staring at the whiskey in the glass. "I *wanted* to. Our mothers always hoped we'd end up together, which was a big part of it. But even if it wasn't for that, we had everything in common. Backgrounds, interests, goals. Everything. We were perfect—"

"On paper," Mason finishes. When I glance up at him, his eyes are burning. "Like me and Bettina. But I'd rather stick my dick in a fire ant hill than in her."

"Charming," I say, though secretly I'm pleased.

"So the matchmaker can't make her own match. That must be awkward for business."

"Excuse me, but I'm not dead yet. I'm only thirty. I've got plenty of time—"

"You're *thirty*?"

He gapes at me like I've confessed I'm really a man.

"Thanks for that. That's exactly what my ego needed today. You're a real pal."

Disgusted, I shake my head and take another swig of whiskey. The glass is now empty, so I fill it again and push it back toward Mason. Who, I realize, hasn't had a sip since I sat down.

"It's not an insult, I just didn't realize you were older than me." Mason lowers his lashes. Running his finger slowly around the edge of the whiskey glass, he says in a husky voice, "It's hot."

It's a good thing I don't have a mouthful of liquid, because I'd spit it all out in a geyser. I wheeze, "*Hot*?"

His gaze flashes back up to mine. He takes one look at my astonished expression, and his face turns to stone. In a flat voice, he says, "Kidding. I'm kidding, Pink. You know I only go for young girls with big tits."

I stare at him, feeling my pulse in every part of my body. I remember the way he looked at my mouth at the restaurant and think maybe, just maybe… he's lying.

14

MASON

If there's a Guinness World Record for Biggest Fucking Idiot, I should enter myself for consideration.

Me and my big mouth.

I clench my jaw, wishing it would lock shut permanently so I wouldn't have to worry about blurting more stupid shit that makes Maddie look like I took a dump on her doorstep.

It's painfully obvious she finds the thought of me being attracted to her about as appealing as an afternoon swim in a pool filled with piss and piranha—

"Do you?" she says quietly.

I jerk my attention away from the whiskey and back to her.

Only a second ago, she looked physically ill when I said it was hot that she was older than me. Now, she looks… fuck. *What is that look?*

I try to keep my voice even when I answer. "Do I what?"

"Only ever go for young women with big boobs."

She sits very still, waiting for my answer, her eyes soft and dark.

My heart stops beating.

Holy fuck.

She's asking if I'm attracted to her.

I want to pull off her glasses and rip her hair out of that stupid fucking bun and kiss her until she's melting. Until she's arching against me, moaning my name.

No, you don't. She's too bossy. Too opinionated. She's a pain in the ass.

Also—spoiler!—she's too damn good for you, so keep your dick in your pants.

My brain is supposed to be in charge, but apparently my mouth is under different management, because I hear myself say, "Historically speaking, yes."

My voice sounds like I just swallowed a handful of gravel.

We stare at each other, gazes locked. Her pulse pounds in the side of her neck. Meanwhile, I'm on the verge of a heart attack.

In the barest of whispers, she says, "What about now?"

FUCK!

I drag in a shaky breath. "Now…"

Don't you dare. Don't you dare fucking do it. You can't be that selfish. There's a million other girls you can bone. You don't have to ruin this, ruin her, just because you wanna get laid.

But the problem is that it's *not* just because I want to get laid.

This has less to do with my dick and more to do with another, more important organ. One higher north in my body.

Which is how I know I have to stop it.

I clear my throat, lean back against the booth, and look at her coldly. "Now I think we should add mute to that list, like you suggested."

There's a long silence as Maddie stares at me. The pink in her cheeks deepens to red. Then she picks up the glass of whiskey and downs the entire thing in one go.

"Okay, superstar. Except you forgot I'm not recruiting women for you anymore."

She refills the glass. Like her voice, her hand trembles slightly.

Disaster averted. Good job, asshole.

I close my eyes and draw a slow breath. When I open my eyes again, Maddie's chugging another whiskey.

"Hey, take it easy there, Pink. That's like three doubles you've had in ten minutes."

She laughs. It's a weird sound, all wrong. "Yeah, who's going to clean all the litter boxes if I get too drunk to do it?"

I lean across the table, take the glass from her hand, and set it down. "Don't do that."

"Do what?"

"Make fun of yourself."

"Oh ho! You're the only one allowed to do that, right?"

"Maddie—"

"Forget it," she says, scooching out of the booth. "I'll see you later."

She stands and immediately wobbles. "Stupid frickin' sticky floor," she mutters, sounding furious. She takes another step and trips.

Before she can fall face first onto the floor, which is obviously contaminated by a wide variety of food droppings, alcohol, and bodily fluids, I stand, pick her up, and toss her over my shoulder.

She bleats like a scared sheep.

The fear lasts exactly one second. Then rage kicks in and she starts to pummel my back with tiny fists.

"Put me down, you beast! Put me down right this minute!"

"Nope." I head toward the door, nodding at the bartender. Unconcerned, he nods back, having probably seen a man carting off an angry drunken woman in his bar a thousand times before.

"Mason!" Maddie nips at my elbow, but misses.

Strangely enjoying myself, I grin. "I had no idea midgets were so bad tempered. Good thing I recently got a tetanus shot."

She gasps. "We *do not* call little people midgets."

"Why not?"

"It's offensive!"

"Since when?" I'm genuinely confused. I had no idea I was being offensive.

"Since forever!"

"But why?"

"Because the term dates back to the late eighteen-hundreds at the height of the so-called 'freak show' era, and it was only applied to people of short stature who were displayed for public amusement, that's why!"

She huffs in outrage.

Fuck, I love it when she does that.

"Oh. Okay. I apologize. I won't use that word again."

I push through the door and wince when the sun blinds me. Then I spot the Benz and head toward it.

In the driver's seat, Dick has a coughing fit as he watches us approach.

When I reach the car, I flip Maddie over and set her onto her feet, steadying her when she starts to lean left.

She looks up at me, squinting. Then she produces a small, ladylike burp.

It might be the single cutest damn thing I've ever heard.

Except she doesn't think so. She slaps her hand over her mouth and stares at me with wide, horrified eyes.

So, of course—being the asshole I am—I laugh.

"Oh, my goodness, please excuse me," she breathes from behind her hand. "That was… oh my. Just *awful* of me. I'm so, so sorry. I cannot *believe* that happened. I swear I'm not normally gassy. And I have *much* better manners than—"

She hiccups, then claps the other hand over her mouth.

Pretending to be stern, I say, "If you fart next, you're so fired. Get in the car, gasbag."

Groaning, she covers her whole face with her hands.

"C'mon, let's go." I open the door and give her a gentle push inside. She collapses into the seat like she wishes it would swallow her. Grinning, I close the door behind her and trot around to the other side.

When I get myself settled, Dick is staring at me over his shoulder.

"What?"

"Nothing," he says innocently. "Nothing at all."

Smiling, he turns around and starts the car.

Beside me, Maddie hiccups again. Hands still covering her face, she slides lower in her seat.

"So this is good information," I muse. "When I'm looking for your next boyfriend, I'll be sure to ask any candidates if they mind if it gets a little windy in bed."

"I don't fart!" she cries, mortified. "And I already said I'm not looking for a boyfriend!"

I try to make my voice sound understanding, but in reality I'm trying hard not to laugh again. "Yeah, and now I get why."

When she peeks at me through her fingers, I smile at her. "You can only blame the weird smells on the litter boxes for so long."

She drops her hands and glares at me. "This is *your* fault! If you hadn't tossed me upside down, I *never* would have—"

"Burped like a sailor after chugging a six-pack of beer? Sure. That's what all the gassy girls say."

She stares at me for a beat, then dissolves into helpless laughter.

Watching her laugh—knowing that *I* made her laugh—makes me want to pound my fists on my chest like Tarzan. But I only sit there beside her, drinking in the musical sound and resisting the violent need to cut it off by crushing my mouth against hers.

Christ. This is getting pathetic. I need to get away from her before I make a complete fool of myself and start spouting poetry.

I must tell Dick to take Maddie home too sharply, because

she stops laughing, and he frowns at me in the rear view mirror like I'm being a total ass.

Which is weird, since he doesn't like her, anyway.

We're silent for the rest of the ride. By the time we pull into Maddie's driveway, she looks like she can't wait to escape from the car.

I'm out of my seat before she can open her door and striding around the back of the car to her side. When I pull her door open and hold out a hand, she hesitates.

She doesn't wanna touch me.

Man, that hurts.

She sees my face darken and smiles. "Don't let the kraken loose. I was just thinking you're a fast learner."

She reaches for my hand. Warm and soft, her fingers slide into my palm. She murmurs, "Thank you," and allows me to help her out of the car.

Then we're standing face to face and I'm trying not to admit to myself how much I like the way she compliments me. How she randomly says these sweet and sincere little things that make me feel good about myself for about five seconds, until I remind myself she doesn't really know me at all.

"I'll walk you to the door," I say gruffly, pulling away and shoving both hands deep into my pockets.

"That's not nec—"

"I said I'll walk you!" I holler. "Are you trying to help me with my manners or not?"

Inside the car, Dick sighs.

But Maddie doesn't react. She only gazes calmly at me, her eyes searching my face. Then she says, "Whatever it is you're angry about, I'd appreciate it if you wouldn't take it out on me."

That's so like her. Straightforward. No BS. She stands her ground but does it politely, with what my therapist would call "respectfully assertive boundaries."

Everyone else freaks out when I get mad. With the exception of Dick, no one has any idea how to handle me.

But this ferocious little steel magnolia knows exactly how to put me in my place without batting an eyelash.

"I'm sorry," I say, meaning it. "I sometimes… it's hard for me to… I have a temper."

When she arches a brow, I rush to clarify. "Not like that. I don't put my hands on women in anger. I'd never, ever do that."

"I know you wouldn't, Mason," she says softly. "But there are a lot of other ways to hurt someone than with your fists."

I blow out a hard breath and drag a hand through my hair. "You're right. I'm sorry."

When she smiles at me, the rush of relief I feel is heady.

"Apology accepted. Now I think maybe you should walk me to the door, because unless gravity is doing something funny and the house is supposed to be tilting like that, I'm very tipsy."

Closing one eye, she squints at her front door.

"I told you drinking all that whiskey so fast was bad."

"Don't be smug, Sparky. It's not a good look on you."

"*Sparky*?"

She takes my arm and leans into me for support, so close her head is right under my chin. "Don't tell me no one's ever called you that before. It's the low-hanging fruit of nicknames for you."

She smells fresh and clean and herbal, the way the air smells when it rains in the mountains.

I love the mountains. I've got a house in Telluride. It's the only place I've ever been happy.

I'm seized in a grip of desire so strong that for a moment I lose my breath.

When I can talk again, I say, "Even if someone did call me that, they wouldn't have the balls to say it to my face."

Maddie tilts her head back and smiles up at me. "Guess my balls must be pretty big, then, huh?"

"Massive."

Stop staring at her mouth. Stop it.

I tear my gaze from her and focus on her front porch instead. "Can you walk or do I need to carry you?"

"Psh. Carry me. As if."

She takes a step, loses her footing, and squawks, grabbing hard onto my arm. "Why is the ground all slippery?"

"That's not the ground, Pink," I say, chuckling. "Up you go."

In one swift motion, I lean over, pick her up, and swing her into my arms.

She's horrified for all of about two seconds, stiff and outraged, then she says, "Well, hell," and slings her arms around my shoulders. Her smile is wide and happy as she relaxes against me. "Home, Jeeves."

I take a moment to examine her fuzzy gaze. "You don't really drink whiskey, do you?"

"Lord, no. That stuff tastes like pure gasoline. How can you stand it?"

"Because I'm so manly."

"Oh, right. I forgot. Are we going to stand here in the driveway all day? Not that I'm complaining. This is surprisingly comfortable. If the football thing doesn't pan out for you, you could start a business carrying tipsy ladies around."

I start up the path to her front door, enjoying her weight in my arms, her smell in my nose, and the feel of her against me, soft and warm. "Like Uber, only more personalized."

"Exactly. And if you took your shirt off, you'd make a killing in tips."

She's noticed my body.

Pretending to be insulted instead of pleased, I say, "I'm more than just a hot bod, lady."

Closing her eyes, she rests her head against my shoulder. "I know. You're smart and funny, too. If only you believed in love and didn't have such a fixation on giant hooters, I could find you a nice girl pretty quick."

"You're smart and funny, too."

Stabbed in the gut. Shot in the chest. Slugged in the face by Mike Tyson.

Never once in my life has anyone said anything nice about my brains, never mind my sense of humor. Probably because I act like I don't have either. It's always my talent at football people are impressed by. That or how much money I make. Or how easily trouble finds me.

But not Maddie.

Maddie who idolizes my arch enemy Tom Brady.

Maddie who calls it like she sees it and doesn't put up with my shit.

Maddie who doesn't give a fuck about money, because she's too busy giving all her fucks about other people's true loves and happily-ever-afters while ignoring her own.

Sweet, sassy, beautiful Maddie, who's drunk at noon on a Sunday because she wouldn't let me drink alone, even though she thinks whiskey is disgusting.

She says, "Are you okay?"

"Yeah. Why?"

"You just made a strange groany noise."

I really wish she'd pass out now. "Maybe you're not the only gassy one."

She giggles. "Maybe, but if I was gassy—and I'm only saying *if*—my farts would smell like rose petals."

"And you accuse *me* of having a big ego?"

"No, seriously. I take vitamin C with rose hips every day. I bet my innards smell like a beautiful rose garden."

"Your *innards*? Woman, you're drunk."

"In the middle of the day, no less," she says happily. "You're a bad influence."

You have no idea.

I walk up the steps of the porch and stop in front of the door. Then I look down at her, nesting comfortably in my arms with her eyes shut. "Hey. Sleepyhead."

"Hmm?"

"Unless you want me to kick down the door, I need a key."

She cracks open an eye and peers up at me. "I'm not falling asleep. I'm trying to stop the world from spinning so much."

"Fascinating. Key?"

Using one hand, she digs around in the small purse slung across her body by a dainty leather strap. She comes up with a single key attached to a ceramic keychain. It's made in the shape of a Harry Potter character.

When I stare at it too long, she says, "Don't look at Hagrid like that. You'll hurt his feelings. He's very soft-hearted."

I say thickly, "I know."

She's a Potterhead.

Because of course she would be. Of course she'd be a fan of the books that saved my sanity as a kid and gave me the only relief I had from the shit show of my adolescence.

Because the universe loves nothing more than to test me over and over and over to see how much I can take before I break.

Swallowing around the lump in my throat, I stand near enough to the handle so she can reach down and insert the key. The door opens, and I nudge it open wider with my knee.

Then I carry my own personal kryptonite across the threshold, my resolve to do the right thing and stay away from her crumbling with every step.

15

MADDIE

So maximum humiliation has been achieved, and it only took a quick mid-day visit to a dive bar to do it.

Me (staring awkwardly): Mason, er, um, *do* you only like young women with big boobs?

Translation: Could you possibly like a dorky, uptight, flat-chested librarian who's constantly barking about your bad manners and to whom you've given exactly zero hint that you might be attracted to, aside from the fact that you stared at her mouth while examining her Meth-Addict Barbie pink lipstick?

Mason (choking back vomit): Yes, I only like young women with big boobs. Mute's good, too.

Translation: You think I'd be interested in old, prim, celibate, opinionated, cat-loving, bun-wearing, pink-obsessed you? Gross.

Me: Commence dying of embarrassment, interrupted at regular intervals by rude bodily noises.

. . .

Yes, it's been a whopper of a day already, and it's not even tea time. Maybe next Bettina will set my house on fire, just to keep the good times rolling.

She'd be doing me a favor. I wouldn't even try to save myself. I'd just lie here on the sofa and cry while I burned.

I'm peeved at the way he looked at my Hagrid keychain, though. You'd think it was naked and vibrating for the way he sneered at it.

"Here. Drink this."

I flip down the corner of the blanket I pulled over my face when Mason laid me on the sofa a few moments ago. He sits on the coffee table across from me, holding a glass of water in his hand, looking huge and handsome and hot.

"It'll help the hangover you're brewing, Pink. You need to stay hydrated."

I concentrate on not slurring my words. "I'm not thirsty, thank you." Then I flip the blanket up again, wishing he'd leave so I could be alone with my crushing shame.

What on earth made me ask him that question?

The idea he'd be attracted to me is ridiculous, as is the idea that I'd care if he's attracted to me or not. I *don't* care. He's not my type. I'm not his type. The two of us have nothing in common.

Even if we did, he's my client! I have a strict rule about not getting involved with clients, or discussing my personal life with them. I've never broken that rule before. Never. I'm a professional, first and foremost. I'm a rock. I'm an impenetrable fortress. I never let down my guard.

Except with this grouchy, egotistical beast of a man who frequently makes me want to put my hands around his thick neck and squeeze the life right out of him.

"It doesn't matter if you're thirsty or not," the beast is growling. "You need to drink the water. Now."

I mutter, "Stubborn much?"

"Trust me, I have a lot of experience with hangovers."

I want to say something tart about other things he has a lot of experience with, but keep my mouth shut. I've done enough damage for one day already.

Besides, I shouldn't judge him. There's no reason he shouldn't enjoy himself with the ladies. He's young, single, and rich. Topped off by gorgeous. It's a lethal combination. I'm surprised he doesn't have a woman crawling out of his underwear right now.

I flip down the blanket and prop myself up on an elbow. Then I take the glass of water from his hand and force myself to drink the whole thing.

Then I burp again, because God hates me.

"Not a word," I warn when Mason's lip twitch. I take the empty glass back under the blanket with me.

When several moments later I hear sniffing, I say, "What are you doing?"

"Seeing if I can detect the scent of roses."

"Shut up."

More sniffing.

"Mason."

"Yeah?"

"You do realize that if I murder you, there's no jury in the world that would convict me, right?"

"You don't wanna murder me. I'm too much fun."

"Fun? Is that what we're having? It feels more like torture."

"You're the one who said your innards smell like roses, Pink. You can't dangle that out there and not expect me to take the bait."

"Point taken. Remind me never to tell you anything personal again."

"You don't have to get all snippy."

"I'm not getting snippy!"

There's a pause, then he says in a stage whisper, "You're getting super snippy."

I sigh heavily. "You're right. I apologize. I'm very embarrassed, that's all."

He sounds surprised. "You don't have to be embarrassed to be yourself around me."

"Thank you for that, but usually being myself doesn't involve unattractive sounds emanating from my body."

Another pause, this one longer. "I don't think your sounds are unattractive."

"You can't see it because of this blanket over my face, but I'm rolling my eyes right now."

"I'm being serious. Your burps are cute."

I know what this is. He's trying to make me feel better for him looking so horrified when I asked him about the young woman/big boob thing. He's hoping I won't fire him.

"I'll add that to your file. 'Enjoys women with robust bodily functions.'"

His voice grows quiet. "I didn't say women. I said you."

My mouth goes dry, and it's not because of the whiskey. "Mason?"

"Yeah?"

"I have to say something now."

"Are you gonna take the blanket off your face?"

"No."

"It's kinda awkward to have a conversation with a blanket."

"It'll be even more awkward to look you in the eye when I'm saying what I have to say, so hopefully you can cut me a break just this once."

I hear him shift around on the coffee table, moving his weight. Then his voice comes from only a few inches away.

"This sounds like it's gonna be juicy. Go ahead."

I like that husky tone in his voice way, way too much for my own good.

I squeeze my eyes shut and grip the glass in my hand so hard it's a miracle it doesn't shatter. "Okay. It's just… the thing is…" I struggle for a second, casting around helplessly for the right words as the world spins slowly underneath my eyelids. "I have an overactive imagination."

Silence.

I hurry on. "And you're… well, I know you're not *intentionally* doing anything, you're just being you, very, um, masculine and whatnot, but… but..."

When I can't work up the courage to go on, he says, "I'm offending you again."

His voice is low and tight and has lost all the teasing from only moments ago.

I flip the blanket off my face to find him leaning close, his elbows on his knees, his expression that of someone who's just been told his grandma died in a tragic knitting accident.

It flips the switch on my tongue-tied problem. I start to gush.

"No! God, no, that's not what I'm saying! You're very charismatic is all—I mean, when you're not being hostile—and my overactive imagination causes me to misinterpret certain things you do and say to mean you're flirting with me—oh, Lord, you're turning green, please don't throw up—and I'm only telling you this so that you won't think you've done something wrong when I start acting like a mental patient, because I really do want to help you, but you were right about me not having much experience with men other than Robert, he was my one serious long-term relationship, and I've been single for a while now, and that's probably making my imagination even worse, and sweet baby Jesus, I'm babbling."

With a whimper, I hide under the blanket again.

Mason lets me lie there in agony for a while, listening to the roar of my heartbeat and praying for the sudden onset of a brain hemorrhage to make it all go away, until he speaks.

"You think I'm charismatic?"

The bastard sounds amused.

"Are you kidding me right now?"

He ignores my outburst. "Masculine, you said, too. And earlier you said I was smart and funny. I sound like the perfect man."

My groan is hopeless. "I've created a monster."

He ignores that, too. "Which is odd, considering you don't like me."

I bolt upright, making the room spin. The glass drops onto the floor and rolls under the couch. "I never said that!"

"So you do like me."

His voice is still light, but his jaw is tight and his eyes are burning, and now I'm utterly confused.

"I'm… I… um…"

"Because you shouldn't."

We stare at each other. It's suddenly very hard to breathe.

His voice lowers an octave. "I'm not a good guy, Pink. You know it. I know it. I'm the bad guy, and that's never gonna change."

I manage to gather enough wits to form a coherent sentence. "I disagree with that."

"Because you don't know me," comes the swift, hard response. "And because you believe in white knights and fairy-tale endings. But I'm the dark knight in this story, the one who kills the prince and sacks the castle and burns the village to the ground. Don't romanticize me. I'm not worth it."

I should be embarrassed. This is a rebuke, after all. He's telling me not to crush on him—which, for the record, I *wasn't*—but this level of sheer ego combined with the stunning depths of his own self-loathing has the opposite effect.

I can't remember the last time I was this mad.

"Number one," I say evenly, staring him down, "if you ever speak about yourself like that in front of me again, I'll fire you, and then I'll smack you silly."

"You'll fire me," he repeats, astonished.

"Be quiet. I wasn't finished. Number two, if you'd stop being so hard on yourself and look at things with some perspective, you'd realize you're no worse than anyone else. Or better, for that matter. You've got your good points and your bad points like the rest of us, but you're not a pedophile or a serial killer or a guy who cuts the tails off puppies."

I pause, realizing I don't know that for sure. "Right?"

His expression sours. "And you were on such a roll."

"Right. Number three, just because I give you a compliment doesn't mean I'm 'romanticizing' you. Friends can tell each other nice things—"

"Friends," he challenges, eyes flashing.

"Fine, business associates. Whatever you want to call it, we're going to be friendly with each other. We're going to have a cordial working relationship—"

"There's that word again," he mutters, rubbing his forehead.

"—because I'm trying to help you," I say over him, "with what you asked me to help you with. Fourth and finally, can we please agree that neither of us is each other's type and there's no flirting or attraction of any sort going on so we can get on with it and find you a wife?"

He tilts his head, examining me with narrowed eyes. "You said you weren't recruiting women for me anymore."

I grimace. "That was an unfortunate turn of phrase."

"So you changed your mind?"

I swing my legs over the edge of the couch and try to ignore the prison riot breaking out inside my stomach. "Everyone deserves a happily-ever-after, especially people who don't believe in them."

He stares at me, thinking so hard he's about to burst a vein.

With my final shred of dignity, I say, "Now, if you'll please excuse me, I need to get to a sink before my Eggs Benedict reappear."

I stand, wobble into the kitchen, and promptly throw up into the sink.

Instantly, Mason is there beside me. He sets a warm, steadying hand between my shoulder blades as I retch.

"That's an insane amount of food," he comments nonchalantly, as if I'm not barfing up my intestines along with several other important organs. I think I see my liver in between the mess of bright yellow yolks and soggy clumps of muffin.

Another wave of nausea hits, producing another violent retch, followed by a stream of undigested Canadian bacon. Or it could be a lung. It's hard to tell, my eyes are watering too much from the alcohol fumes.

"I'm so gonna use this against you later," says Mason, sounding tickled by the prospect.

Shaking and panting and still bending over the sink, I say hoarsely, "If you do, I'll set you up with a girl who secretly loves the Patriots, and you'll have to listen to her call out Tom Brady's name in bed."

"Wow, that was evil! Good for you, Pink. I didn't think you had it in you."

"Yes, you better watch out. I'm chock full of evilness."

"And vomit," he says as I retch again.

When it's all over and I'm slumped against the counter, sweaty and disheveled and moaning faintly like a ghost, Mason says cheerfully, "Hey, when are you gonna introduce me to your cats?"

If I don't end up stabbing this man repeatedly with a sharp object, I'll be shocked.

When I lift my head and glare at him, he chuckles.

"You're cute when you're contemplating murder."

"Call me cute one more time and see how far you can get with smashed kneecaps."

He says innocently, "I thought friends were allowed to compliment one another?"

"Are you always this subversive, or am I special?"

"I have no idea what you mean," he says, still with that air of innocence, though it's obvious he's lying.

"You're lucky that in my post-vomity state, I'm too weak to kick you in the shin."

He rubs a slow circle over my back. He voice turns soft, and so do his eyes. "You're not gonna kick me in the shin, tiny violent one. Now do you want me to help you to your bedroom, or do you wanna go lie back on the couch?"

"Bedroom, I think. But I don't need any hel—"

Mason does a ninja-quick bendy move and picks me up in his arms. Too wrung out to protest, I rest my head on his broad shoulder and try not to breathe barf fumes into his face.

"You're never going to listen to a thing I say, are you?"

"Of course I am. Here, let me prove it to you: where's your bedroom?"

"Down the hall and to the left. But directions don't count."

He strides out of the kitchen, carrying me as if I'm as light as air. "Directions totally count."

"They don't."

"Do so."

"You're proving my point here, Sparky."

"I don't know how I feel about that nickname." He turns the corner into my bedroom, being careful not to bang my feet against the door frame.

"What's wrong with it?"

"It sounds kinda Christmasy."

"Bah humbug. "

"I just don't wanna be called a name that sounds like it belongs on an elf or a reindeer, that's all."

"But elves and reindeer are adorable!"

"Exactly. I don't do adorable. You wanna call me Thor or Rambo, go right ahead."

He bends over the bed and eases me down onto it, adjusting

the pillow under my head. Then he pulls off my shoes and drops them on the floor, ignoring my feeble protests that I can do it. Finally, he shakes out the folded blanket I keep at the foot of my bed and settles it over me, tucking it under my feet.

Then he catches a glimpse of my face.

"What?"

"Nothing."

"Really? Because that's a whole lot of nothing."

He's repeating my words again. I wonder if he has whatever the audio equivalent of a photographic memory is. "It's just that for such a big macho swaggery dude, you're quite maternal."

He pulls a face. "Great. What every guy wants to hear, that he reminds you of a mother."

"What's wrong with being compared to a mother?"

"Nothing, if you don't have a dick."

Despite my weakness, fuzzy head, and overall feeling of ickyness, I smile. I'd make another smart crack about the size of his ego, but I don't want to hurt his feelings.

I'm starting to get that he's much more sensitive than he'd ever admit.

He disappears into my bathroom. I hear some rummaging around, then he returns with two aspirin and sets them on the nightstand next to the bed. "Water," he says, then disappears again, this time to the kitchen. I hear the faucet turn on and off. He reappears with a full glass of water, which he sets next to the aspirin.

Then he stares down at me with his hands propped on his hips. "Take a nap. You'll feel better when you wake up."

"Promise?"

"Pinky swear."

I'm oddly comforted by that. "Will you promise me something else?"

"Yeah, but only because you're in a weakened condition.

Don't try this when you're back up to 100% feisty mode, because I'll say no."

"Okay, but don't get mad."

He arches his brows. "Why would I get mad?"

"Um, it could be a tad insulting."

His brows slowly lower over his eyes. He folds his arms over his chest and stares down at me.

"Don't try to intimidate me. I'm still going to say it."

"What a surprise," he growls.

I blurt it out before the top of his head can explode. "I want you to call me the next time you have the urge to visit a bar."

There's a long, thundering silence. His gray eyes glitter like ice in the slanted light. He gives his jaw a workout for a while, then says through gritted teeth, "Why?"

Too sick to roll my eyes at him, I smile instead. It takes fewer muscles. "Because those places are feeding grounds for women like Bettina, and I can't have you running off with some gold-digging wench before I can get you your happily-ever-after."

He considers it for a moment. "Why did you think that would be insulting?"

"That was only the first part."

He looks at the ceiling, muttering, "I shoulda guessed."

"The second part is that I suspect the way you deal with your anger is to drown it, and I hate to think of you angry and alone shooting whiskey when you could be angry and with me doing something more productive. We could go bowling. Work off some of that rage. Stop staring at me like I just landed on your lawn in my spacecraft."

He exhales slowly, shakes his head, and uncrosses his arms. Leaning down over me, he gently removes my glasses. He folds them and sets them on the nightstand next to the bed.

I close my eyes because the bed is swaying.

He murmurs, "I can't picture you bowling, Pink."

"I don't. But I'd learn for you. Will you please draw the curtains?"

I hear him moving to the windows, then I hear the swish of the drapes across the rod. The red light beyond my lids dims to a more comfortable gray.

Then I feel the lightest touch at my temple, the barest brush of a fingertip across my skin.

"Sweet dreams," whispers Mason, pushing a stray lock of hair off my forehead.

Then he's gone, and I'm drifting into queasy slumber, recalling something troubling from our conversation before I fall asleep.

"Can we please agree that neither of us is each other's type and there's no flirting or attraction of any sort going on?"

He never answered my question.

16

DICK

When Mason comes outta Maddie's house and I see his expression, I feel the kind of fear I haven't felt since the day I opened my front door twenty years ago to the sight of two grim-faced cops who wanted to have a word with me about my son.

His step is slow and heavy. His gaze is fixed on the ground. His normally proud, straight shoulders are slumped in defeat. The boy looks like he's carryin' the weight of the entire world on his back.

I've seen him enraged a thousand times. Seen him drunk and disorderly, too, and every good and bad emotion in between.

But I've never seen him look like he's walkin' outta his own funeral.

He opens the passenger door and gets inside. We sit in heavy silence for a minute, until he speaks, his voice tight.

"You're the only person I can halfway trust, and I'm grateful for everything you've done for me. But if you say a single bad word about that girl from now on, I'll never talk to you again."

Knowin' him like I do, I know he needs a minute to work through whatever's got him tied up in such knots before he comes out with it. So I start the car without a word and head back to the house, keepin' my mouth sewed up and my eyes on the road.

Finally, when we're turnin' down the street to his place, he speaks.

"She's an innocent."

I ain't exactly sure what that means, so I keep my trap shut and wait.

Mason takes a breath. "She's just… good. Kind. She wants other people to be happy. That's like her whole fucking thing. Her whole life. Getting people together, helping them find someone to take care of them, making sure they're okay. She actually believes all that stuff about true love."

He pauses, then says faintly, wonder in his voice, "She really *believes* it."

Unsure how to answer, I decide to be Switzerland and stay neutral. "Yep."

When he speaks again, his voice sounds tortured. "And it's not like she's had this perfect fairytale life, either. Did you know her parents were killed in a car crash when she was a teenager?"

When I look at him in surprise, he nods. "Yeah. And she was in the back seat. How'd you like to survive the crash that killed both your parents?" His voice rises. "And how do you walk away from something like that and not have it ruin you? How can you still be so positive?"

His volume goes up another notch. "How can life fuck you over like that and you still want to take some asshole you just met bowling so he doesn't have a drink?" He roars, "*And you don't even know how to bowl!*"

"Uh…"

"And she sticks up for midgets who aren't even there!"

"Uh…" Shit. I got nothin'.

"And she sticks up for *you* when you're tearing yourself down! And she's funny and real and likes Harry Potter and is one of only two people in the whole world who isn't afraid of you!"

He turns to me, eyes wild. "What am I supposed to do with all that?"

Oh boy. We got a meltdown on our hands. We just slammed right into DEFCON 1. Nuclear war is imminent.

I count to three and say a prayer to the holy trinity of Joe Montana, Johnny Unitas and Peyton Manning before I answer. "If she bothers you so much, the best thing is to stay away from her."

He stares at me with crazy eyes for a long, tense moment, until finally all the anger drains out of him. He exhales, turning to look out the window.

"You're right," he says quietly. "That's it, then. Call her tomorrow and tell her we're going with a different matchmaker."

"Will do, champ."

Oh, I'm gonna make a call, all right. Except not to Little Miss Sunshine.

Here's how it works, ladies and gents. You tell yourself a story long enough, you start to believe it. Even if it's not true. Even if it's absolute bullshit. And the story Mason's been tellin' himself his whole life is that he deserves all the bad shit that's happened to him. That he's rotten to the core, a magnet for disaster, unloved and unlovable, despite any evidence to the contrary.

Because hating yourself is the only acceptable option if the alternative is hating the person who was supposed to love you the most.

So no matter how much he might want to turn toward the light and let a kind and soft-hearted girl into his life, he's not gonna let it happen without a fight.

Which I knew goin' in.

Lucky for him, he's got fairy godfather Dick on his side.

And I'm about to wave my magic wand and sprinkle a shitload of pixie dust all over the place.

17

MADDIE

When I walk into the office on Monday morning, Auntie Waldine is already there, sitting behind the reception desk. She's hunched over the phone with the intense concentration of a hostage negotiator.

"Uh-huh," she says, sending me a distracted wave as she continues her conversation. "Goodness. I see. Honestly, I have to confess it doesn't surprise me one bit." A short pause is followed by a cryptic, "I have my ways."

I bypass her desk and enter my office. As is her custom, my aunt has already poured me a mug of hot coffee. It waits for me, steaming, on my desk.

One of the benefits of sticking to an inflexible schedule is that others can always rely on you to arrive exactly on time.

As I get myself settled and fire up the computer, Auntie Waldine continues her conversation. Her answers are spaced with pauses as she listens to whomever is talking on the other end.

"I agree, but Lord knows, looks can be deceivin'. Mmhmm. Oh, no, she'd have a dyin' duck fit." A delighted cackle. "Land's end, you're so right!"

She's gossiping with her best friend, Celia, no doubt. The two of them are thicker than thieves. When the other line rings, I pick it up so she can continue talking.

"Good morning, Perfect Pairings. This is Maddie speaking. How may I help?"

"Good morning, Madison," says a male voice I recognize. "Did I catch you at a convenient time?"

I lean back in my office chair, pick up my mug of coffee, and blow across the surface. "You did. I just walked in. How are you, Bobby?"

"Excellent, thank you. Glorious weather we're having, isn't it? Perfect day for croquet."

He tries, Lord knows he tries, but the man is hopeless.

"Yes, it is. How's your mother?"

His bright tone falters. "There isn't much the doctors can do except make her comfortable. She's in hospice care now. At this point, it's only a matter of time."

I know how difficult this must be for him and feel terrible about it. He and his mother have always had a close relationship. She's a sweet woman. And being an only child, he's going through this alone.

At least I had my older brothers to lean on when my parents died. Bobby has no one.

"I'm so sorry to hear that," I say gently. "Is there anything you need? Can I help with something?"

He clears his throat. "Actually, I was hoping we could have lunch together today. I've been at the hospital since right after church yesterday, and I could use a break."

I was thinking more along the lines baking him a casserole, but lunch works, too. "Of course. Should we do Antonio's? That's near the hospital. About noon?"

"That would be so great," he says warmly, relief echoing in his voice. "I'll pick you up at your office."

Picking me up sounds a little too close to a date for my

liking. The last thing I want to do is give him the wrong idea, and Mason's comment about Bobby being an addict and me being crack has stuck with me. "Oh. Um. Or I could meet you there?"

"Nonsense. I'll see you at noon."

He disconnects without waiting for my answer or saying goodbye, which isn't like him. His manners are always impeccable. Then again, his mother is dying. He's bound to be out of sorts.

"Who are you havin' lunch with at Antonio's?"

I jump at the sound of Auntie Waldine's voice. When I look up, she's hovering over my desk like a vulture.

"Bobby," I say, taken aback at her sudden appearance. "Weren't you just on the phone?"

She sails right past my question, perching on the edge of my desk to more comfortably continue the frontal assault. "So tell me all about brunch yesterday, child. Did Mason and Bettina hit it off?"

I put the phone down and take a sip of coffee before answering. "Believe it or not… no."

"*Really*?" Wide-eyed, she ponders that for a moment. "And here I thought they'd be two peas in a pod."

"You and me both. But for some bizarre reason, he wasn't interested."

When she stares at me like I'm as dense as a block of cement, I say, "What?"

She makes a motion with her hand like she's swatting away a fly. "I had an idea about another candidate for him—"

"No," I interrupt firmly. "No more of your 'ideas'. Matchmaking is a delicate science, requiring considerable thought and a logical, methodical approach. You can't just throw people together and see what sticks. And you definitely can't rely on the superficial. You have to know what people really *need*, which isn't necessarily what they say they want."

"You're saying you have to look beyond the surface to see what's in people's true hearts."

"Exactly."

Auntie Waldine's smile is small and mysterious. "Sounds more like magic than science to me."

I gaze at her sternly. "Don't go there. I haven't even had my coffee yet."

She rises and heads back to her desk, saying over her shoulder, "One of these days, dear girl. One of these days."

I call after her, "Whatever the heck that means!"

But she's already picking up the phone again and dialing.

When Bobby arrives at my office at noon, he brings a bouquet of flowers with him. I try not to feel like it's a bad omen.

"How thoughtful," I say, taking the flowers from his hand. "Thank you."

He stands in the reception area, looking like an ad for Brooks Brothers in a beautiful gray cashmere sweater with a dress shirt and tie underneath. A pair of black slacks and leather loafers complete the look. Though I suspect he must've come straight from the hospital, he doesn't look like a man who's been sitting in an uncomfortable chair beside his dying mother's bedside for days on end.

If Bobby has any flaws, it's vanity. He's too concerned with appearances and what other people think. He wasn't that way when he was younger, but I suppose a career in politics could bring out the inner narcissist in anyone.

"You're welcome," he says, smiling at me. Then he leans in and gives me a dry peck on the cheek.

Sitting at her desk, Auntie Waldine calls out, "Mornin', Bobby!"

"Hello, Waldine," says Bobby, turning to her. "How are you today?"

"Finer than frog's hair," she replies enthusiastically, grinning like a maniac.

I'm immediately suspicious. The last time she looked this happy, she'd been in contact with her great-grandmother's ghost.

Ignoring my narrow-eyed look, she rises and rounds her desk.

Today she's wearing a nuclear green tunic over stretchy black leggings. Her sandals have multi-colored, chunky fake jewels on the straps. Her toenails are painted a searing shade of yellow to match her fingernails, and a series of strategically placed glittery combs hold up her curly red hair.

This mass of color and sparkle engulfs a startled Bobby in a hug.

"Oh, honey," she says, patting him on the back. "You're such a dear. Don't you worry, it'll all work out for you in the end. Capricorn is in your eighth house. Very auspicious."

Oh, for fig's sake. She did his astrological chart before he got here.

"Leave him alone, Auntie Waldine."

But Bobby isn't bothered. When he pulls away, he's smiling. "Good to know." He glances at me. "What about Madison? What's in her eighth house?"

When she looks at me, I shake my head. "Don't even think about it."

She smiles like a buddha.

Bobby says politely, "Would you like to join us for lunch?"

"Don't I wish!" She laughs. "But, no, thank you. I brought a bologna sandwich today that I simply can't *wait* to dig into."

Without another word, she takes the flowers from my hands and disappears down the hall that leads to the office kitchen, cackling to herself with the glee of an evil mastermind as she goes.

Bobby looks at me. "That must be some special bologna."

I know there's more to it than the dang lunch meat, but shrug it off as another of her peculiarities. She's probably off to cast a spell on some pesky neighbor.

"It was kind of you to extend the invitation."

His gaze softens. "I didn't do it for her."

Oh dear.

We head off to lunch, while I try my best to ignore the feeling there's a black cloud following us as we go.

Antonio's is an upscale Mexican restaurant in the heart of midtown and is famous for its Cadillac margaritas. I've enjoyed quite a few over the years, and order one as soon as we're seated to settle my nerves.

I keep telling myself it's my aunt's strange behavior that's got me jittery, but don't quite believe it. There's a tension in the environment I can't put my finger on, the electric feeling of a storm approaching, as if the air itself is holding its breath.

"This is nice," says Bobby, folding his napkin over his lap. "I'd forgotten how much I like this place."

"Are you still enjoying DC?"

His chuckle is dry. "Aside from the crime, the traffic, the smog, and the outrageous cost of real estate? Yes. It's a very vibrant city. And the culture is fantastic. It seems like there's a new ballet, opera, art exhibit, or restaurant opening every night. And, of course, the history can't be beat."

"It's always been on my bucket list."

"You'd love it." He picks up the menu and starts to study it. "You'll come visit me and see."

I'm not sure how to respond to that, so I take a sip of my margarita to buy some time. Fortunately, I get a reprieve when the waitress arrives to tell us the daily specials.

As soon as we order and she leaves, however, Bobby picks up right where he left off.

"My condo overlooks the Potomac. I've got three bedrooms, but there's a guest suite in the building, too, if you prefer."

It hangs there like a dare.

I wonder if this is something he picked up in Congress. This way of asking without asking, with a not-so-subtle assumption that the answer is yes.

It feels slick. I don't like it.

I take another swig of my margarita and set it down on the white linen tablecloth. Then I look at him and decide to bite the bullet. "Why did you really ask me to lunch today?"

He looks surprised.

"I only ask because I'm getting a strange vibe."

"Vibe? You're starting to sound like your aunt."

I'm starting to feel like her too, because I could swear that cloud I sensed following us earlier has settled around his head and shoulders like a dingy gray fog.

I blink several times to clear my vision and it's gone.

Time for new glasses.

"So there are no ulterior motives here? You really only wanted to catch up?"

He gazes at me for a beat, then a small smile curves the corners of his mouth. Looking pleased, he nods.

"This," he says, his voice warm. "This is why I wanted to have lunch with you. You can't imagine how difficult it's been to adjust to spending all my time with people who never say what's really on their minds."

"I'll take that as a compliment."

"Believe me, it is." His smile grows wider. I can tell it's genuine.

I'm relieved for all of about two seconds, until he starts to talk again.

"Now that I'm thirty, I'm eligible to run for the Senate when my current term in the House is up. And this situation with my mother has forced me to confront my own mortality."

Uh-oh. It's never good when a man realizes he isn't going to live forever.

Bobby takes a breath. "I've been thinking a lot about my future... and who I want to spend it with."

Off in the distance, I hear a dull boom of thunder. Or maybe it's my imagination. Either way, I'm officially freaked out. "Please tell me you're saying you want to hire me to help find you a wife."

He takes the margarita from my hand, sets it aside, and clasps my cold hand between his own. "No, Madison," he says gently, staring deep into my eyes. "What I'm saying is that since we broke up two years ago—"

"Nineteen months." I'm desperate to interrupt this oncoming disaster. But it's like trying to stop the Hoover Dam from bursting by sticking a toothpick into the gushing crack in the side.

"My mistake. As I was saying, I haven't found anyone I'm as compatible with, and I doubt I ever will. We just mesh. We have so much in common. We come from the same place. We've known each other all our lives. We *get* each other. And you're a wonderful, intelligent woman who would be such an asset to my career. You're so sensible."

Sensible. Like a pair of orthopedic shoes.

I say, "I'm overcome with emotion. Get the smelling salts ready, the swooning's scheduled to start any second."

But my sarcasm doesn't deter him. He soars straight over the edge of Niagara Falls in his leaky barrel.

"Marry me, Madison. It's the logical thing for us both."

My expression must betray my complete lack of enthusiasm for the idea, because he gets defensive. "It's not like you're in a relationship. I asked around."

"Brilliant. I don't have anything else going on, so I might as well marry you?"

"Not to toot my own horn, but I'm told I'm quite a catch."

"I'm not fishing. And how the heck did we go straight from an invitation to visit you to a marriage proposal? My head is spinning."

"I've had a long time to think about it."

I make a face at him. "Like from the car to the table? Before yesterday, we hadn't even spoken since the last time we broke up."

"That connection's always been there. It's why we keep getting back together. We should make it permanent this time. I'm ready to settle down."

How convenient for him that he's unconcerned what *I'm* ready for. "You're forgetting what I told you when we last broke up, Bobby."

He gives my hands an encouraging squeeze. "I know the importance you put on romantic love, but there are other kinds of love that are just as important. The love between two best friends, for instance. The love that comes from knowing you can always rely on someone. The solid, enduring kind of love built on a shared past and similar dreams of the future. Not every relationship needs passion to make it work. In fact, many married couples are happily sexless."

I pause to give him some serious stink eye. "Have you discovered I've inherited a large amount of money I don't know about?"

Failing to move me with his highbrow arguments, he goes low.

"You're not getting any younger, either. Tick-tock."

"Holy… why do you assume I won't clobber you with one of my shoes for saying something so offensive?"

He shakes his head. "You're too sensible for that."

"Bobby?"

"Yes?"

"I dare you to call me sensible again."

I get the feeling he wants to drop his head into his hands and groan.

Then I get another feeling, an intense and crackly one that reminds me of the time I stuck a paperclip into an electrical outlet when I was a kid to see what would happen.

When I turn my head toward the source, the electrical crackle detonates over every inch of my skin.

In the foyer, next to the restaurant's mascot of a toothy paper-mache burro wearing a sombrero, Mason stands staring at me.

18

MASON

As if from far away, I hear Dick say, "Aw, shit. That's Maddie over there. I'm sorry, champ. Let's go to a different restaurant."

My brain agrees, but every other part of my body is in revolt.

My feet won't turn me around.

My mouth refuses to give an affirmative answer.

My stomach has dropped to somewhere around my ankles, and my dick…

Let's just say my dick thinks he's a gladiator and has drawn his sword.

Seeing Maddie sitting at that table across the restaurant holding hands with Robert the robot and gazing deep into his eyes has made nerves I didn't even know I had bristle like porcupine quills.

Any second now, I'm gonna start pawing the ground and snorting.

Dick's voice comes from that distant place again. But now, instead of apologetic, it's soothing. "Easy, Mace. Take a deep breath."

"I'm fine."

Funny, but it sounded like I said, "She's mine."

I need to start scheduling my therapy sessions for more than once a week.

Maddie turns her head. We lock eyes across the restaurant. I'm instantly juiced by a thousand volts of energy.

I'm electric. I'm on fire. I'm Frankenstein's monster with lightning scorching through his reanimated veins.

Without looking away from Maddie, I say to Dick, "We're staying. Get us a table. I gotta hit the head."

I turn and walk to the restroom before he can answer. Once inside, I take out my cell and send Maddie a text. ***Meet me in the men's room.***

I have to pace to manage the adrenaline lashing through me until she answers back a few minutes later.

Did you mean to send this to Bettina?

I send her the emoji that looks like an angry face with the top of its head exploding.

She texts back: ***You blew me off last night. Now suddenly we're meeting in the toilet?***

She texted me three times yesterday, starting from a few hours after I left her house. The first one was an apology for ruining my Sunday. The second one was a request that I call her so she could apologize over the phone. The third one, a few hours later, was only ***Hello?***

A while after that is when she called. In her voicemail, she used words like "ashamed" "mortified" and "inexcusable." It sounded more like a confession of murder than an apology for throwing up in the sink.

It took every ounce of willpower I had not to call her back, but I stayed firm.

I was proud of my self-control.

Now here I am, less than a full day later, sending her panicked texts from a restaurant john sixty seconds after I see her face.

Pathetic.

I text her a lie in a last-ditch effort to get her in here so we can talk. ***My phone was off. Didn't know you were trying to reach me until now.***

Then I stand there staring at the phone in my hand, cursing silently at it when it fails to produce a response.

"I was under the impression we'd agreed about the honesty thing, Sparky."

I jerk my head up and see Maddie standing inside the men's room door, her arms folded over her chest. I was so preoccupied with the stupid phone, I didn't hear her come in.

"We did."

"For the record, texts count in that agreement."

"What makes you think I wasn't being honest about my phone?"

She eyes me. "Were you?"

Fuck. "No."

She exhales a slow breath and unfolds her arms. "I don't blame you for avoiding me. Yesterday was a hot mess, and that's my fault. But I would've preferred getting fired via text than in a men's room."

She glances at the wall behind me. Her eyes widen. "A men's room with a disturbing painting hanging over the urinals of Jesus and Elvis Presley sharing a platter of nachos at a bullfight. Dear God."

Dick already told me in the car coming here that he hadn't made the call yet to tell her we were going with a different service, so I know her comment about getting fired is based on guilt, not fact.

Which makes me feel like an asshole.

"I wasn't gonna fire you."

She turns her attention away from the painting and examines my face. Then she folds her arms across her chest again, tilts her head down, and looks at me over the top rim of her glasses.

I'm in for it.

Before she can rag on me for being the degenerate liar I am, I turn the tables.

"But I am curious about your lunch date. Looks pretty hot and heavy, considering you said you weren't in love with him. Is that standard procedure, fibbing to your clients about your love life?"

My attempt to distract her works, because she groans. "What you saw out there isn't my love life. That's the Titanic right after they discovered they ran out of lifeboats."

From her obvious misery, I realize I misinterpreted what I saw. She wasn't gazing deeply into the robot's eyes… *he* was gazing deeply into *hers*.

Instantly, my hackles go up. All my protective instincts slam into overdrive.

I step closer to her. "What's going on? Is he bothering you? Do you need me to go out there and set him straight?"

Startled, she glances up at me. "Oh, look, we're growling again. Have you thought of taking one of those DNA tests to see if there's a bear somewhere in your family tree?"

"I'm serious, Maddie. If that guy's bothering you, I'll break his teeth."

She gazes at me for a moment in silence, then smiles. "I can't believe I'm going to say this, but that's actually very sweet."

I feel myself bristle again, getting ready to smash something. "Is that a yes?"

Her sigh is exasperated. "Calm down, Hulk. It's a no." She mutters to herself, "A marriage proposal is hardly cause for ruining twenty grand worth of dental veneers."

"He asked you to marry him?"

I know my tone was way too loud because an aggravated male voice says from one of the stalls, "Hey, pal, you mind keepin' it down? I'm tryin' to take a crap in peace over here."

Maddie gapes at the closed stall door with that queasy look

like she's about to barf again, so I take her by the arm and lead her out of the john.

Once we're in the hallway, I steer her to a quiet area behind a bunch of potted palms.

"Sorry about that."

She says smartly, "Which part? Calling a meeting in a public restroom so our conversation can be eavesdropped on by a stranger emptying his bowels, or acting like a man proposing marriage to me makes about as much sense as that painting over the urinals?"

A flare of anger tightens my stomach. "Why do you always have to take things I say about you the negative way?"

"Why do you always have to have conversations near a row of toilets?"

"I *don't*."

"Neither do *I*."

Standing a foot apart, we stare at each other, unblinking, breathing hard. She's pissed off and so am I, but I can't remember exactly what happened to get us this way, because there's a voice inside my head screaming *Kiss her! Kiss her! Kiss her!* and it's taking all my concentration to ignore it.

Eyes blazing, she says, "You know, before I met you, I hadn't argued with anyone in fifteen years."

"Doubtful. That tongue of yours is way too sharp to be outta practice."

Her face flushes. Her eyes flash. Her mouth makes that angry, puckered shape, and holy fuck, I want to kiss this woman so bad I can taste it.

She says, "I'm going to walk away now."

"Go ahead. No one's stopping you."

We keep staring at each other. Neither one of us blinks or moves.

"Am I fired?"

"No."

More staring. I want to latch my mouth onto that pulse pounding in the side of her neck and suck on it, hard.

She says, "Okay, then."

"Fine."

"Good."

"Yeah."

"Fine."

"That's what I just said."

"I know."

"Fantastic."

"Yep."

"Thought you were leaving, Pink."

When she moistens her lips, I almost groan out loud.

There's a moment, a long, breathless moment when I'm sure she's gonna go up on her toes and kiss me. A crackle grows between us, a strong sense of pull. A gravitational, irresistible attraction, hot and elemental, like superheated magnets.

Like magic.

On instinct, I lean closer to her. My hands shake. My heart pounds so hard it hurts.

Then a concerned voice says, "Madison?" and the spell is broken.

We look over, and there he stands in all his baffled, over-groomed, robotic glory.

"Is everything all right?"

"Yes, Bobby," says Madison, blinking like she just woke up from a dream. "Um. Yes." She slowly exhales. "We were just… I was just…"

"Talking to Mason." His gaze sharpens. "Yes, I see. Hello, Mason. How are you?"

Bobby approaches us warily. Maddie jerks away from me like we've been caught plotting the overthrow of the government. I have to force myself to drop my hand to my side and not reach for her again.

"Swell. You?"

"Excellent, thank you."

We size each other up while Maddie stands to the side, looking shell-shocked.

She wanted to kiss me. I know she did. I fucking *know* it.

What I don't know is if that makes everything better, or so much worse.

Bobby asks pleasantly, "Are you here alone?"

"Having lunch with my agent."

"Ah. That's unfortunate. I would've invited you to join us."

He smiles at me. We both know he's lying.

Glancing at Maddie, he says, "Madison, why don't you go back to the table? Your entrée has arrived. It'll be getting cold."

"Good idea. Bye, Mason." She turns and flees.

Someone being chased by a tiger couldn't run any faster.

When she's gone, Bobby's veneer of civility vanishes. With cold disdain, he says, "She's too good to see what you are, but I see you loud and clear, friend."

I actually appreciate this. At least when the gloves come off, we can talk man to man. I despise all that bullshit polite small talk required in normal social interactions.

"'See you loud and clear' doesn't make any fucking sense, genius."

His cheeks turn ruddy. "Pardon me, but I refuse to have a battle of the wits with an unarmed opponent."

"Good one. How long you been waiting to use that in a conversation?"

"Just stay away from her," he says more loudly.

"Tried that. It lasted exactly twenty-one hours."

"Then try harder."

I take a step toward him. My voice comes out deadly soft. "Or what?"

I see him fighting himself not to step back, and I almost feel sorry for him.

Almost.

Until he says, "You don't deserve a woman like Madison."

This fucking asshole.

"Agreed."

He doesn't know what to make of that. But it only takes him a second to dust himself off and get right back up on his high horse.

"Even if she had a momentary lapse of judgment and consorted with the likes of you, it would be temporary. She'd come to her senses and dump you back into the gutter where you belong. Your notoriety can't hide the fact that you're nothing but trash. You're beneath her."

The class card. I really love that one.

I heard a lot of it when I was growing up. It used to make me feel ashamed. Dirty, like I carried my poverty on my skin so everyone could see my ugly layer of grime.

Now it doesn't make me feel ashamed so much as it makes me feel like breaking something.

Shaking with fury, I take another step toward him. This time he does take a step back. His eyes widen in fear.

I snarl, "The only reason you're not lying in a pool of your own blood right now, you pretentious little prick, is because I know Maddie wouldn't want me to hurt you. But let me tell you this: if you upset her again, if I find out if you've made her even a tiny bit *miffed*, I'll make it my personal mission to fuck you up so bad you won't ever be able to upset anyone about anything ever again."

I walk away from him before I slam my fist into his nose and head out to find something else to slam it into.

19

MADDIE

By the time Bobby returns to the table, my post-Mason nuclear glow has worn off, and I feel like lying down somewhere cool, quiet, and dark where I won't be disturbed.

The morgue, for instance.

I almost kissed him.

No—strike that. I almost threw myself at him and ripped off all his clothes with my teeth.

I honestly have no idea what came over me. Nothing like it has ever happened to me before. One moment I was so mad I could spit, the next my panties were on fire and the two of us were starring in our own personal porno inside my head.

And he was doing the dirtiest things to me. The *filthiest.*

Things I couldn't even tell my pastor about because he would probably drop dead on the spot.

"You didn't have to wait for me to start eating." Smiling, Bobby takes his seat and drapes his napkin over his lap. He picks up his knife and fork and methodically starts to deconstruct his order of chicken tacos.

There are few things he finds more distasteful than eating with his hands.

I pick up my fork, too, and pretend to remember how to use it.

"I'm going to walk away now."

"Go ahead. No one's stopping you."

Infuriating. That's the word for Mason. He's bossy, grouchy, mystifying, moody, and utterly infuriating.

And gorgeous.

And complex.

And protective.

And masculine, in the best sense of the word. If I were stranded on a desert island, he'd be the one I'd want with me. I have no doubt he'd know how to hunt for food and make a fire and build us shelter from the rain, all while fending off wild animals with tools he made with his own hands. Or, if he didn't know how to do any of that, he'd easily figure it out.

Because he's that guy. Shaky with social graces. Solid where it really counts.

Or maybe I'm romanticizing him again.

Realizing Bobby has asked me a question, I focus on him and push my thoughts of Mason aside. "Excuse me?"

Bobby's pleasant smile doesn't falter. "I was just asking if you've known Mason Spark for long."

"Not really."

He waits for me to provide more detail, utensils hovering over his plate. Because of the non-disclosure agreement, I can't tell him how we really met, so instead I try deflection. "How are your tacos?"

"I haven't tried them yet." He takes a bite, chews thoughtfully, then says, "Interesting guy. He's not at all what I thought he'd be like."

I know I don't have to ask. Even if I tried to change the subject again, his opinion will be forthcoming in five, four, three, two—

"Much nicer that his reputation suggests." He chuckles,

shaking his head. "Though it seems his reputation with the ladies is spot on."

I have to take a sip of water to calm my nerves before I speak. "There's nothing going on between us."

I'm not sure if that's technically the truth or not, considering what's mainly going on is an escalating exchange of hostilities. But I forget about the technicalities when Bobby looks up at me, appearing surprised.

"Of course there's not. I know you're much too smart to date someone like him. I was talking about his phone call."

I'm caught between curiosity and irritation. The "someone like him" comment doesn't sit well with me. I know what he means, and I don't like it. But curiosity wins out. "What phone call?"

Bobby turns his attention back to his plate of food. "After you left, we chatted for a moment, but then he took a call from a woman. It sounded quite steamy."

I stare at him. "Woman? Steamy?"

He shrugs. "I was standing close enough to hear a woman's voice on the other end of the line. I thought he might excuse himself to take the call privately, but as soon as he heard her voice, he forgot I was there. When it became apparent they were about to engage in phone sex, I excused myself."

I want to ask what exactly the imminent arrival of phone sex sounds like, but I find myself unable to speak. My face stings as if I've been slapped.

Bobby continues, oblivious to my sudden stillness.

"When I came out of the restroom a few moments later, he was gone." He chuckles. "I assume he had more pressing things to attend to than lunch."

I look toward the entrance of the restaurant, but don't see Mason or Dick. They're not sitting at any of the other tables, either.

A wave of heat starts in my chest and rises all the way to my hairline.

Mason got a booty call. In the middle of the day. *And left to go hit it.*

That son of a goat.

But I can't blame him for anything. He's done nothing wrong.

I'm the idiot here, not him.

If it wasn't obvious enough how laughable Mason thought it was that a man proposed to me, his lies about his cell phone dying and not wanting to fire me should have been a clue how he felt.

I remember every moment of our recent bathroom encounter in excruciating detail and feel like a moron.

He didn't offer to knock Bobby's teeth out because he was being protective. He did it because he knocks people's teeth out on a regular basis. That's his thing.

That and dive bars and young, big-breasted women.

Abruptly, I'm angry with myself. Here I am fantasizing over a man with whom I have nothing in common, a man who's given me no indication he's interested in me, a man I argue with constantly and have never even kissed.

A man who flat out told me not to like him.

A man who's simply paying me to do a job.

Which, so far, I've utterly failed at.

The verdict is in: I'm being ridiculous.

I set down my knife and fork slowly. I turn my plate clockwise until the pattern on the rim aligns with the edges of the table. I straighten the salt and pepper shakers, move my margarita next to my water glass, and fold my napkin into perfect thirds on my lap.

Then I eat my lunch, listening to Bobby's pleasant chit-chat while I count backward from one thousand in my head until the rock in my throat and the fist in my stomach have gone and I feel nothing.

~

That day comes and goes. I force my temporary insanity over Mason to go with it. Bobby drives me back to the office after lunch. We part on good terms, and I wish him good luck.

When he brings up the marriage idea again, I tell him it's not going to happen.

He reminds me how much my mother loved him and how much his mother loves me, and I tell him it's still not going to happen.

Then he gives me another dry peck on the cheek and says he'll be there for me when I change my mind.

The confidence he has that I won't be getting any other offers of marriage leaves me feeling like wilted lettuce. I go home and stare at myself in the mirror until I can't tell if I'm pretty, plain, or as ugly as a donkey's behind.

It never mattered much to me before. Mainly, I try to look professional. My father used to tell me I was pretty as a peach, but boosting a child's self-confidence is right up there on the scale of parental responsibilities.

This was also a man who thought fried banana and peanut butter sandwiches were the height of human achievement, so his opinion is obviously suspect.

I know I'm not a beautiful sex bomb like Bettina, but I'm not a garbage can, either.

I also know that most of my clients are what would generally be considered attractive, but not gorgeous. Not even close. They're somewhere in the middle, like me. Like most people, I suppose.

So if all these nice people of average attractiveness can find love and get married, why does Bobby think he's my only hope?

The worst thing about it is that he knows me better than almost anyone.

Which means he might be right.

Which is more depressing than all the memories of how I've behaved with Mason combined.

"The matchmaker can't make her own match. That must be awkward for business."

Over the next few days, Mason's words come back to haunt me with such irritating frequency, I start to wonder if he had a point.

I'm at my desk late on Friday afternoon, having spent most of the day in meetings with new clients, when Auntie Waldine wanders in, eating a dill pickle. She settles into the chair opposite my desk and smiles.

"How you doin', child?"

"Peachy keen, thanks for asking."

Staring at me with an air of contemplation, she crunches on her pickle while I tap on the keyboard, trying to will her away. The woman has to be the world's loudest eater. She could be snacking on a marshmallow and somehow make it sound like she's grinding her molars on a mouthful of rocks.

Finally, she says lightly, "Oh, I nearly forgot."

It sounds like she really means, "I've been thinking for days of exactly the right way to say this." With a sigh, I settle back into my chair and wait.

Smacking her lips, she swallows the last bite of pickle. "Did you see there's a Harry Potter marathon goin' on over at the AMC?"

I jolt upright, almost knocking the jar of pens off my desk in the process. "No, I didn't see that! When does it start?"

"Tonight, I think." She licks pickle juice from her fingers, one by one, then sits there with her hands in the air like she's waiting for a genie to appear and blow dry them.

I hand her a tissue. "Thanks for letting me know. I'll go online right now and buy tickets. Would you like to join me?"

She gives me a look like I need to seek medical attention. "No, thank you. I've already seen every one of them blasted movies a million times. If I have to hear the name Hermione again, my brain will turn to jelly."

"You're assuming it hasn't already."

She tuts. "Careful, now. I've still got a key to your house. I'll de-militarize your pantry and rearrange everything by calorie content instead of size, shape, and color."

I think about that for a moment. "That's not a bad idea."

She crosses herself then beseeches the ceiling. "Heavenly Father, where did I go wrong?"

My parents took me to see the Harry Potter movies when they first came out when I was a kid. But after they died and Auntie Waldine moved in to take care of me and my two brothers who were still living at home, I played the videos on TV in what she complained was a continuous loop.

I know now that my obsession with those characters is part of how I dealt with my parents' death, that in some dark room of my adolescent subconscious I believed watching the movies religiously might bring them back. But over the years Harry, Hermione, and Ron became my closest friends. I cheered their victories and agonized with them in their defeats.

I loved them more than most people made of flesh and bone.

Especially Hermione. I still think she's the real hero of the story. Without her fearlessness, brilliant mind, and loyal companionship, Harry would've never defeated Voldemort. He probably would've been killed off in the first book.

As I go onto the movie site to buy a ticket, Auntie Waldine asks how my meetings went.

"Really well. All three of the ladies were referrals from past clients, and the older gentleman found us from that ad you placed in the American Airlines magazine."

"Did they all sign up?"

I nod, clicking on show times. "I was thinking the tall blonde, Stephanie, might be a good match for Mason Spark."

"Did you now."

Her tone is oddly indulgent, a verbal pat on the head, but I'm too busy selecting my seat in the theater to give it more than a passing thought.

"Yes. She ticks most of the boxes on his list, but more importantly, she seems patient and kind. And down to earth, which is a non-negotiable. He needs someone with real values, not a Bettina clone. And in Stephanie's job as an independent mediator, she's also got a lot of experience in conflict resolution."

I smile, thinking of the sound of Mason's growly voice. "I'm sure that skill will come in handy."

"Oh, yes, I reckon that boy'll be mighty impressed with her work experience."

I can hear the eye roll in my aunt's voice. A twinge of irritation tightens my stomach. "Don't mock him."

She chuckles. "I wasn't, child. I was mocking you."

I look askance at her. "Why?"

But just then the phone rings. She rises from her chair and saunters out of my office to answer it at her desk, whistling "Witchcraft" by Sinatra as she goes.

I complete the ticket purchase and get back to work, wondering if everyone has relatives as strange as mine.

Four hours later, I'm happily munching on buttered popcorn in a dark theater. It's only one quarter full, which is nice because I don't have to shush people around me or tell them to stop texting like I usually do. By the time the credits roll, I've got a happy buzz from the supersized soda I drank and the company of my dear friends at Hogwarts.

I'm gathering up my coat and purse when I spot a familiar figure walking up the aisle.

I'd recognize those broad shoulders and bulging biceps anywhere.

Almost simultaneously, Mason recognizes me. He stops dead a few rows down and stares at me.

I recover first. Making my way slowly out of my aisle, I pause at the last seat and wait for him to stop looking like he's been hit in the face with a shovel. Then he shoves his hands into the front pocket of his jeans and says gruffly, "Hey."

"Hey, yourself." I look past him, expecting to see a woman walking up, but everyone else has already filed out. He's alone.

"What're you doing here?"

I'm irritated by his tone, which seems to indicate he thinks I'm stalking him. "Watching a movie. You?"

"Same. What're the odds?"

"Pretty good, considering movie theaters are where they usually show movies."

A corner of his mouth quirks. "Smartass."

"Yes, but you have to take some responsibility. You make it so easy for me."

The quirk turns into a full-blown smile. I try not to notice how handsome he looks with a few day's scruff darkening his jaw, his hair in need of the attention of a comb, and wearing a grayish T-shirt that could pass for a dishrag, but fail.

The man could be naked and covered in motor oil and still look incredible.

Now that I think of it, that's a bad example.

He walks closer with his long, easy stride, still smiling. "Are you in the wrong theater? I think *Cats* is playing next door."

"Very funny. You missed your true calling as a comedian." My tone is sour, but I'm not mad. In fact, the irritation has vanished and suddenly I'm so happy I could burst into hysterical giggles.

Lord, this is so bad.

To manage the hormonal surge seeing him has unleashed, I say, "I think I found a girl for you."

His smile vanishes. He cocks his head and examines my expression for a moment, then says softly, "Oh, yeah? Who?"

"Her name's Stephanie. She just signed on with Perfect Pairings today, but I think you'll really like her. I was going to send you an email about her next week after I vetted everything."

"Next week," he repeats, sounding doubtful, like maybe he already has plans to be out of town. Or maybe I'm misreading that, and he's hoping I'll send him the information sooner.

"I suppose I could expedite things."

For a moment he seems deep in thought, working his jaw and gazing at me steadily. Wheels turn behind his eyes. Then he seems to decide something, because his shoulders relax and he exhales.

"You doing anything right now? We could grab a quick bite and go over it."

"Well, I did have important plans to bathe my herd of kitties and read them *The Cat in the Hat* by Dr. Seuss before bed, but I suppose I could reschedule."

Gray eyes alight, Mason says with a straight face, "A group of cats is called a clowder. Or, if you're talking about kittens, a kindle."

When I merely blink at him, he says, "But I give you credit for the excellent customer service. You're really going above and beyond."

"Don't you forget it, pal. When I find you a wife, I expect a fantastic reference letter."

He looks like he's about to say something. Whatever it is, he decides against it and holds out his arm instead.

I take it, pretending I have no desire at all to squeeze the bulging muscles under my hand, and we head out of the theater into the balmy spring night.

20

MADDIE

Mason leads me away from the theater and we start down the street, arm in arm. "No Dick tonight?"

He chuckles. "That sounded all kinds of wrong. But no. I took a taxi here. Dick's at home. Probably watching Sports Center in his underwear and eating a frozen dinner in front of the television."

"He lives alone?"

"Yep. Got divorced twenty years ago. Never remarried."

"Oh no! I'll have to think of someone for him. What's his type?"

Mason glances down at me. The streetlights cast a lovely golden glow on his hair. "You ever think some people might not like being married?"

"Meh. Those people just married the wrong person. Everyone has a true soul mate somewhere out in the world. That one person who gets you," I snap my fingers, "like that. Who you feel at home with. The hard part is finding them. After that, marriage is a walk in the park."

"You sound like you're speaking from personal experience."

I inhale, enjoying the scent of night blooming jasmine in the air. "My parents had the best marriage I've ever seen, so I suppose I am. Living with two people who loved each other more than anything else was definitely an experience. Don't get me wrong, they loved us kids, too, but…"

"But what?" Mason prompts, riveted.

I try to think of the right way to put it. "Some people make their children the center of their universe. But in my parent's case, they were the sun and we were the planets that revolved around them. They were complete unto themselves. Even if we'd never been born, nothing would have been missing from their world. We were a welcome addition, but not a necessary one."

My sigh is wistful. "That's what true love is: your own private galaxy where you're whole and happy, everything makes perfect sense, and you never have to feel alone again."

We walk for a moment in silence, until Mason says, "Bullshit."

His hard tone startles me. "Excuse me?"

An elderly couple passes us, bickering. Mason waits until they're out of earshot to speak again.

"Just what I said. That definition of true love is a fantasy fueled by romance novels and Disney movies. Nothing is perfect, especially not relationships, and there isn't a person alive who can make another person whole."

Insulted, I say, "What's your definition, then?"

He stops and turns so we're facing each other on the sidewalk. Looking down at me, he's all burning eyes and blazing intensity, anger rolling off him in waves.

"I wouldn't know. I've never experienced it. But I sure as hell do know that the higher the pedestal is that you set your idea of love on, the more you'll be disappointed when reality fails to meet it."

"People fall in love every day."

"They fall out of it every day, too."

"There are plenty of marriages that last entire lifetimes!"

"There are way more that die within a few years."

I'm so riled up I want to stamp my foot, but I know that would be silly. And driving my heel down onto his toes would be downright rude. Instead, I try to convey my anger with my eyes.

If only they had a pair of built-in lasers.

"So you're going to go into a marriage expecting it to be temporary? I'm trying to find you a wife so you can dump her in a few years? Why are we even bothering?"

"I already told you."

Exasperated, I throw my arms in the air. "To make your dang agent happy?"

He looks at me long and hard, his jaw clenched and his nostrils flaring. "Sometimes we do things we don't want to do for other people because it makes them happy. Or it keeps them safe." Looking me up and down, his eyes flash. "Or because it's the right thing to do for *them*, despite your own feelings."

His voice grows tight. "You know what? *That's* my definition of love. Putting someone else's best interests before your own, no matter what it costs you."

"And what about your future wife? What about her best interests?"

He snaps, "She'll be well compensated for her time."

I snap back, "What if she doesn't want your money, Mason? What if what she really wants is *you*?"

His voice rises. "Then she's got something wrong with her head."

I say through gritted teeth, "You blind, stubborn, impossible man. There are a million women out there who would love nothing more than to be with you and share a life with you, and not because of your blasted money!"

I hate it that my voice shakes, but I keep on, because if I don't get this out, I'm liable to explode.

"You're intelligent, handsome, funny, and talented. You're kind and sensitive, too, even though you go to great lengths to hide it. Yes, you've got a problem with your temper, and your manners are rough, and maybe you've got other problems I don't know about, but like you said—nothing is perfect. And nobody is, either.

"And if you would just pull your dang head out of your dang butt and stop being so committed to the idea that you're a piece of crap, you'd see that any woman would be lucky to have you!"

We stare at each other. The air between us is living fire.

Then I whirl away and continue down the sidewalk, sucking in deep gulps of air and trying my hardest not to scream in frustration.

One of these days, the man is going to give me a coronary.

In a few moments, Mason catches up to me. His legs are so long he doesn't even have to change his stride as I storm full steam ahead.

We barge down the sidewalk for a while until we come to a small Italian restaurant. It has a green awning and a red neon sign that reads, "Cassinari's." Mason grabs my arm and steers me off the sidewalk and down the steps to the entrance. He pulls open the door and swings me through it, following right behind.

"Table for two," he barks at the young hostess standing inside.

She makes a small peep of terror. Wide-eyed, she grabs a pair of menus, then skitters away.

We follow her to a table in the back corner. The hostess tosses the menus on the table, then runs away in fear, leaving us sitting across from each other in blistering silence.

We grab the menus and glare at them for a while, until a smiling brunette waitress appears at our tableside.

"Good evening," she says pleasantly, addressing me. "Welcome to—"

Mason shouts, "We'll have the spaghetti carbonara and the chicken scaloppini with two house salads and a carafe of red wine."

The waitress pauses a moment, waiting for her hair to settle back around her shoulders. The she says calmly, "I take it you're not interested in hearing this evening's specials."

I like this girl.

"No, thank you," I say, before Mason can blast her again.

We hand her our menus and she leaves.

When it becomes apparent we could spend the entire meal in hostile silence, I decide to be a grown up and speak first. "I'm sorry I yelled at you."

His answer is immediate. "I'm sorry, too."

"Truce?"

"Truce." His lips twitch. "Though I'm sure it will last all of two minutes."

"If that, considering I'm about to tell you I wanted the lasagna."

He covers his mouth with his fist, trying not to laugh. "And here I was trying to be a gentleman."

"I applaud the effort. But for future reference, women don't need to have a man order their meals for them. It's infantilizing and patronizing."

"So many rules."

"You have no idea. Wait until we get to advanced etiquette and you have to identify which fork is for oysters and which is for shellfish."

He crinkles his nose. "Oysters are shellfish."

I smile at him. "Correct. You just passed your first etiquette test. But don't get too cocky, because the dessert fork looks a lot like the shellfish fork."

This time he doesn't hide his laugh behind his fist. "And here I thought a single fork was all I needed to eat a meal. Silly me."

God, he's handsome when he's smiling. He's got a face that was made to melt panties, and that's a fact.

He says, "What?"

I realize I've been gazing dreamily at him and redirect my

attention to unfolding my napkin and arranging it on my lap. "I was just wondering what happened to your hand."

I glance up at him. When his smile vanishes, I'm sorry I asked.

He flexes open his right hand and examines his scraped and bruised knuckles with a dark, dangerous look in his eyes. "I started working out with a heavy bag."

"How interesting. Now how about you tell me the truth?'

He mutters, "*Jesus*, you're a pain in my ass."

"The Lord has nothing to do with it. Spill, Sparky, or I'll tell your future wife you have a fetish for ladies underwear."

"I do have a fetish for ladies underwear."

"I meant wearing it."

His quicksilver mood changes again. He smiles, pausing to consider me. "You would've made a great spy."

"How so?"

"You look so innocent, but there's this whole mob boss thing going on under the wholesome exterior."

"*Wholesome*? You make me sound like a loaf of multigrain bread."

He says drily, "It's a compliment, Pink."

"Psh. I'd hate to hear what your insults sound like. Oh, wait. I already know."

"Are you trying to pick a fight with me? Because you know I'm up for it."

Now it's my turn to laugh. "Yes, that I do know for sure."

The waitress returns with a basket of rolls. Before setting it on the table, she looks at Mason for approval, her brows arched.

He gestures at the tabletop. "Please."

"Just checking. One learns to tread lightly in minefields." With a wink in my direction, she turns and leaves.

"I take it you come here often," I say.

"At least a few times a week. And Lauren takes every opportunity to abuse me."

The way he says it indicates he enjoys the friendly abuse. My curiosity is piqued. "Is this where you take your dates?"

He pauses for a beat, then starts to fiddle with his knife. "I don't take anyone here."

That's right. He already told me what his normal "dates" consist of, and they don't involve going to restaurants. "You eat here that often alone?"

Looking at his knife, he answers. His tone is quiet and dry. "In case you haven't noticed, I'm not the kind of person who has a lot of friends."

I'm seized by the irrational urge to pull him into a hug and pet his big dark head while murmuring things to comfort him. I sit with it for a moment, amazed how he can bring out my maternal side only a few minutes after I wanted to push him into traffic.

He gives me emotional whiplash.

"I usually eat alone, too. Unless Auntie Waldine comes over, but she's got a big group of very social lady friends who are attached at the hip. They're always going dancing or trying the hot new restaurants. She calls them her coven."

I smile, thinking of her. "I'm not completely sure if she's being ironic."

"How many of them are there all together?"

"Eleven. No, wait. Including my aunt, there's twelve."

Mason nods. "Yep. That's a full coven all right. If you see any glass jars at her house labeled 'eye of newt,' back away slowly." He glances up at me and catches my expression. "*Now* what?"

"You said 'eye of newt.'"

"And?"

"I was just wondering how many people would have any idea at all what that means. Or where the reference comes from."

He sits back in his chair, folds his arms over his chest, and sends me one of his superior, down-his-nose looks. "Was that last part a challenge?"

"No, Thor, it wasn't a challenge. I was complimenting you. Put your ego back in its booster seat."

"Because I do know where the reference comes from."

"I have no doubt. Can we move on?"

"Macbeth."

"Congratulations. You've read Shakespeare."

He studies my expression. "You don't seem surprised."

"Remember that time, like ten minutes ago, when I said you were intelligent?"

"Yeah."

"Did you think I was lying?"

He takes a moment to think about it. "No. But for some reason you have a blind spot when it comes to me."

I drop my head into my hands and sigh. "You could make the pope go on a killing spree."

"Though from what I can tell, you think too much of people in general. Everyone is good in your eyes."

I lift my head and say tartly, "You're forgetting about Satan."

He snorts. "Even Helen Keller could tell Bettina is no good."

I wag my finger at him. "Don't say anything mean about Helen Keller. That woman is a national treasure. And it's not right to make fun of people with disabilities. Their lives are challenging enough as it is without being the butt of jokes."

He gazes at me for a quiet moment, his eyes growing warm. "You're right, Pink," he says softly. "My bad."

It seems like he's saying something else than the words that came out of his mouth, but I don't know what it might be. Still, the look in his eyes flusters me. I have to look away before my face starts to redden.

The waitress returns with our carafe of wine. As she's filling our wineglasses, she says, "You guys officially started practice yet?"

"We start OTAs on Sunday," says Mason. "Training camp starts next month."

"Cool. I'm going to draft you for my fantasy football league, so make sure you kick ass this season."

He puts a hand over his heart. "I'm flattered."

She gives him a sour look. "Don't be. You're my third choice for QB after Drew Brees and Baker Mayfield, but I figure since you tip so well, I'll move you up. But if you suck on the field this year, don't come back here expecting to get good service. Your entrees might get dropped onto the kitchen floor a couple times before they make it to your table."

He says to me, "You said that was a cockroach you saw on the carpet? We should give the health department a call."

The waitress smiles. "Don't forget to tell them about the cockroach you're going to find in your spaghetti." She turns and leaves.

I *really* like this girl.

I lean in and say in a lowered voice, "Have you ever thought about dating Lauren? She seems great."

In response, he simply stares at me.

"Right. I forgot about your infamous List of Ideal Female Attributes. She doesn't have the blonde hair, giant boobs, or pretty much anything else. Wait, where were the sense of humor and sharp intellect on that list?" I pretend to think. "That's right —they were *missing*."

He mutters, "Here we go."

"Along with honesty, integrity, responsibility—"

"Oh, please," he says, rolling his eyes. "I'm not looking for an accountant."

"—compassion, kindness, respect—"

"Or a nurse."

"—spirituality, wisdom, inner harmony—"

"Or a guru. Just a wife, Pink. That's all I need. Let's keep it simple."

I pick up my knife and point it at him. "Okay. *That*. That right there is probably the single most offensive thing I've heard lately, and I've been hearing a lot of offensive things from you men."

He adopts an air of strained patience. "Is this gonna take long? If so, I should visit the restroom first."

I ignore him. "'Just' a wife is insulting on so many levels. Shall I name them for you?"

"No. Not that you're gonna listen to me."

I have to decide whether or not to launch into an explanation, considering he's expecting me to do just that. Ultimately, I arrive at the conclusion that nothing I say or do will change his mind. It's not my job to change anything about him, anyway.

I set my knife down and take a swallow of the wine. It's dry, full-bodied, and very good. Unlike my mood, which has taken a nosedive.

"Uh-oh," says Mason, smiling a lopsided smile. "The lips are pinched. I'm in trouble now."

I sniff disapprovingly. "I'm sure I have no idea what you're talking about."

His smile turns heated. "God, I love it when you get prissy."

"And I hate it when you call me that."

"I've never called you that before."

"Oh, *excuse* me. Prim and puritanical were the other two P-words I've been the lucky recipient of." I eye the knife longingly, imagining myself embedding it into his chest.

"But since we're on the topic of prissiness, I noticed you weren't wearing an engagement ring."

Ugh. He's talking about Robert. "I think I'll need to have a lot more of this wine before we broach that particular subject."

He stares at me like a police interrogator, waiting for me to break, until I sigh in defeat. "Okay. You win. What do you want to know?"

He leans forward, resting his elbows on the table. "You said no to his proposal?"

"Bingo! Give the man a prize."

"But you said he was so perfect for you. That you had so much in common, blah, blah, blah."

That elephant's memory of his is started to get annoying. Especially because it's selective. "I also said I wasn't in love with him, remember?"

His gaze sharpens. "So, what you're really saying is that all that nonsense about shared goals, dreams, and backgrounds is just the undercard. The main event is *twue wuv*."

"Wow. You just mixed boxing metaphors, blistering sarcasm, and a classic movie quote in one neat package. Truly, you have a dizzying intellect."

He pauses. "Did you just quote the same movie back to me?'

With a straight face, I say, "Mawwiage. It's what bwings us togevah today."

For some strange reason, me quoting the lisping clergyman from *The Princess Bride* makes Mason look anguished. He sags back into his seat, scrubs his hands over his face, and softly groans.

I watch all that, wondering what on earth is wrong with him. "Am I giving you heartburn?"

He exhales deeply, shaking his head. "You have no idea."

"I'll leave if it will make you feel better."

"Here, gone, it's all the same. I'm screwed."

I scrunch up my face and stare at him. "I'd ask if you're drunk, but you haven't even had a sip of your wine yet."

Looking morose, he stares at his wine glass. "You're right." He picks up the glass and downs the entire thing in one big swallow.

"Oh, we're doing this again? Good times. Remind me not to text you later to apologize after I throw up. Inevitably, we'll end up in a restroom somewhere shouting at each other."

He gazes at me, his empty wine glass gripped in his big hand. Then he starts chuckling. "Don't forget the guy taking a dump."

"How could I? I'm scarred for life."

The waitress arrives with our salads. We're quiet as she sets down the plates and wishes us *buon appetito*. She refills Mason's wine glass, then leaves.

We munch for a while, until I can't hold my tongue any longer. "There's something I need to say to you."

He freezes. "Oh God."

"Don't be such a wuss. It's not bad."

"I'll be the judge of that." He sits back, bracing his arms against the table. "Go ahead, then."

"Look at you, drama queen. You're sitting over there like you're facing a firing squad."

His tone is bone dry. "You say that like you're *not* a firing squad."

I wave him off impatiently. "What I need to say is this: I can't in good conscience set you up with anyone if you can't promise me that you'll give her a real chance."

When his face darkens, I say, "Hold on, you can yell at me after I'm done. I meant what I told you the day we met about not being in the business of fake relationships. I want to help you find someone, but you have to give me your word that you'll go into it with an open heart."

"*An open heart*?"

He looks like he's suffering from the sudden onset of acid indigestion.

"Sorry, macho man. I meant open mind."

He glares balefully at me.

"You can stare daggers at me all you want, but I'm serious about this. I know how cynical you are, but it's not fair to pretend to be looking for something permanent if all you really want is someone to twiddle your dingwallace while shoring up your bad reputation for a while before you send her off with a golden parachute."

After about thirty seconds of silence, he says, "I don't even know where to start. No, wait. I do. *Dingwallace*?"

"Can we just agree that you'll consider it?"

He narrows his eyes. "Consider what, exactly?"

"I'll spell it out for you." I lean forward over my salad plate and pin him in an unblinking gaze. "Falling. In. Love."

He stares at me with matching intensity, his gaze roving over my face. I can see his internal struggle, how hard he's thinking, how many times he starts to say something but stops.

Finally, he says in a husky voice, "All right. I'll consider it."

I'm so surprised by that, it takes me a moment to recover. "You will? For real?"

He moistens his lips. Then he swallows, hard, his Adam's apple bobbing. "Yeah. For real."

"Great. Wow. I'm…I think I'm speechless."

"Give it a few seconds. You'll recover."

I'm too thrilled to be put off by his sarcasm, so I beam at him instead. "This is exciting! I feel like I just saved you from throwing yourself off a cliff!"

"When actually it's the exact opposite."

"Don't ruin my fun. Moments like these are literally what I live for."

"I know, Pink," he murmurs, smiling gently at me. "I know."

21

MADDIE

I'm so excited by Mason's willingness to be open to the possibility of falling in love for real that I spend the rest of dinner selling him on how great Stephanie is. By the time we've finished eating, I've built her up so much Mason says he doesn't believe a word of it.

"What's wrong with her?"

"Nothing's wrong with her! She's wonderful!"

Walking beside me back to the theater where my car is parked, he shakes his head. "I'm not buying it. If she's as amazing as you say, why does she need a matchmaker?"

"Because she's a career girl. She's busy. And she doesn't want to deal with Gumble or Pinder or any of the other internet dating stuff where that cute guy you swipe on is probably skinning cats in his spare time."

Mason chuckles. "I think you mean Bumble and Tinder."

"Potato, potahtoe, whatever. My point is that hiring a matchmaker is a much more safe and customized experience. Wait a minute, why do I have to explain this to *you*? You hired me!"

"Dick hired you," he says drily. "I went along with it kicking and screaming."

I harrumph. "Like the big baby you are."

He slants me a look. His smile is suggestive. "Oh, I'm big all right."

"I'd roll my eyes, but I don't want to encourage you. Here's my car."

Mason stops short, gaping at my car. It gleams under the parking lot lights like a black pearl. "This? *This* is what you drive?"

"Don't be sexist. A woman is perfectly capable of handling a muscle car."

He stares at it like he's just made a sighting of Bigfoot. "This isn't a mere muscle car, Pink. This is a 1966 Shelby Cobra Super Snake."

"So?"

Looking around like he's expecting armed robbers to pounce out of the bushes any second, he hisses, "So do you have any idea how much this is worth?"

"A lot, apparently, because everywhere I go random dudes throw themselves onto the hood and beg me to sell it to them."

His voice rises an octave. "Why don't you? How do you have this? What the hell is happening right now?"

Digging my keys from my purse, I say, "Calm down. Why are you acting like a lunatic?"

"*This is my dream car*."

I stop digging and look at him. "Really?"

He thunders, "*Yes*!"

"Then why don't you buy one?"

He roars, "*Because there are only two of these in existence*!"

"Huh. I didn't know that." I shrug. "Or maybe I did and I forgot."

He grabs his head and makes a garbled noise, as if he's choking on something.

"Relax, will you? I'll let you drive it if you want."

I reach for the driver's door to unlock it, but Mason leaps on me, grabbing my hand.

"No! Nobody is driving this! You can't put more mileage on her. She's too precious. We'll call a flatbed tow truck." When I stare at him in disbelief, he adds, "Your storage facility is climate controlled, right?"

"What the heck are you talking about? I keep this in my garage!"

He looks like I've just told him the Patriots won the Super Bowl again.

I shake him off, unlock the door, and settle myself into the driver's seat. Mason stands outside with his hands on top of his head, staring wide-eyed at me.

"Get in, Sparky."

"I can't let you drive this home."

"Why on earth not?"

He thinks for a second in panic, casting around for an excuse, until he blurts, "You've been drinking!"

"Nice try. I had three sips of wine with dinner."

"You could still be over the legal limit!"

I sigh, because this is getting ridiculous. "If I was driving a Toyota, would you be worried about my blood alcohol level?"

He tries to look indignant but totally fails. "Of course I would."

I squint up at him, standing there unhinged, and have an epiphany. "Oh shoot."

"What?"

"There's a reason Dick always drives you everywhere. Your license is suspended."

As if he's won the argument, he says enthusiastically, "Yes!"

"For a DUI?"

"No, for considering things like the speed limit and red lights as suggestions." Then, after a pause: "Why did you think he was driving me?"

I make a face, not wanting to admit it. "Your ego?"

"Seriously?"

"Don't act like it's out of the realm of possibility."

He folds his arms over his chest and stares down at me. "I'm disappointed you would think that about me."

"Get in the car."

He gives the car a thorough once-over, then looks back at me, his gaze dubious. "Are you a good driver? You don't tailgate, do you? That front bumper is original. I don't want it getting scratched."

"Get your behind in this car before I peel out of this parking lot in a plume of smoke and run over your giant feet." I lean over and open his door. "*Now.*"

With a grudging grunt, he gives up and ambles around the rear. He gets in the passenger seat so slowly and carefully I could have time for a nap.

"I'm dying of old age over here."

He settles in, sighing in pleasure. "God. Look at the condition of the leather. Pristine. I've had blow jobs less exciting than this." He looks as if he's about to get naked and roll around on the floor like a dog.

I warn, "If you start removing your clothes, I'll kick you out. Even if we're on the freeway."

When I gun the engine, he lets out a little moan.

"Okay, it's getting weird now, Sparky."

Running his hands reverently over the dash, he says, "How do you have this car, Pink?"

"It was my dad's. He loved cars. He was a race car driver."

He stops fondling the dashboard and looks at me. "Your father was a race car driver?"

I put the Cobra into reverse and pull out of the parking spot. "Why does everything I'm saying make you act like you're having a religious experience?"

"I wanted to be a race car driver when I was a kid."

Surprised, I glance at him. "Me too."

He does that cartoon character thing where it looks like his eyes are about to pop out of his skull. "What? *You*? No."

"Please stop talking before I'm forced to physically harm you."

"I just… can't…" He shakes his head as if to clear it. "You're blowing my mind."

"Well, believe it or not, yes. I wanted to race cars, just like my dad. Two of my brothers were into computers and photography. Another was pre-med. Another was an artist. None of them thought cars were cool. But I did. I thought racing was the coolest job in the world. I thought my dad was cooler than Steve McQueen. That's why I got this instead of them when my parents died."

I pause for a moment, awash in memories. "But after the accident, I didn't want to race cars anymore. In fact, I couldn't get into a car for more than four years. All my friends were getting their driver's licenses in high school and I was still riding my bike. It took a lot of therapy before the nightmares stopped."

We drive in silence. I feel Mason looking at me, but don't glance over at him.

"By the way, where am I going? I don't know where you live."

"I'm in Buckhead."

"Of course you are."

"Don't judge me for being rich."

That makes me smile. "You're right. I'm sorry. Life must be terribly difficult for you."

"Snob."

"Rich guy."

"You say that like having money is a bad thing."

"Money itself isn't good or bad. It's what you do with it that matters."

After a moment of silence, he says, "I take it you've never been poor."

He gets quiet after that, and so do I. We drive through the city lost in our own thoughts, until we come to the swanky part of town known as Buckhead.

Mason says, "Left here. Follow it up four blocks, then make another left. I'll direct you from there."

As we go, the houses get bigger and bigger and farther apart. Mason tells me which streets to turn on, until finally we're idling in front of a massive stone wall interrupted by a wrought-iron gate so large and elaborate it could pass as the entrance to heaven.

"Punch one-nine into that keypad." Mason nods to the small black box on a stand on the left side of the driveway. I pull forward a bit, then lean out and key in the numbers.

"What else?"

"That's it."

I turn to look at him. "Your passcode is only two digits?"

"It's my jersey number. Why are you staring at me like that?"

"Because that's got to be the least secure entry code in the history of entry codes."

He shrugs, as if security doesn't matter. "I wanted something I wouldn't forget."

The gates swing open. I press my foot on the accelerator pedal, shaking my head in disbelief.

The disbelief turns to shock when, after what seems like a mile long drive down a beautiful gravel driveway flanked on either side by huge willows, an enormous estate comes into view. It looks like a palace.

"Oh my God. Is that where you *live*?"

"Yep."

"How many people live there with you?"

"None."

We drive closer. I lean over the steering wheel to look up and take it all in. It's the hugest residence I've seen in my life. "How big is this place?"

"Thirty-four-thousand square feet on seventeen acres."

I burst out laughing. "I've visited theme parks smaller than this!"

He stares at it through the windshield with a faint air of distaste. "I told my real estate agent I wanted the biggest place available. This is what I got."

"Wow. Your electric bill must be a killer."

He smiles, but it doesn't look like a happy smile. "I wouldn't know. Everything gets paid through my money manager."

"Well. That must be great."

"You'd think."

The undercurrent of dissatisfaction in his tone is so strong, I want to ask him why he lives here if he dislikes it so much. But I hold my tongue and keep driving, until he tells me where to stop. I put the car in park and thank him for dinner.

He turns to me, startled. "You're not coming in?"

It's my turn to be startled. "Oh. Um. Did you want me to come in?"

He jerks his thumb at his mansion. "Don't you want a tour?"

"Of Hearst Castle? No, thanks."

His expression tells me how incomprehensible that is. "Everyone always wants a tour. Always."

"I mean, it's a very nice place, I'm sure."

Now he looks insulted. He turns to stare at the house, then turns back to me. "*Nice*?"

"Please don't take it personally. I'm not trying to start World War III here. A house like that just isn't my thing."

"Your *thing*?"

"Will you stop repeating everything I say?"

"It's just that I'm having trouble with the fact that you don't like my house. Everybody likes it. Everybody. Especially women."

I sign in exasperation. "Oh, for goodness' sake, Mason, I could give a flying fig what everyone else thinks. I'll take my cozy little cottage over this place any day."

"*But why?*"

I fold my arms across my chest and turn my torso toward him. "Why are you so upset that I don't like it when you don't like it, either?"

He shouts, "I never said I didn't like it!"

"You didn't have to. The closer we got to it, the more you constipated you looked."

"That's just my face!"

"Baloney. You hate your house. Admit it."

Wild-eyed and wound up, he stares at me for a long, silent moment. Then he exhales in a huge gust and drops his head into his hands.

He says miserably, "I totally hate it. It's awful, isn't it?"

I pat his shoulder. "It's beautiful, elegant, and absolutely ridiculous. Have you thought about asking the state legislature if they need new headquarters?"

He moans into his hands. "I don't even have any furniture except a bed. You should hear how bad it echoes in there. And everything is marble, so it's always freezing cold. Sometimes I wake up in the middle of the night and think I'm sleeping in a mausoleum!"

I can't help myself. I start laughing again.

He lifts his head and glares at me. "It's not funny!"

"It's so funny I can't stand it."

"Do you have any idea what I paid for this place?"

"Your gargantuan mausoleum?" I squint at it through the window. "I dunno. Bazillions?"

"Exactly! Bazillions!"

"I'm no financial whiz, Sparky, but I think they saw you coming."

When he groans and drops his head against the head rest,

closing his eyes, I try to reassure him. "I'm sure there's some oil baron with twelve ex-wives and a hundred kids who'd love to move into it. With all the members of his country club. And their housekeeping staff."

Mason opens his eyes and glares at me.

I try to stifle another laugh, but fail. "And the entire population of Portugal."

"Ha ha."

"Oh, lighten up. It's not like you can't sell it."

Sounding panicked, he says, "But where would I *live*?"

"You say that like there are zero options between here and a cardboard box."

"Name one."

"There's a house for sale at the end of my block."

That astonishes him so much it leaves him speechless.

"You're right," I say solemnly. "It's only a three-bedroom. There's not enough space for both you and your ego."

He looks away. "I'm just surprised you'd want me living on the same street as you."

"Are you kidding? Imagine how much fun we could have screaming obscenities at each other over the backyard fences. The neighbors would love it."

When he glances back at me and sees me smiling, he smiles, too. "Yeah, especially when they hear your PG version of cursing. 'Dingwaddle' this and 'flying fig' that. They won't even know what language we're speaking."

We smile at each other so long it starts to get uncomfortable. I look away, patting my hair to make sure no stray strands have escaped from my bun.

After a rough throat clearing, Mason says, "I guess I'll go in, then."

"Okay. Goodnight. And thanks again for dinner. I love that place."

When he doesn't respond, I glance over at him. He's staring

back at me with the same warm look that flustered me at the restaurant. "You're welcome, Pink. Anytime."

"So I'll send you all the information on Stephanie as soon as I vet her file. Okay?"

"Sure. Looking forward to it."

An awkward silence follows. Finally, Mason breaks it by saying, "Sweet dreams." He opens the door and starts to get out.

"Wait."

He turns to me, his hand on the door and a question in his eyes.

"I, um, I need to say something."

He groans. "You're killing me, you know that?"

"No, this isn't anything about you. You haven't done anything wrong. This is about me."

Eyes alight, he settles back into his seat. "This should be interesting."

I search his face before I speak, because I want to be sure I don't miss any change in his expression. "I'm sorry for teasing you about your ego. It's not nice. And I don't want you to think that I think there's anything wrong with you, because I don't."

His face goes through several different emotions before it settles on something I can't identify. It's part pain and part pleasure, with a whole lot of ambivalence thrown in.

He says softly, "I know you don't think there's anything wrong with me. Which is what makes me assume your parents must've dropped you on your head a lot when you were a baby."

"Oh, for crying out loud. I'm trying to apologize here!"

He grins. "You did. I heard you. And you don't have to do it again, because I like it when you give me shit."

When I quirk my lips, he amends quickly, "The business. I meant I like it when you give me the business. Nobody else mouths off to me the way you do."

"Good to know," I say, smiling. "Now that I know you like it, the gloves will come off, pal, so you better watch out."

"I can hardly wait."

We sit there grinning at each other, until Mason says, "Get outta here. I'll talk to you next week."

"Aye-aye, Captain."

Then it all falls apart in slow motion.

I don't know what makes me do it. I honestly don't. One minute we're smiling and saying goodbye, the next minute I'm impulsively leaning over to give him a kiss on the cheek.

Only he's turning his head, so my target moves.

Where his cheek was supposed to be, suddenly his lips are there instead.

His warm, soft, beautiful lips, which part when they meet mine.

22

MASON

UCK.

She's kissing me.

Oh God, her mouth.

I'm dying. I'm fucking dying. This is it.

I might be dying, but my dick isn't. The instant Maddie's lips meet mine, my dick wakes up, roaring. My blood turns to fire in my veins. Our tongues meet with an electric shock, and I suck in a hard breath through my nose.

When she makes a small, surprised sound of pleasure in the back of her throat, my brain throws its hands in the air and gives up all hope of managing the situation.

I grasp her head in my hands, close my eyes, and kiss her back like I'm starving.

Because I am. I'm starving for her, and have been since the day we met.

She makes another sound, this one longer and deeper, closer to a moan. I've never heard anything so hot in my life.

In response, my dick throbs. I'm not sure I won't come in my pants.

Her hand flattens on my chest. The other makes a fist in my

hair at the scruff of my neck. She melts against me, pulling me closer, arching her back, and holy fucking shit I want this woman so bad I'd burn down the White House to have her.

Her mouth is sweet and lush, giving me what I need, letting me have everything I'm demanding. I feel like I'm tumbling through space. Freefalling. I'm so jacked up my hands are shaking. I can't catch my breath.

I want to rip off all her clothes and take her like an animal.

I want to see her naked skin.

I want to feel it, kiss it, bite it, mark it.

I want to—

She gasps, pulling away abruptly. Her eyes are wide and horrified. She covers her mouth with a trembling hand and breathes, "Oh God. I'm so, so sorry."

I'm so stunned by the loss of her mouth that I can't talk. I just stare at her, breathing hard and shaking, my dick straining for release from my pants.

"I didn't mean…" She shakes her head. She looks disoriented. Her eyes are hazy and her face is flushed.

Finally I manage to speak, but it comes out in a husky growl. "Yes, you did. You meant every fucking second of it."

She did, too. I know she did. But hearing me say it pisses her off.

Because who couldn't see that coming?

She withdraws to her side of the car until she's practically melded to the driver's door. Looking haunted, she grabs the steering wheel and stares out the windshield, her eyes big and her knuckles white.

She says stiffly, "I apologize. That was so unprofessional of me. I don't even know where to begin."

"Really? That's how you're gonna handle it? Act like you made mistake?'

"I did make a mistake!" she cries. "I meant to kiss you on the cheek!"

"Look at me."

She squeezes her eyes shut. "I can't."

Getting angry, I growl, "For fuck's sake, Maddie. *Look at me*."

"Stop cursing at me!"

I take her face in my hands and turn her head, forcing her to meet my eyes. "Okay. You've got a choice here. Go left or go right. It's totally your decision."

She waits, staring at me, chewing on her lip.

I say, "Left is we pretend this didn't happen—"

"Left."

Bad things are happening in my stomach. I feel like I just swallowed a bunch of poisonous snakes. "You didn't wait to hear what right was."

She whispers, "I don't need to. I just want to erase it."

That hurts so much it leaves me breathless. "Why do you want to erase it?"

"Because you're my *client*. I *never* get involved with clients. It's a breach of ethics. It's completely unprofessional. It's just wrong!"

"Oh," I say, my heart pounding with relief. "In that case, you're fired."

She pulls her face from my hands and turns her attention back to the windshield. With thinned lips and the snippiness of a schoolmarm, she says, "No, I'm not. Now please get out of the car."

She's being so absurd, I almost laugh. But I'm too mad. I holler instead.

"You can't stop me from firing you!"

Her voice rises. "Mason, I'm going to find you a wife, whether I'm fired or not. Now please *get out of the car*."

This woman. This stubborn, smart-mouthed, pain in my ass. I stare at her, wanting to rip the steering wheel off and throw it through one of my stupid, overpriced windows.

Irritated that I'm only sitting there staring at her and not following her demand to get out, she tries to rationalize with me. "Look. You finally agreed to give falling in love for real a chance."

I say loudly, "Yeah, I did. You wanna know why?"

She ignores me. "And you've paid me a large amount of money to find you a compatible partner."

I dig my hands into my hair and exhale angrily at the ceiling.

She ignores that, too. Her voice rising, she says, "And I'm going to find you someone who makes you happy, Mason, even if it kills us both."

I look at her, sitting there so angry and proud and beautiful. So hell-bent on doing her job.

So blind.

A kind of desolation overtakes me. Because I know deep down that even if I told her how I feel, she'd just think I was trying to sleep with her.

I'm her polar opposite, her cynical, horn dog client who she thinks could, maybe, fall in love with someone else, but never with her.

I'm also the guy who knows better than to try to convince her she's wrong. Because if there's one thing life's taught me, it's that love is for other people.

People who aren't me.

All the anger drains out of me. Now all I feel is hollow, like a shell.

"Okay, Maddie," I say, my voice dull. "Good luck with that."

I throw open the door and climb out. I'm about to leave, but I can't resist leaning down through the window to tell her one last thing.

"You know, for such a smart girl, you can be really clueless."

She looks at me. Our gazes lock and hold.

Then I turn around and walk away, vowing I'll never see her again.

23

WALDINE

I'm right in the middle of askin' the spirit of Celia's aunt Gertrude to bless the circle with her presence when I feel it.

A disruption in the energy field. A big one. Dark and powerful and movin' fast, like an ocean wave.

My eyes fly open. One by one, the eyes of every person around the table open, too, and look around in alarm.

"What in the Sam Hill was that?"

Sittin' directly across from me at my silk-draped dining table is Delilah. She's holdin' hands on either side with Charlotte and Veraminta May, who everyone just calls May for obvious reasons. The room is dark except for the twelve candles flickerin' in the center of the table, and it's quiet, except for the sudden loud beating of my heart.

With the kind of dread I haven't felt in years, I tell Delilah, "That was Maddie. Somethin's wrong."

The table erupts in worried chatter. Eleven women start squawkin' at each other like chickens in a hen house when they smell a fox moochin' up to the door.

I say above the noise, "Quiet, y'all! Jabberin' won't do any good. Let me give her a call and see what's goin' on."

I release the cool, dry hand of Bernice on my left and the warm, plump hand of Cassidy on my right, and rise from my chair, breaking the circle. Everyone else rises, too. May turns on the dining room lights and Celia blows out the candles.

Then the entire group follows me nervously into the kitchen, where I grab the phone off the wall and start dialin'.

Maddie doesn't pick up her cell. There's no answer at her house, either. I set the receiver back on the hook and think for a moment.

Then I pick it up again and punch in a number.

"Hello?" says a sleepy male voice.

"Dick! It's Waldine! I think we got ourselves a problem!"

There's a long pause. Then his gruff New Yawk accent kicks in, along with the attitude.

"Yeah, we gotta problem, all right. You're callin' me in the middle of the night and screamin' at me like a crazy person. Do you have any idea what time it is?"

"Of course I do," I answer, aggravated. "You think I hold a séance any other time than midnight? You're not dealin' with an amateur, here!"

Around me, I hear a chorus of "Mmhmm" and "That's right" from the ladies.

There's another pause. Then Dick says somethin' that shocks me right out of my slippers.

"Did you make sure the number of candles on the table is divisible by three?"

I'm sure my lower jaw hits the floor. I spend a while blinkin' in surprise, then say defensively, "Of course I did."

"Hmm. Did you put any bread out?"

My temper snaps. Who does this damn Yankee think he is? "Can you interrogate me about my skill in communin' with the other side *after* we find out what's happened to my niece and Mason?"

That gets his attention. I hear him rustlin' around, wrestlin' with his bed sheets, then he comes back on the line all hot and bothered, hollerin' like a stuck pig. "What're you talkin' about, woman? What's happened to Mason?"

"That's what I'm callin' to find out! Have you heard from him?"

"No! The last time we talked was when I told him about the Harry Potter marathon, like we agreed! He said he was gonna take a cab to the theater, but that was hours and hours ago!"

"Criminy," I mutter, propping a hand on my hip. "That means they could be anywhere right now."

"If they even saw each other. That theater complex is huge. They coulda passed right by each other like ships in the night."

I chuckle darkly. "Oh, they saw each other all right."

"How do you know?"

"Because if they didn't, Maddie would be at home by now and pickin' up my call, instead of out somewhere creatin' giant wormholes in the ether!"

"Wormholes? *Ether*?"

"Oh forget it," I say, exasperated. "Just call me the minute you hear anything from your boy."

"What're you gonna do?"

I look around at all the ladies hangin' on my every word. Ladies who've known and loved my niece all her life. Ladies who knew and loved my sister, too, God rest her blessed soul.

I tell Dick, "We're gonna go find Maddie."

We all pile into my Caravan and take off with Charlotte on phone patrol, redialin' Maddie's house and cell every so often.

First stop is the theater. We cruise the parking lot, looking for her car, but it's nowhere to be seen. It's not parked outside any of the nearby bars or restaurants, either, where she and Mason might've gone together.

Next up is the office. But when we roll into the parking lot, all the lights are out at Perfect Pairings.

Then we hit the all-night coffee shop Maddie goes to when she can't sleep. She's not in there, either.

But we end up stayin' for pecan pie and coffee spiked with Southern Comfort as we sit around two pushed-together tables and think, which no right-minded person can do on an empty stomach.

I say to Charlotte, "Did you call all the hospitals again?"

"I did, Waldine. Nothin'."

Delilah pipes up. "What about urgent care?"

I shake my head, thinking. "It's bigger than that."

The girls start to throw out options willy-nilly where Maddie might be.

"The library?"

"Closes at seven."

"A club?"

"Not her style."

"The park?"

"She's too smart to sit on a park bench in the middle of the night like serial killer bait."

Then, around a mouthful of pecan pie, Delilah says, "Maybe she's at home and just isn't pickin' up the phone."

Everyone stops what they're doing and looks at each other.

I say, "Jesus, Mary, and Joseph, you'd think a group of twelve women would have half a brain between them."

At the speed of a herd of turtles, we all jump up and run out. When we get to Maddie's, I screech to a stop at the curb. The lights are all on inside the house. The curtains in the front windows are wide open.

And there's Maddie, vaccumin' the living room carpet like it's noon instead of the middle of the night.

Charlotte says, "Well, that's a relief!"

"Don't be relieved yet," I say, watching Maddie through the windows. "This looks worse than I thought."

"But she's home and safe, Waldine."

Delilah sums up the severity of the situation with two simple words. "She's cleaning."

Then everybody gets quiet, because we all know what that means.

24

MADDIE

I think that knocking sound is in my head until I look up and see Auntie Waldine outside at the living room windows, rapping on the glass. She's wearing all white, as are the eleven women gathered around her.

Oh no. This is so not the time for a visit from the Sisterhood of the Traveling Ouija Board.

I shut off the vacuum reluctantly and go to the front door. When I open it, everyone has moved to my front porch and are crowded around the door with the zeal of missionaries who'd like to inquire about the health of my soul.

I say warily, "Hi?"

"Child!" says my auntie, looking panicked. "What's happened?"

I want to be surprised by that. I should be surprised. But it's taking all my energy just to concentrate on the list of things that still need to get cleaned in the house. I can't deal with the mysteries of the universe at the moment.

I say calmly, "Nothing's happened. I had dinner with Mason and now I'm cleaning. Would anyone care for some sweet tea?"

Eyeballs ping pong back and forth as the ladies share knowing glances.

Then, with the hushed tones and slow movements nurses use with psychiatric patients, they turn me around and usher me to my kitchen table, where they ease me into a chair.

I watch them glance at the open cupboards—still empty and drying from the hot water and vinegar scrub I gave the shelves and doors—the jumble of jars, boxes, and cans colonizing all the countertops that I pulled from the pantry and cupboards that need to get dusted and alphabetized before they're put back in, and the stacks of china I've already hand washed and laid out on the kitchen table, awaiting their return to the dining room breakfront.

After I polish the wood and Windex the glass.

And re-line the shelves with fresh liner paper.

I say, "Nobody touch anything, please. I've got a system. I've also got whiskey instead of sweet tea if you prefer."

I've had a bottle of whiskey unopened in the cupboard for years. I only bought it for guests, because I can't stand the stuff. At the moment, it seems of utmost importance that I get that bottle out of my house.

It's just sitting there on the counter, mocking me. Reminding me of Mason.

"You don't really drink whiskey, do you, Pink?"

Can you be haunted by someone who's still alive?

I don't realize I've said that aloud until Auntie Waldine sits in the chair beside me and clasps my hands in hers. Very seriously, she says, "There are some people who can project their astral body across great distances. So the answer is yes."

Everyone in my kitchen is solemnly nodding. I wonder if there are cameras hidden somewhere, and I'm soon going to be starring on reality TV.

"Good to know. So, as you can see, I'm very busy. Maybe we can pick up this intervention or whatever it is at another time? Like never?"

"The vacuum can wait, child. What you need right now is to talk it out."

"It?" I say suspiciously.

"Your emotional reaction to seein' that tattooed hunk of man of yours."

More nodding from the group. One of the ladies titters. "Ooh, *tattooed*."

This is absurd.

"He's not 'mine.' He's just a client. And I appreciate your concern, but as you can see, I'm perfectly fine."

"Fine?" says May from behind Waldine. She eyeballs me. "Honey, your energy earlier was so disruptive it almost knocked loose the new filling in my back tooth. You are *not* fine."

"Ah. My energy. Now it all makes perfect sense."

Ignoring my sarcasm, Waldine turns to the group. "Does anybody have any sage? We need to clear out the air in this place."

"This isn't California," I say sternly. "No one is lighting dried herbs on fire in my kitchen. Can't you see I just mopped the floors?"

"Yes," says Delilah. "And you should really do that last, after your other cleaning is finished."

When all the other women give her sour looks, Delilah turns sheepish. "Sorry."

"Now, look here," says my auntie, turning back to me. "I know that therapist you had said it was healthier for you to talk about your feelings instead of doin' all this cleaning nonsense. And we're not leavin' until you get everything off your chest. Are we, ladies?"

They answer as one with variations on the theme of *We're staying here until we annoy you to death*. Heat starts to crawl up my neck.

"My feelings? Well, since you asked…right now I'm feeling ambushed."

"Okay, good. How about before that?"

"Before that I was feeling *not* ambushed."

"Go on," urges Auntie Waldine, nodding in a therapeutic way that makes me exasperated.

"I was just here, minding my own business, cleaning my house. Because it was filthy. It was a complete mess. It's always such a mess!"

I see everyone glancing doubtfully at my shining cupboards and gleaming floor, and my chest constricts.

"It is," I insist, my voice climbing. "I have to stay on top of it or it gets out of control. You have no idea how much dirt can accumulate if you're not vigilant. You have to stay vigilant or everything falls apart!"

Along with the heat crawling up my neck, my hands have started to shake and my heart is pounding. The room feels like it's closing in around me.

"I can't let it fall apart. I have to keep it all together. Keep it…together."

I'm sweating now. Panting.

Panicking.

Cradling my hands in hers, Auntie Waldine looks into my eyes. "Sometimes the only way to keep yourself together is to let everything else fall apart. Now tell me what happened with Mason."

There's a long, breathless moment when everyone stares at me and the only sound I hear are my rapid, shallow breaths. Pressure builds inside me. Inside my chest, within my veins, behind my eyes. I feel like a balloon filled past capacity. A dam with a roaring river at its back.

Then the dam breaks, and I burst into tears.

"I kissed him!" I sob, collapsing over our joined hands. "I kissed him and he kissed me back and it was wonderful and horrible at the same time because we're nothing alike and he's the most aggravating man on the planet and he doesn't listen to a word I say and he thinks I'm a librarian and he left lunch to go have sex with some woman and it HURT and Bobby is the only man who'll ever want to marry me and Mason doesn't believe in love and this whole thing is a big, stupid catastrophe *and now I have to go find that idiot a wife*!"

"There, there," croons my auntie, stroking my hair. "Let it out, child, just let it out."

She lets me cry for a while, then says, "But you're wrong about him not believin' in love."

I lift my head and stare at her through my tears. "Did your magic eight ball tell you that?"

She scolds, "Don't you sass me, Madison McRae."

"I'm sorry." I sniffle, feeling twelve years old.

When she sees that I'm sufficiently contrite, her tone softens. "You're also wrong about the two of you bein' nothin' alike."

I want to tell her she doesn't know what she's talking about, but also don't want to get a smack in front of a group of people who may or may not have frequent conversations with the dead, so I keep my mouth shut.

"Do you remember how I was after your mama and daddy died and I moved in with you and your brothers to take care of y'all?"

I'm startled by the change in direction, and take a moment to compose myself before I answer. "I remember…um, sorry, but what I remember most is that there seemed to be a lot of men coming and going from the house."

"Exactly," she says, nodding.

Since she doesn't seem insulted by that gem of a memory, I keep going. "And, um, there were a lot of empty wine bottles lying around the kitchen."

"Mmm. That there were, indeed."

Delilah pipes in. "Remember how her hair looked?"

Charlotte clucks her tongue. "Like a hornet's nest."

May says, "And remember how she never showered?"

"Or changed her clothes," says Celia, shaking her head.

"She looked like she was livin' under a bridge," adds Bernice. "With a family of rodents."

"Thank you," says Waldine loudly, looking around. "May I continue?"

"What's your point, Auntie Waldine?"

She turns her attention back to me. "My point is that everyone deals with grief in their own way. You turned yours inside." She taps my chest gently with her finger. "You held it all in, and made rules on top of rules to guide your life from then on out so you'd feel in control. So you wouldn't be in danger. So nothin' as bad could ever happen to you again."

I feel myself getting choked up and have to take a lot of deep breaths.

"But me, on the other hand, I went the other way. I drank and took lovers and smashed things and raged and went through all the stages of grief about a hundred times. But, eventually, I healed. I was able to move on with my life."

Her gaze turns penetrating. "Not everyone heals. Not everyone moves on. Sometimes they stay stuck right where they are, like a plane in a holding pattern, flyin' round and round in circles and never bein' able to land because they can't let go of whatever broke them."

"You're saying I'm in a holding pattern."

"Yes. And so is your friend Mason. Your plane's flyin' one way and his is flyin' another, but you're both still off the ground because landing means lettin' go and lettin' go means maybe lettin' something in that could break you all over again. This time for good.

"Now, I don't know what happened to that boy, but I do know that him bein' crabby and shouty comes from the same place as you bein' the dirt police. And dressin' like a nun. And actin' like you're tryin' to hold a dime between your butt cheeks when you walk. And—"

"I got it," I interrupt in a loud voice.

"My point is that you *are* the same," she says gently. "You've both got a lot of broken pieces. But if you give it a chance, you might find that all your broken pieces fit together perfectly to make a beautiful whole."

I stare at her for a long time. In a strangled voice, I say, "I'm going to cry again now."

Then I burst into tears with renewed vigor, because that's just how my day is going.

I wring myself dry, blubbering and boo-hooing until I'm sure the neighbors will call the police to report a banshee at large in the neighborhood. When I'm good and tuckered out, the ladies make me hot chocolate and put me to bed with a cold washcloth over my eyes. Then they set about cleaning up the mess I made in the kitchen, putting everything back into the pantry and cupboards.

I'm sure they don't arrange things with any kind of system. And the labels on all the cans are probably facing in every direction except front. I'm too tired to care.

As I'm falling asleep, I promise myself I'll fix it tomorrow.

But in the morning, I'm shocked to find everything arranged in perfect rows by height and color *and* alphabetized. And the rest of the house is sparkling, clean, too. I feel overwhelmed with gratitude and love, and so lucky to have such wonderful women in my life.

Until I see the note on the kitchen table.

Mercury is going into retrograde today, honey, so if you're still a soggy lump of existential despair when you read this, dry your tears and buckle up. Things are about to get bumpy.

Auntie Waldine can always be counted on to add a dash of whacky to the situation.

In the light of day, my mind is much clearer than it was last night. I had an emotional reaction to kissing Mason, yes, but I know it was only momentary. Regardless of my aunt's airplane metaphors, Mason and me together just doesn't make sense. I lost my head, but now I've found it, and I've still got a job to do.

I've got to find Mason a wife.

I go into the office and spend the rest of the day vetting Stephanie's file. I run the background and credit check, call her references, and review her social media profiles. There are two other men I think she might be interested in, but I really want her to meet Mason, so after thinking how best to approach the subject, I give her a call.

"Hi, Maddie!" she says when she picks up the phone. "It's funny you called, I was just thinking about calling you to thank you for our meeting!"

She's got one of those bright, bubbly personalities that seem bulletproof against negativity. When I asked her during our meeting to describe her worst date, she laughed, waved it off, and said, "There are no bad dates. There are only learning experiences that lead us to where we're supposed to be going and the partner we're supposed to be with."

I thought that was so good I wanted put it on my website.

I say, "Is now a good time for us to chat?"

"Sure! What's up?"

"Well, I have three potential matches for you that I'd like to talk to you about."

She's thrilled. "Really? That fast? Wow, I'm impressed!"

I tell her about the first two guys. One's a university professor, the other's a top executive at a media company. She's not interested in either.

Which leads us to bachelor number three.

"Do you want to hear the good news or the bad news first?"

She pauses. "He's not in prison, is he?"

That makes me laugh. Then I remember Mason's scraped knuckles and stop laughing.

"No. He's been fully vetted, and I think he's an incredible guy. But I'll be honest with you. It's going to take a special kind of woman to handle him. He's not all sunshine and rainbows."

She sounds intrigued. "Go on."

"We'll do the good stuff first. He's very smart, and he's got a really sharp sense of humor. He's extremely successful, driven, and talented. He's also very sensitive, much more than he lets on. He notices everything. He's not the guy who'll be clueless when you're upset. He'll want to know what's wrong. He'll get in your face about it. If you're the type that likes to gloss it over and move on when you're mad, that will be a problem."

"For such a smart girl, you can be really clueless."

I push aside the memory of Mason's confusing words and keep going.

"His job is very high profile, so he's recognized in public often."

"He's a celebrity?"

"Not to the point where you'd be mobbed at McDonald's, but he does get asked for autographs."

"Is he on TV?"

"I can't get into the details yet. But you'd have to sign a non-disclosure agreement if you wanted to be matched with him. You wouldn't be able to speak publicly about your dates or tell anyone you'd met him." I pause for effect. "If you did, you'd be subject to legal action."

She laughs, which I take as a good sign. "So if we fell in love and got married, I'd have to pretend he didn't exist?"

"No, the NDA only covers your initial match, phone conversations, and first dates, and my company's part in the process. If a relationship develops, you're free to negotiate further."

"Negotiate? What, like a prenup?"

"If it got that far, there would definitely be a prenup," I say, nodding. "So you should consider how you feel about that before moving forward."

She mulls it over for a moment. “It’s not my favorite idea, but I get it. Wealthy people need to protect their assets from unscrupulous scammers and gold-diggers.”

“Precisely.”

“So is that the bad news?”

I make a face. “Um, no.”

“Is he ugly?”

A square jaw, full lips, and a pair of blistering gray eyes swim into my mind’s eye. “He’s the opposite of ugly. He’s incredibly handsome. In fact, he might be the most attractive man I’ve ever met.”

I say that so forcefully it surprises both of us. We sit in silence for a moment, until Stephanie says, “That could pose its own set of problems, too.”

I knew this girl was smart.

“Yes. He gets a lot of attention from women. Whoever ends up with him will have to have a strong sense of her own self worth and be mature enough to deal with it. If you’re the jealous type, it won’t work.”

Stephanie sounds doubtful. “I don’t know, Maddie. I’ve been cheated on before. A guy who has women hitting on him all the time doesn’t sound like my cup of tea.”

“I hear you. It would concern me, too. But I’m convinced that if he met the right person, he’d be a goner. If he gave his heart, he’d never look at another woman again.”

She’s silent for a while, thinking. Then she says, “I can tell you like him, and I trust your judgment, so he can’t be all bad.”

“I do like him,” I say softly, thinking of his face. Thinking of that kiss, which likely will be branded on my brain forever. Then I think of him growling at me, and sigh. “But I haven’t gotten to the other stuff yet.”

“That sounds ominous.”

“I won’t sugar coat it. He’s a hot head. His default volume is a shout. He's bossy and moody and uses very colorful language to express himself. His manners also leave a lot to be desired."

She says drily, "Sounds like a charmer."

"That's the thing. He *is* a charmer. He can acknowledge when he does something wrong, and apologize for it. He wants to do better. He's got a good heart. Underneath his scary exterior—"

"Scary?" says Stephanie, alarmed.

"Intimidating is a better word. Underneath his intimidating exterior, he's just a big softie. He's actually very sweet."

Her tone turns doubtful. "He sounds complicated."

"He is."

"Like a lot."

"He absolutely is."

She exhales. "So give me the bottom line here. With everything you know about him, do you think the good outweighs the bad? In other words, is he worth the risk?"

I answer without hesitation, conviction ringing in my words.

"Yes. You might want to kick him in the teeth six days out of seven, but if he was yours, he'd fight to the death to protect you. He's ridiculously loyal to the point of self-sacrificing. He's got depth, soul, and passion. He'll make you contemplate murder so often it will become habit, but more often than that, he'll make you laugh. He's a diamond in the rough, but his shine outweighs his rough edges by a million to one."

I take a breath and boil it down to its essence.

"He won't be an easy man to love, but he's definitely worth it. Any woman would be lucky to have him."

A long silence follows. When Stephanie speaks again, her voice has changed somehow, but I can't put my finger on what it is.

"In that case, I'd like to speak with him. Let's set up a meet and greet phone call, and we'll go from there."

I'm limp with relief. "Fantastic! I'll get back to you as soon as I hear from him."

We say our goodbyes and hang up, and if there's a hollow feeling in my stomach at the thought of what will happen if Mason and Stephanie hit it off, I ignore it.

I'm a matchmaker. Getting other people their happily-ever-afters is what I do.

It's not about me.

I need to keep my own feelings out of it.

25

MASON

Maddie's smart, I'll give her that. She doesn't call me. She knows I won't answer.

She sends an email instead.

Sunday morning, bright and early, just as I'm about to leave for the first official training practice of the off-season.

Because the woman is all about bad timing and busting my balls.

Dear Mason,

Good morning! I hope this email finds you well. I spoke to Stephanie about you, and she'd like to set up a phone call. Her details are attached. Please let me know when you're available to speak with her.

PS – This is a recent picture of her. Yes, she's also that pretty in person.

Warm regards,

Maddie

"Warm regards," I mutter, staring at the attached picture of an attractive blonde. "I'll give you warm regards."

I email back with no salutation and no signoff. ***Not interested. And you're still fired.***

Maddie's response arrives not even two minutes later.

Am not. But if you don't like her, I'll let you fire me and I'll refund your money.

Blessings,

Madison

"Ha! We've graduated to blessings now! And *Madison*!" Set to the soundtrack of the growls rumbling through my chest, my fingers fly over the keyboard.

If it means you'll stop badgering me, then set up the phone call.

But I won't like her.

Bon voyage, bienvenue, and sayonara,

M

When her next email arrives, I have to restrain myself from picking up my laptop and throwing it across the room.

You'll like her.

If you don't, think of Dick. "Sometimes we do things we don't want to do for other people because it makes them happy." Sound familiar?

Go Patriots!

Madison

PS - Bienvenue means welcome, Sparky, not goodbye.

"She's trying to kill me," I say, glaring at the screen as steam pours from my ears. "Silk Hiding Steel Pink Pixie Girl is trying to irritate me into an early grave."

Fine. You win, Capone. Tomorrow. Have her call my cell at 6pm.

She writes back, ***Excellent! And I'm not a gangster, thank you very much. I'm a Southern lady.***

I write back, ***Same thing.***

Then I slam the laptop closed and head out to practice, trying to wipe the memory of that kiss from my brain so I can get back to forgetting what happens inside my chest every time I think about it.

Spoiler alert: it doesn't work.

Practice is a disaster.

I can't get my mind off Maddie. Every time I call a play or throw a pass, she's there in my head. She scolds me when I yell at the punter for missing the snap. She rolls her eyes when I curse over a botched play. By the time practice ends and I'm headed to a meeting with Coach, I've had a full day's worth of lectures on my temper, my sportsmanship, and my leadership skills, all of which she finds lacking.

It's a special kind of nightmare having Miss Manners living inside your skull.

Especially when all you want to do to Miss Manners is kiss her again.

And again.

And again.

"Have a seat, Mason."

Sweaty and still in my practice gear, I sit across from Coach's old, beat up metal desk in his otherwise new and modern office at our training facility.

I know the reason he doesn't throw out that dumb desk is because he's superstitious. It's the same desk he had when he first won a Super Bowl as coach with the Giants twelve years ago.

Then, when we were conference champs my rookie year and every year after that, he practically had the thing sainted.

People and their mental guardrails.

He's too old to still believe in good luck.

At least bad luck is reliable. That bitch will never let you down.

I drop my helmet on the floor next to my chair and meet Coach's eyes. "You don't have to say it. I know I sucked."

He leans back in his chair and folds his hands over his stomach. Bald and thin as a rail, he's got piercing blue eyes and deeply tanned and leathered skin from too many decades standing in the sun shouting from the sidelines.

His blue eyes do their thing and go right through me.

"You did suck. Big time. You're outta shape and unfocused. And your aim is for shit. I thought you were gonna bean the water boy with that whackadoodle pass thirty yards past the receiver on the first play. Poor kid almost shit his pants.

"And you didn't follow your own play calls. You say we're gonna do *this*, then you wind up doing *that*. The whole team was running around in total confusion all day. It was like watching the Dementia Bowl."

"Yep."

He looks surprised that I didn't argue with him. This is a man who's seen my head explode every time I've been criticized over the past six years, so I can't blame him.

"So we're on the same page?" he says, eyeing me. "That's a first."

Normally, right about now I'd be really pissed off. I'd take everything he said as a challenge. An insult.

Now it just makes me depressed.

Life was so much easier before I had to think about anyone else.

I blow out a hard breath and drag a hand through my sweaty hair. Then I meet Coach's wary gaze and get ready to eat some crow.

"I, uh…" *Fuck.* "I think I probably owe you an apology for my past behavior."

If I didn't know better, I'd think Coach was about to slide out of his chair.

He narrows his eyes. "*Excuse me*?"

This is how much of a dick I've been. This right here.

I can't even say I'm sorry without him thinking he's gone deaf.

"I said I owe you an apology. Full stop."

The silence in Coach's office echoes for a long, tense time. He stares at me like he's never seen me before in his life. Then he says, "You ever see that movie *Invasion of the Body Snatchers*?"

Sighing, I look at the ceiling. "I haven't been replaced by a pod person."

"You sure? Because you sound like an alien."

"I'm not an alien."

He doesn't look convinced. "If you're not an alien, answer me this: which is the most important thing in life? Money, sex, fame, family, or the ability to manipulate the space-time continuum?"

I say automatically, "Love."

He lifts his brows. "That wasn't one of the choices."

I frown, thinking back. "It wasn't?'

"No. And now I definitely know you're an alien, because the Mason Spark *I* know would never allow that particular four letter word out of his mouth."

Christ. What the hell is wrong with me? Make a joke, idiot.

"Yeah. Sorry. Still getting used to this body." I stretch my lips over my teeth in an attempt at a grin.

Coach sees my weird smile and goes ballistic. He hollers, "Are you on drugs?"

"Does oxytocin count?'

"Yes!" he roars, jumping up from his seat to pound a fist on his battered metal desk. "Get your ass into rehab, son! We've got a Super Bowl to win!"

"Oxtytocin is the cuddle hormone, Coach. I don't need rehab."

Coach drops abruptly into his chair and stares at me. "Did you just say cuddle?"

"Yeah."

"What in God's green acre are you talking about?"

Groaning, I drop my head into my hands and rest my elbows on my knees. "I don't even know. I've lost my fucking mind. I have no fucking idea what I'm doing."

After a long silence, Coach says, "It's a girl, isn't it?"

"Girl? She's more like the Genghis Khan of etiquette. The Tony Soprano of manners." Thinking of Maddie, my sigh is wistful. "The Bugsy Siegel of true love."

"Is she also the Michael Corleone of circumcisions? Because you sound like you've lost your balls."

"Circumcisions are for foreskins, not balls."

"This conversation is a circumcision for my brain."

I lift my head and look at him. I must look really pitiful, because he says, "Whoa."

"Yeah."

After a while, he says, "Well, it can't be all bad if she's got you apologizing out of the blue for your past behavior." His expression sours. "Though that's a pretty big canvas to cover with one little apology. You might need to buy me some flowers and send me a box of chocolates, too."

"Gimme a break, will you?"

"What do you want from me here, son? You show up looking like a bag of smashed assholes, outta shape, unfocused, and talking some ridiculous shit about ancient emperors, mob bosses, and true love. I don't even know where to start."

"You can start by explaining what the fuck a bag of smashed assholes is."

Aggravated, he waves a hand in the air. "It's an old military term. It means something really bad that you don't want to see. The only thing worse is a *clear* bag of smashed assholes, and you're almost there."

I say forlornly, "I know."

"So did you get this girl pregnant, or what?"

"No! God, no. Nothing like that." I add sheepishly, "We haven't even… you know."

He lifts his brows, making the wrinkles in his forehead multiply like rabbits. "You're joking."

"Nope."

"You're telling me you're this worked up over a broad you haven't even slept with?"

We stare at each other for a while. Then I say, "It's bad, isn't it?"

"You bet your ass it's bad, son! If you ever get her naked, you'll probably burst into tears! You'll start listening to Kenny G and watching Ellen DeGeneres and wearing frilly shirts made of macrobiotic hemp!"

I say defensively, "I love Ellen."

He hollers, "Say the word 'love' one more time and I'll make you run a hundred goddamn laps around the field!"

He stands, props his hands on his hips, and starts to pace in agitation behind his desk. "All right. Talk to me about this love gangster of yours. What's the situation?"

I lean back in my chair and look at my hands. Hands that only a few days ago were cradled around Maddie's beautiful head as I kissed her. "The situation is that she's too good for me."

He barks out a laugh. "Every woman is too good for every man, idiot. You just have to find one that doesn't lord it over you too much."

I think of his wife, a fiery Italian-American woman he's been married to for about a hundred years. "Is that what you found with Carla?"

"Are you kidding? That woman tells me she's better than me every chance she gets. I can't even take a piss without her hollering about how I always leave the seat up and spray pee everywhere and she should've married Joe Scalia like her mother said."

"Have you ever asked her why she didn't?"

He laughs again, only this time it's warmer. "Because Joe Scalia didn't make her lady bits tingle, that's why."

I grimace. "I can already tell I'm gonna be traumatized by this little talk."

"My point is all that bullshit about you not being good enough is just that: bullshit."

I keep staring at my hands. My voice drops lower. "Yeah, except it isn't. You know my story."

He stops pacing. I know he's staring at me, but I don't look up. Shame makes my ears grow hot.

Then he sits down behind his desk again and props his feet up on the top. "Is that what this is about, son? Your past?"

"What's past is prologue."

He sounds irritated by me quoting Shakespeare. "No, what's past is just that: *past*. I'm not your goddamn therapist, son, but let me give you a piece of advice earned over many years of living."

I glance up to find him gazing straight at me, his blue eyes sharp as icicles.

"Don't let the worst things that happen to you be the benchmark for your self-respect. Don't give bad people the power to hurt you again by believing you deserved what they did in the first place. You didn't deserve it. You were just a kid. Life can be horrible sometimes, but it only has to stay horrible if you let it.

"Do yourself a kindness and let the past go. The only thing you'll get by holding onto it is more of what you've got now. Anger. Depression. Loneliness. Is that how you want to live the next fifty years of your life?"

"Until you learn to open your heart, you'll always be as lonely as you are now."

Remembering Maddie's words the day we met, I have to swallow a few times so I can talk around the rock in my throat.

"I don't know how to let it go. I don't know how to move forward."

"Yes, you do."

When I only stare at him in silence, he says, "You can't change the past, but the future's up to you. So make it a better one. Write yourself a new story."

"But *how*?"

His voice grows softer. "Be the man you think would deserve her."

That hits me like a grenade.

I sit there stunned, staring at him, and trying to blink fast enough to get the water gathering in my eyes to evaporate so he doesn't have to worry about me playing Kenny G during our pre-game meetings.

Coach takes pity on me. He returns to his usual tough and gruff self, dismissing me with a jerk of his thumb toward the door.

"Now get your ass outta here. And pull yourself together before you go into the locker room and see your teammates. You look like you've been anally probed by those aliens who abducted you."

"Yes, Coach," I say, my voice thick. I pick up my helmet and stand. "Thank you, Coach."

"Anytime, son. Anytime."

Before I turn away to leave, I see his small, satisfied smile.

26

MASON

I forget all about my scheduled call with Stephanie until my cell rings at six the next afternoon.

I just got home from practice. It was better than yesterday's, but not by much. On the field, my concentration is shot. I'm huffing and puffing like an old man because, as usual, I swapped partying for training during the off-season.

Guess I'm not eighteen anymore.

Worse, I never realized how much my teammates distrust me, but it's painfully obvious now that I've bothered to notice it. When I approached my wide receiver to ask if we could talk about modifying one of our standard plays, he flinched when he turned around and saw me standing there.

Flinched. Like I was holding a gun in my hand.

Okay, full disclosure, we *may* have had one or two little spats that came to blows in the past.

It looks like I've got a shitload of bridge building to do this season.

Or a fuckton.

Either way, it's a lot.

"Yeah."

"Hello, Mason? This is Stephanie Scott."

I'm blank. Standing there in my big, echoing kitchen, I'm drawing a total blank on that name. "Who?"

"From Perfect Pairings? Maddie set up our call?"

Oh fuck. *This*.

"Yeah," I say gruffly, going to the fridge to hunt for something to eat that isn't an inch thick with mold. "About that. Listen, I'm sorry, Stephanie, but I don't think this is a good idea."

"Neither do I," she agrees, her voice warm. "Considering our matchmaker is in love with you."

I almost drop the phone.

When my mouth remembers how to work again, I say, "*What*?"

She laughs. "That was pretty much my initial reaction, too. But then I thought about it, and I have to be honest, I think it's incredibly romantic."

I stand there with the refrigerator door open, blasting cold air into my unblinking eyeballs.

Stephanie blithely continues, either oblivious to or uncaring about the bomb she just dropped onto my head.

"I mean, she's so obviously gaga over you—you should have heard her, Yellowstone's geysers don't gush half as much—but she's setting her own feelings aside to find someone she thinks *you* will fall in love with. Your happiness is more important to her than her own!"

She sighs. "Oh, it's just lovely."

I manage to gather my wits enough to sputter, "That's nuts."

She laughs again.

It's a nice laugh, a sweet and happy one, not like she's making fun of me. She really just sounds delighted.

Still, I can't help the way it makes anger explode in my veins or how my voice comes out like I'm ordering my arch enemy's execution.

"Is this a fucking joke? Who put you up to this? Was it Dick? If it was Dick, I'll wring that old buzzard's neck and throw him down a flight of stairs!"

After my outburst, Stephanie is taken aback. She mutters, "She wasn't kidding about that temper."

"Listen, lady, I don't know what the hell kind of BS this is, but I do know that Maddie is NOT in love with me."

"Oh, really? How can you be so sure?"

I slam the refrigerator door shut with so much force the kitchen windows rattle. "This is ridiculous."

Stephanie is insistent. "Did you *ask* her if she's in love with you?"

"Of course not!"

"Perhaps you should."

She has that same snippy, disapproving tone Maddie gets when she's lecturing me on my manners. It drives me nuts.

Especially considering I wish it was Maddie herself giving me the lecture. Even after the absence of only a few days, I miss her voice.

"I'm not asking anyone if they're in love with me, all right? Jesus, you women are off your rockers, you know that?"

"Ah, yes. The 'crazy' argument. Anytime a woman says something to a man that rattles his cage, we're labeled mentally unstable. Are you aware how patronizing that is?"

Her disapproving tone has intensified. Now she sounds like somebody's intolerant elderly aunt condemning the evils of same-sex marriage.

I want to tear my hair out with both hands, but I'd have to put the phone down to do it.

So instead I stand in the middle of my kitchen making rabid wolf noises and hoping my heart doesn't burst and kill me before I can call Dick and ream him a new asshole for setting this Doberman on me.

"Listen, Mason. I didn't tell you this to upset you. And

maybe I'm wrong." She pauses. "I'm not, but since you're getting so bent out of shape, I'm throwing it out there."

"How kind."

"I can't have a meltdown by America's favorite athlete on my conscience."

Despite my irritation, I grudgingly smile. "America's favorite athlete? That's the first sensible thing you've said."

"I meant aside from Tom Brady."

"*Wow.*"

"You'll live. Listen, why don't we get together for coffee and I can tell you everything?"

When I hesitate, still wondering if it's a setup, she adds, "I've already signed the non-disclosure agreement. This will be only between us. And we can meet wherever you're comfortable."

She pauses. "Unless you're not interested in dating Maddie, in which case you're an idiot. She's *darling*."

I say through gritted teeth, "I'm aware."

She breezes on as if I haven't spoken. "If you say no, I'm calling my brother-in-law next, because he's got this gorgeous single friend who owns a software company. He's *so* bright and accomplished. And funny. And rich. Did I mention he was gorgeous?"

I try to call her bluff. "If he's so perfect, why aren't you dating him?"

"He's too nerdy for me. His collection of movie memorabilia is probably worth a lot, but it's not my thing. He's got a whole room in his house dedicated to Harry Potter, if you can imagine."

I think of Maddie's Hagrid keychain and the framed movie posters of Harry and Hermione in her bedroom, and all the hair on the back of my neck stands on end.

I growl, "What're you doing right now?"

I can hear the smile in her voice when she answers. "Name the place."

27

MADDIE

All the next day at work, I've got my fingers crossed that the call with Stephanie and Mason went well. So when Auntie Waldine buzzes through a few minutes before closing to say Stephanie is on the line, I answer it eagerly.

"Hi, Stephanie! How did it go?"

"*Amazing*. God, you were so right about Mason. Everything you said was spot on. He's incredible."

She sounds like she's lying in bed smoking a cigarette, naked and glowing from the dozen orgasms she just had. Considering I thought there was a good chance I'd have to talk her off a ledge, it's unexpected, to say the least.

"Oh. Um. Really?"

"Yes. We had such a great connection on the phone, we made a date for coffee right after. At his house. Boy, were you right about him being handsome. And calling him a charmer is an understatement!"

She giggles.

It's soft and knowing and satisfied, that giggle, and conveys her meaning better than a thousand words would.

She slept with him.

The room disappears. My focus narrows to a tunnel. Suddenly, I can't breathe.

Calm down. Don't jump to conclusions. You could be reading something into her tone that's not there. I take a deep breath. "How do you mean?"

Her laugh is coy. "Oh, come on, now. You know I can't give any details! I signed an NDA, remember?" She drops her voice. "But let's just say that bed of his is extremely comfortable."

I was right. Stephanie and Mason had sex last night.

And I'm the one who made it happen.

"Maddie, are you there? Hello?"

I whisper, "I'm here."

"Are you okay? You sound funny."

My hands are clammy and shaking. There's a crushing pressure inside my chest. I want nothing more than to throw the phone across the room and scream, but that's so stupid.

I'm so stupid.

What did I think would happen if they hit it off? If he's the guy who'll leave a restaurant in the middle of the day for a booty call, he's also the guy who'll have sex on the first date.

Wait, *I knew this*!

So why the heck am I so upset? This is what I wanted. I wanted to find a girl for him…

And by God, I did.

"Maddie? Did I lose you?"

"Sorry, Stephanie. Something just came up. An emergency. Um, the, uh, the building is on fire. I'll have to give you a call back tomorrow."

I slam the phone down, not caring that I sounded like an absolute madwoman. It doesn't matter what I sounded like to Stephanie, anyway. She got her money's worth.

She and Mason both did.

I realize with a cold, smothering sense of horror that I've become exactly what I argued against the day I first met Mason at my office. He sat right there in that chair across from my desk when I told him I wasn't running an escort service.

And look at me now.

I'm nothing more than a booty call middle man.

I grab my purse and head out of the office. Startled, Auntie Waldine looks up from her desk when I fly past.

"Maddie? What's wrong? Where are you goin'?"

"I've got things to clean," I say, feeling like I'm drowning.

I'm elbow-deep in soap suds when someone starts banging on my front door.

"Go away, Auntie Waldine," I mutter, scrubbing my favorite sauce pan with so much force the Teflon should be peeling off, but it still doesn't look clean enough.

I realized I hadn't gotten to the pots and pans the other night, so as soon as I arrived home from the office, I removed them from the drawers and started in. I might have to go over everything a few times to make sure they're—

BAM BAM BAM.

"Nobody's home!" I shout over my shoulder, scrubbing furiously.

Ten seconds later, a deep voice from behind me says, "That's funny, 'cause you look like you're home to me."

I whirl around and find Mason standing in my kitchen. All six-foot-five, six, seven *plus* of him, big and brawny and wearing a wild, dangerous expression like he's come to perform an exorcism.

Heart hammering, I demand, "How did you get in?"

He doesn't answer. He simply lets his gaze drift slowly over me, from the top of my head down to my bare feet. His eyes are hot, his jaw is set, and his nostrils are flaring.

It's his crazy look. The one he gets right before he gets unhinged.

Dripping suds onto the floor, I point my finger at him. "Don't you dare stand in my kitchen glaring at me after breaking in uninvited! Get out!"

"No."

"What? What do you mean *no*?"

"Just what I said."

He takes a step toward me. He's wearing tight black jeans and a tight black T-shirt. Muscles bulge out all over the place. Tattoos swim in my vision.

Less forcefully, I say, "Get out."

"You're not listening, Pink." He shakes his head, tutting. "You just. Don't. Listen."

He takes another step toward me, then another, then he's standing an arm's length away, staring down at me in all his blistering masculinity.

I swallow, shrinking back against the sink. I whisper, "I want you to go now."

"It's interesting," he says, gazing at my mouth. "The things you say."

"W-what?"

He ignores my stammering. "Even more interesting are the things you don't say."

"I have no idea what you're talking about."

"Don't you?" His smile is small, wicked, and dangerous.

My heart flutters around under my ribcage like a panicked little bird. "No, I don't. Stop talking in riddles. But first get out."

He chuckles. "Why are you so mad at me right now?"

I say indignantly, "I'm not!"

His dangerous smile widens. "That's what I'm talking about,

Pink. That right there." He leans in, braces his arms on the counter on either side of me, and stares into my eyes.

I'm trapped.

I'm also having some bizarre combination of a panic attack and a hot flash. I can't catch my breath, and I've started sweating.

"Okay," he says, his voice husky. "We're gonna play a little game."

I didn't realize I was holding my breath until it all comes out in a gust. "You've lost your mind. Is that it? You've had a hard hit on the head during practice, and now your brain is dislodged. I'll call a doctor."

"It's called Twenty Questions," he goes on, leaning slightly closer until our noses are almost touching. "Question one: where's the fire?"

My hysterical inner voice screams *In my underwear!* But I've retained enough presence of mind not to repeat that. Instead I say, "What fire? There's no fire. You're being ridiculous."

When he moistens his lips, I think I'll pass out.

"It is ridiculous, isn't it?" he muses. He leans closer, brushing his cheek against mine. Then he whispers into my ear, "So I wonder… why would you say there's a fire at your office when there wasn't one? I went by there first, just to make sure."

I freeze in horror.

No. Oh no.

She didn't.

I squeak, "Stephanie told you that?"

His husky laugh raises goosebumps all down my arms. His voice is so close to my ear I feel his breath, a hot, silky whisper of air down my neck when he speaks.

"No, sweetheart. I heard you tell that whopper myself." He pulls away and gazes into my eyes again. "I was on the other line with her when she called you. She was trying to prove something to me that I didn't believe."

He called me sweetheart. Why would he do that? I can't think. I can't breathe. Wait, he was on the phone, too? Oh God, WHAT'S HAPPENING?

"Question two."

He leans to my other side to inhale a slow, deep breath against my neck, just under my jaw. Feather light, his lips brush over the sensitive skin there. I stiffen. All my nerve endings moan. I have to bite my tongue to stop from screaming.

He whispers, "Why would you care if I slept with Stephanie?"

I blurt, "I don't care, why would I care, that's just silly, it's none of my business who you sleep with."

His chuckle sounds devilishly satisfied. "Very convincing."

He straightens, takes my face between his big rough hands, and stares down at me with entire cities burning in his beautiful eyes.

"Question three. And you better tell me the truth this time."

I stand there frozen, breathless, my mind spinning and my blood in flames, waiting for him to speak with the terror of a convict with her head in the guillotine waiting for the sharp, glinting blade to fall.

He says, "Do you have feelings for me?"

An involuntary sound escapes my throat. A sound of shock, disbelief, euphoria, terror.

If this is only question three, I'll be dead by number twenty.

"Answer me."

"I'm… I… um…"

"Yes or no, Pink. It's a simple question."

I'm gripping the counter so hard it's a miracle it doesn't shatter. I wonder if he can hear my knees knocking, but then can't wonder anything else because he lowers his head and very lightly brushes his lips over mine, and my brain stops working altogether.

Against my mouth, he whispers, "Yes or no."

I whimper.

"*Yes or no*."

He's hot and hard against me, a wall of a man who could crush me so easily, but he's holding my face so tenderly it makes me want to cry.

"I j-just want you to be h-happy."

"I'm beginning to get that." He presses a soft, small kiss to one side of my mouth, then the other. "Now answer the question."

"I… I…"

"Come on," he breathes. He stares at me with so much intensity, so much desire, I feel like he's breaking my heart.

I ask desperately, "Did you sleep with Stephanie?"

His answer comes fast and unequivocal. "No."

I'm swamped with relief, until he fires a question back at me. "Would you care if I did?"

I squeeze my eyes shut and reluctantly tell him the truth. "Yes. I'd hate it. I'd hate *you*. I'd never want to see you again."

His chuckle is low and warm and utterly smug. "Now we're getting somewhere."

My God, I'd like to introduce his skull to a sharp object.

I open my eyes and cry, "Fine! Yes, I have feelings for you! Violent, murderous feelings!"

"Getting warmer. Keep going."

"This doesn't make any sense! Why are you even asking me this? I'm bossy and mouthy and a pain in your butt and you don't believe in love and only like girls with big boobs!"

He nods. "We definitely don't work on paper. And don't forget you can't stand my manners."

"Exactly!"

"Plus, you're hell on my blood pressure."

"*I'm* bad for *your* blood pressure? Ha! I've been flirting with heart failure since the day we met! You're the most aggravating man on the planet! Do you have any idea how hard it's going to be for me to find you a wife!"

His eyes burn like two hot coals. His voice comes out in a throaty growl. "How many times do I have to tell you, Maddie? You're fired."

He pulls me against his chest and crushes his mouth to mine.

28

MADDIE

I realize not even five seconds in that I've never been properly kissed in my entire life.

Not by Timmy Reid, the first boy I kissed at summer camp when I was eleven.

Not by Bobby during our entire relationship.

Not even by Mason himself, because that was an accident and he obviously wasn't prepared for it and so couldn't do his absolute best.

But *this*.

This kiss is a gold medal winner, a heart breaker, a soul stealer, a dream.

This kiss is everything I never knew I needed.

This is the kiss that will ruin me, I know it is, but because it's so brain-meltingly decadent, I don't care. I'll worry about my ruination later.

At the moment, my hormones are in charge, and they're burning down every wall I built and rule I made to keep me safe all these years.

Helpless to resist the sheer pleasure of the kiss, I sag against him, closing my eyes and moaning into his mouth. His hot, wonderful mouth, which quickly turns all my limbs to Jell-O. He clasps an arm around my back when my knees start to fail and wraps one hand on my jaw, holding my head in place so he can plunder my mouth.

And plunder he does. His kiss is demanding, an unspoken but clear command of *Give everything to me, and don't you dare hold back.*

It goes on and on and on, until I'm squirming and sweating, going up on my toes to get closer and rubbing my breasts against his chest.

He comes up for air with a soft groan. "Fuck. Oh, fuck. Maddie."

"Quiet," I say, pulling his head down. "We're not finished."

Our mouths meet again. Things go from heated to desperate. We're both breathing hard through our noses and grasping at each other, our bodies straining and our hearts pounding, each making small noises of need.

My nipples are so hard it's almost painful. A dull, heavy ache is growing between my legs.

Then a loud voice says, "Well, isn't this a pretty picture."

Disoriented, I jerk away from Mason.

In my kitchen doorway stands Bobby, a bouquet of flowers in his hands and a look of cold fury on his face.

I can barely string a sentence together because of the hormones making scrambled eggs of my brain, but I manage. "Bobby. What are you doing here?"

"I went by the office to see if you'd like to go to the hospital with me this evening. Your aunt said you'd left in a big hurry, and when I got here, your front door was wide open, so I was worried something was wrong." His cold gaze cuts to Mason. "Obviously, I was correct."

Mason stares back at Bobby, thunderclouds gathering over his head.

Oh dear.

Instinctively, I move between them and stand facing Bobby with my back to Mason. I feel him simmering behind me, see the anger in Bobby's eyes, and pray this visit doesn't end with a chalk outline on my kitchen floor.

"Nothing's wrong. But this isn't a good time—"

"You told me nothing was happening between you two, Madison," Bobby cuts in accusingly, still looking at Mason. There's a look of disgust on his face, faint but unmistakable. His upper lip is curled as if he smells something bad.

Mason says quietly, "And I told you what would happen if you upset her again. But if you've forgotten, I'll happily give you a demonstration."

I have no idea what he's talking about, but the tone in Mason's voice sends chills down my spine. If I were Bobby, I'd be backing away slowly right now, swallowing a scream, my sphincter clenched in fear.

But if Bobby is affected by the threat in Mason's voice, he doesn't show it. Ignoring Mason's statement, he turns his gaze to me.

And starts firing.

"This man is a criminal. Did you know that?"

I feel Mason's energy ratchet up several more degrees toward explosion mode, but I don't turn to look at him. Keeping my voice calm, I say, "I think it's time for you to go."

"A *violent* criminal," Bobby says. "I know because I took a look into his background. I had a bad feeling about him, and I was right."

And I have a feeling you're blowing smoke.

If Mason had any criminal convictions, they would've shown up in his background check when he signed up with Perfect Pairings. This is just posturing. Mud slinging.

And I don't like it one bit.

My tone firmer, I say, "Please go now. I don't want to have to ask you again."

But Bobby isn't interested in what I have to say. He's too interested in making a point.

"He hasn't told you about his past? Well, it doesn't surprise me. I wouldn't want any woman I was trying to seduce to know how sordid it is, either."

His tone deadly soft, Mason says, "Your next words might be your last, so choose them carefully."

"More threats," sneers Bobby. "That's all you're good for isn't it?"

"That wasn't a threat. It was a promise."

"Really? You're going to assault me in front of a witness?" Bobby jerks the bouquet of flowers in my direction. "You might get away with threatening me in private, but you're insane if you think Maddie would lie to the police on your behalf. Lay a finger on me, and she'll tell them everything."

"What private threats?" I demand, my patience unraveling. "What are you talking about?"

"He warned me to stay away from you," says Bobby. "Ask him."

Startled, I turn to give Mason a look. "What? When?"

Mason's eyes blaze with anger as he gazes down at me, his jaw clenched. "It was the other way around. *He* warned *me* to stay away." When I don't say anything for too long, Mason prompts, "You don't believe me?"

Bobby laughs. It sounds cruel. "Why would she believe you—a serial womanizer with a reputation for arrogance, bar fights, and hard drinking—over me, *who she's known all her life*?"

Mason swallows. Still looking at me, he says, "Do you?"

With a sinking feeling in my stomach, I say slowly, "You said a minute ago, 'I told you what would happen if you upset her again.' So… what did you tell him would happen?"

When Mason stands silent, grinding his jaw, Bobby provides the answer.

"He said, and I quote, 'I'll make it my personal mission to

fuck you up so bad, you won't be able to bother anyone about anything ever again.' If that's not a threat, I don't know what is."

Mason and I stare into each other's eyes. I wait for him to deny it, but he doesn't.

"When was this?"

Sounding triumphant, Bobby says, "At Antonio's. The day we had lunch."

Remembering our conversation at the table after Bobby came back from the restroom that day, my stomach falls. I say, "The day you got the booty call."

Mason's brows knit. "What booty call? What're you talking about?"

"The woman who called you when you and Bobby were talking near the restrooms at Antonio's. The woman you left to go meet."

Mason's lips part. He glances at Bobby, then back at me. He exhales a short, hard breath, part laugh and part sound of disbelief. "He told you I left to go meet someone?"

"Are you saying it didn't happen?"

There's a long, tense moment of silence where Mason simply stares at me, examining my face. Then he shakes his head, as if he can't believe something. As if he's been wrong about something all along.

He says bitterly, "I guess if he said it happened, it did. Right, Maddie?"

"No," I say, exasperated. "I'm *asking* you."

"Why don't you ask him? He seems to have all the answers."

"Mason, please. Just be honest with me!"

"You want honesty, Maddie?" he says, his voice rough and his face turning red. "Okay. You got it." When he looks at Bobby, all the veins are standing out in his neck. "Go ahead. Tell her what you found out about me."

The strangest expression crosses Bobby's face. I've never seen it on a person's face before, and I hope I never will again.

It's a look of greed, madness, and victory. A bloodthirsty look, dark and chilling, one that might be worn by a warrior during a battle right before he swings his sword and chops off his enemy's head.

He says with spiteful glee, "Your new friend here spent two years in a juvenile detention center for aggravated assault. He nearly beat one of his foster parents to death with a baseball bat."

Juvenile. He wasn't an adult. The records would have been sealed by the court.

They wouldn't have shown up on a background check.

I stare into Mason's beautiful, angry eyes with a feeling like I've been shoved off a tall building and am tumbling far out into space.

"When they found the man, his face was so badly damaged, the police couldn't identify him. He spent three months in the hospital fighting for his life."

Mason isn't saying anything in his own defense. He's just looking at me.

In his eyes is a goodbye.

"Before that, your friend spent almost ten years in the system. In and out of dozens of foster care homes. He never stayed at any of them very long. Fighting, stealing, acting out… nobody could handle him. You were a problem from the start, weren't you, buddy? A bad seed, right out of the gate."

Mason makes no effort to refute Bobby's words, nor does he flinch at the cruel tone in which they're spoken. He simply stares at me and lets his silence tell the truth.

Bobby laughs, warming up to the subject. "Yes, you're a real—"

"Shut up." I rip my gaze from Mason's and whirl on Bobby.

He blinks when he sees my expression. His laugh hangs in the air for a moment, slowly dying. "Excuse me?"

Shaking with anger, I say, "I said *shut up*. What you're doing right now is disgusting."

His cheeks redden. He starts to sputter in outrage. "What-what I'm doing is-is trying to keep you safe! I'm only thinking of your best interests!"

"Baloney. You're only thinking of trying to tear him down in front of me, and I won't have it."

Scandalized that I'd be arguing with him about this, he says, "*Madison*!"

"Don't you 'Madison' me!" I say loudly, advancing toward him a step. "You know what, Bobby? I've got half a mind to call your boss in Washington and tell him that you've illegally used your political power to try to discredit an honest citizen—a *voter*—because of a romantic rivalry. How do you think that would go over, huh?"

I mimic making a phone call. "Hi, Mr. President? Yes, I just thought you should know the House of Representatives has a law-breaking rapscallion in its midst."

Eyes bugging, Bobby screeches, "*What*?"

I advance on him another step. He takes a step back to match it.

"I know that it would take a formal court order to access a sealed juvenile record. And considering you have no good legal reason to get such a court order, your request would've been denied. Which means you must've had a friendly judge who owed you a favor. Which means you broke the rules."

My volume goes up a notch. "Can you say *official misconduct*?"

Bobby's so horrified, he can't speak. He stands there clutching the bouquet of flowers so tightly the poor things are gasping.

"Now, I'm only going to say this once, so you better listen up." I fold my arms over my chest and glare at him. "Apologize to Mason."

Bobby's jaw comes unhinged. He stares at me in disbelief, mouth hanging open, color draining from his cheeks.

"Okay, I'll say it twice, because it looks like your brain has hit the pause button: Apologize to Mason. If you don't, so help me God, I'm going to call the Commander In Chief." I narrow my eyes. "*And then I'm going to call your mama.*"

In the following silence, the kitchen faucet drips mournfully into the sink. Finally, Bobby gets hold of himself. Looking at Mason, he says stiffly, "I apologize."

"Good." I point toward the front door. "Now turn your sorry butt around and leave."

He can't decide whether to holler in frustration or stomp his foot, so he does both.

I roll my eyes and sigh. "Pitch your hissy fit in your own house, Bobby. *Go.*"

Nearly bursting with fury, Bobby throws the flowers onto the floor, spins on his heel, and storms off, slamming the front door behind him.

Exhaling in relief, I turn back to Mason. He's staring at me with the same look of shocked disbelief Bobby had.

I ask gently, "Are you okay?"

His voice comes very faint. "Are *you* okay?"

"Yes. That was unpleasant, but it's not the end of the world."

He glances toward the front door, then back at me. All his anger from a few moments ago is gone, and now he seems nothing but confused. "But… what he just told you about me… you're not…"

"What?"

"Freaked out? Upset? Worried?"

"Worried about what? That you'll brain me with a baseball bat? Of course not."

When he just keeps staring at me like he doesn't understand what language I'm speaking, I sigh.

"Look, Mason. I'm not going to say I'm happy to hear it. I'm not. It makes me sad for you. I hate that you had such a rough childhood. But it also helps me understand where your anger comes from. All those foster homes… I can't even imagine."

He opens his mouth but closes it again, unable to speak.

Apparently, I need to do more explaining.

"Yes, the aggravated assault charge is bad. But knowing you like I do, I'm guessing that had to do with protecting someone else. Tell me if I'm wrong."

Mason's shock is deepening with every word I say. His eyes are wide and his lips are parted. Resting at his sides, his hands shake. He whispers, "How could you possibly know that?"

Sometimes my gut feelings are uncannily correct, that's how. The same intuition that gave me the tingles the day we met and he said he "needed" a wife was busy tingling when Bobby was telling his story.

But I can't say that out loud. I'll sound like a crazy person.

Or—worse—my aunt.

"You don't have to tell me what happened—"

"He was raping my foster sister. She was eleven years old."

Horrified, I cover my hand with my mouth. "Oh God."

He goes on, still in a whisper. "Because of my history of problems in the system, the judge went hard on me."

"Oh, Mason. I'm so sorry."

He stares at me as if horns are growing out of my head. "*You're* sorry," he repeats, astonished.

"Yes. It's awful you had to go through all that. It's even worse that you're still living with the after-effects. But I'm proud of you for going to therapy. I'm even prouder that you've managed to make such a success of yourself." My voice grows quiet. "And you should be proud of yourself, too."

He gawks at me so long I start to lose my patience. "If you thought me hearing about the terrible things that have happened to you would make me like you less, then I'm insulted."

"Like me? So you admit it. You *do* have feelings for me."

"*So* many feelings."

His voice turns rough. “Yeah? Like what?”

I try to hide my smile. “Annoyance. Frustration. Exasperation. The list is long.”

He gazes down at me, his eyes blazing with emotion. “I think we should go over that long list in the bedroom.”

He swings me up into his arms and strides out of the kitchen, headed down the hall.

29

MADDIE

We enter my bedroom. He takes us down to the bed. His weight on top of me is heavy, so heavy, but perfect and wonderful, too. So is his mouth, which clamps onto mine with renewed passion.

I do what I've wanted to do since the first day I saw him and sink my fingers deep into his mass of thick, dark hair. When I make a delirious noise of pleasure against his mouth, he pulls back to stare down at me.

In a guttural voice, he says, "You're laughing."

In between panted breaths, I answer. "No, I'm just losing my mind."

"In a good way?"

"In the best way," I whisper. "Don't stop."

His gaze turns from concerned to molten. "Bossing me around, even now."

"You're the bossy one!"

"Am not."

"Are too."

"God, you're annoying."

"At least I know what a dessert fork looks like."

We pause for a moment to grin at each other, then go back to kissing. He adjusts his weight, shifting his pelvis slightly so he's settled between my spread thighs, my skirt riding up around my hips.

He pulls away again when he hears the noise I make.

"What now?" he demands, glaring down at me.

My laugh is small and weak. "Don't be mad. It's just that I think there's a football stuck in your pants."

Mason lowers his head to my ear and gently bites my earlobe. "That's not a football, sweetheart," he breathes into my ear. "That's all me."

When I whimper, he chuckles.

He moves his mouth to my neck and starts kissing me there, gently sucking and nibbling, making his way down my throat while I writhe under him, scratching my fingernails against his scalp and trying not to burst into flames.

Sliding a hand down my waist to my bare thigh, he nuzzles his nose into the open collar of my blouse. When he kisses my chest, I freeze.

He glances up at me, his eyes hot, dark, and questioning.

My cheeks flaming, I bite my lip and turn my head so I don't have to meet his eyes. "Um. I'm not, um…"

"You're not what?"

Suddenly miserable, I squeeze my eyes shut. I whisper, "If you're expecting to see thirty-six double Ds, you're going to be disappointed."

He presses another kiss to my chest, this one lower and softer, into my cleavage.

Well, let's be honest. Into my non-cleavage. So basically just my bony sternum, where any other woman's cleavage would be.

Mason whispers, "I'm expecting to see *you*, sweetheart. Sexy, beautiful, perfect you, who could never in a million fucking years disappoint me."

I'm about to make a comment about his cursing, but he

distracts me by biting my hard nipple, right through my shirt and bra.

It's not painful, but it is completely shocking. Literally. A jolt of electricity sizzles through my body. I gasp and jerk.

"Too hard?" Mason murmurs, squeezing my thigh.

My response is a breathless babble. "No God not too hard I love it I love it please do it again don't stop."

"Since you said 'I love it' twice…"

He bites down again. A bolt of pleasure shoots from my breast straight down between my legs. I arch, moaning, my eyes rolling back into my head.

"God, yes," he says in a husky, pleased voice. "Let's see if we can do even better."

Before I have a chance to feel self-conscious, Mason pops open the remaining buttons on my blouse, pushes aside my bra, and latches onto my nipple, drawing it into the wet heat of his mouth.

The sound I make isn't human.

He sucks a little harder. In response, I wrap my legs around his waist and start to rock my hips against him, whimpering helplessly in pleasure and pulling on his hair.

"Wow," he says, chuckling. "This really makes up for all those jabs you took at my ego."

A dangerous kind of elation is building inside me. A wild recklessness, like I'm an animal with no fear of the future and no memory of the past. All I want is for him to put his mouth on me again, all over my body. I want his hands on my bare skin. I want him inside me, and for the moment I don't care at all what the consequences might be.

I just want him, consequences be damned.

I roll out from under him, push him onto his back, straddle him, and pull my fingers through my bun. I shake my hair out, letting it fall around my shoulders, and toss the elastic onto the floor.

Mason gazes up at me in frozen, stunned silence. Looking at my loose hair and flushed cheeks, his eyes flare hot with desire.

I like his expression so much I decide to let my reckless feeling take the reins.

I set my glasses on the nightstand and shrug out of my blouse. That gets tossed to the floor atop the hair elastic. Smiling, I unhook my bra and let it dangle from my fingertips.

"You're looking a little electrocuted down there, Sparky. Do I need to give you a minute to recover?"

"Maybe a lifetime," he answers, dazed. He trails his fingertips up my ribcage, making me shiver. Then he cups his big, warm hands over my breasts.

"So perfect," he murmurs to himself as he caresses me. "Just so pretty and perfect."

The look of awe in his eyes gives me a lump in my throat. I drop the bra and hide my face behind my hair, trying not to show how overwhelmed his tenderness and appreciation makes me feel.

It doesn't work. Mason sits up abruptly and hugs me.

With his face buried in my neck and his arms tight around my body, he whispers, "You can't hide. I see you. *I see you*, do you hear me?"

"I see you, too," I whisper, fighting tears.

"I know you do." He lifts his head and gazes into my eyes with a look of wonderment. "And you can't imagine what that means to me."

Closing my eyes, I exhale. He steals it from me, sealing his mouth over mine and cupping his hand around the back of my head. He kisses me like that, tenderly, cradling me, until I can't take the emotion of it and break away with a hitching breath.

He whispers my name, pressing his cheek against my chest. We stay like that for a moment, silent, him listening to the crashing of my heartbeat, until he turns his head and starts to kiss my breasts again.

I groan. "Your mouth."

"Tell me you love it." He suckles on a nipple, digging his fingers into my hips and flexing his own hips up, grinding me against his erection.

"I love it," I say breathlessly, starting to shake.

He moves his mouth to the other nipple, sucking harder, testing it gently with his teeth until I moan.

Then he slides a hand between my spread thighs and strokes me.

Over my panties.

Up and down.

There.

When I shudder in pleasure, he demands, "Tell me you love that, too."

"You know I do."

He slips his thumb under the cotton and finds the center of me, the swollen, rigid bud, so sensitive and—

"Wet," he growls. He strokes his thumb up and down again, then around in circles.

I gasp and tremble, falling apart in his arms.

In a whipcrack movement, he flips me over onto my back. Then he bends down between my legs, pulls my panties off, applies his mouth to that sensitive nub, and sucks on it.

Gasping, I sink my fingers into his hair.

He slides his thumb inside me. I moan, loudly, arching against the mattress. When he reaches up with his other hand and pinches one of my throbbing nipples, I completely lose it.

I start to buck against his face.

Then the begging starts.

"Yes, Mason, God, yes, please don't stop, please, that's so good, Oh God, *please*."

He makes a humming sound that reverberates all the way through me. I take it to mean he won't stop.

I rock against his mouth, moaning and panting, so turned on

by the shockingly carnal sounds his mouth is making against my wet flesh that I'm delirious. I've lost myself. I don't care how I might sound or look, all I care about is the bright and burning pleasure between my legs and the white hot peak he's driving me to, closer and closer with every confident swirl of his tongue.

That he knows exactly how to please a woman this way is abundantly clear.

Just as clear is my total lack of caring how much experience he's had to obtain this particular talent. All I know is that it's amazing, and I never, ever want it to stop.

Which is what I scream at the top of my lungs just before I reach that white hot peak and explode.

30

MASON

Pulling my hair and screaming, her back stiff and her thighs shaking, Maddie comes against my mouth.

I've never seen anything as beautiful as her, unbound. Her beauty is made all the more sharp at this moment because the rest of the time, she's always so controlled. Formal. Body contained within buttoned-up blouses and sensible skirts, hair wound tightly in businesslike buns.

But now she's unraveled…

Because of me.

I did this.

I feel like a god.

And I want more.

When her convulsions have stopped and her breathing has slowed to shallow panting, I turn my face to her naked thigh and kiss her there. Then I give her a bite, because her flesh is too succulent to resist.

I say, "I think you loved that, too."

One arm flung over her eyes, her naked breasts gleaming, she laughs. A low, satisfied laugh that I want to hear every day for forever.

"Someone's fishing for compliments."

I pull myself up her body and kiss her deeply. Letting her taste herself, how sweet she is.

She curves around me, sighing. "I admit it," she whispers. "I loved that, too." Then, after a pause: "Egozilla."

Feeling like I'm flying, I chuckle and nuzzle her neck. "Guilty. But we're not done yet."

I stand and pull off my T-shirt, dropping it to the floor. I'm rewarded by a pair of brown eyes going wide. Her gaze travels over my bare torso. Her lips part, but she says nothing. She only blinks.

Finally she manages, "Your… muscles… holy…"

Grinning, I say, "Thank you."

Then I kick off my boots, strip off my jeans, socks, and briefs, and stare there waiting.

Her gaze drops to my stiff dick, jutting out at right angles from my body. She opens her mouth. She closes it. She clears her throat, turning red in the face. "Mason."

"Yes, Maddie?"

"Are you seriously standing there waiting for me to gush over your big penis?"

"Well, librarians do have excellent vocabularies. I'm sure you can do much better than *big*. And *penis*, for that matter."

She throws an arm over her eyes again, muttering, "Unbelievable."

I take a moment to fish a condom out of my wallet and roll it on before I lower myself into the cradle of her thighs.

I love the feel of her underneath me. Love the way she winds her arms around my shoulders and tries to hide her smile. Love most of all the way she gasps quietly when the head of my dick nudges her wet folds.

Kissing her breasts gently and keeping myself right at her entrance but not pushing further inside, I say in a conversational tone, "Here, I'll start. 'Mason, your dick is huge.'"

She says drily, "Not nearly as huge as your infatuation with it."

"Tsk. Wrong answer." I flex my hips slightly, sliding the crown of my cock into wet heat then stopping.

She sucks in a breath and stiffens.

I go back to licking and sucking on her nipples, trying to pretend my arms aren't shaking and ignoring that steady drumbeat of *more, deeper, now* growing louder inside my body.

"Let's try again, sweetheart." I lazily lap at a pebbled nipple. "'Mason, your cock is enormous.'"

She makes a noise of discontent, shifting restlessly underneath me, pushing her breasts closer to my face. Arching her back.

"Sorry, I'm not hearing anything yet."

Her voice breathy, she says, "I can't believe you're aggravating me at a time like this."

I whisper, "Is this aggravating you?" and rock my hips in very small, controlled motions, withdrawing only to immediately push forward shallowly again.

When she moans and wraps her legs around my back, I almost lose it. But I manage not to drive hard into her and start pounding, like the beast inside my veins is roaring for me to do.

I balance on my elbows and remain motionless as she starts to buck her hips, trying to slide me deeper inside.

"Tell me, sweetheart," I breathe into her ear. "Talk to me."

She whines in frustration. "Please. Please."

"What do you want?"

She grabs my ass and tries to pull me inside her. I suck on the throbbing vein in her neck, but don't give in. I need to hear her tell me explicitly what she wants.

Then she blows the game out of the water and completely blows my mind.

She turns her head, looks into my eyes, and says very deliberately, "Mason, I want you to make love to me, I want you to do it hard, and I want you to do it *right now*."

Well, all rightie, then.

I fist my hands into her hair and drive hard into her, balls-deep.

She arches, crying out.

For a moment I'm panicked, thinking I've hurt her, but then she digs her nails into my back with a pleasure-filled "*Yes*" and I know she isn't hurt at all.

She loves it just as much as I do.

That snaps the leash on the animal inside me I've been trying to keep under control.

I grab a handful of her ass and drive into her again and again, thrusting deep and grunting, biting her neck and riding a wave of euphoria as I listen to her helpless moans of pleasure.

She raises her hips to meet my every thrust. She scratches her fingernails down my back. She says my name over and over, chanting it like a prayer, and I can't remember ever feeling so happy.

Or so terrified.

This is everything I could ever want. This connection. This fire. This honesty, too, the knowledge that I'm seen and accepted, even appreciated, despite all my shit and my failings.

She's the only person who's challenged me in years. The only one who's gotten under my skin.

The only one who can hurt me.

Groaning, I bury my face in the space between her neck and shoulder.

"I know," she whispers. "Me too."

With those words, I know my fate is sealed. There's nothing left to do but surrender.

With a long, low moan, she shudders beneath me. She's close again.

I lift my head and look at her. Her head is tipped back onto the pillow. Her eyes are closed. Her face is flushed and her lips are parted, and I don't think I've ever seen anything as beautiful in my life.

"Maddie," I say hoarsely, fighting to hold on.

"Yes," she says, bucking her hips wildly. "God, yes, Mason, *yes*—"

She stiffens, arching her back. I feel a hard contraction around my dick, and another, then I lose it on the third.

I throw my head back on a shout and come, jerking, sweating, helplessly thrusting as I spill myself inside her, my heart beating like a hammer.

Beating out the tempo of her name.

Snuggled against my side with one slender leg thrown over both of mine, Maddie has a small, blissful smile on her face that does more for my ego than a million compliments would.

The golden afternoon light has faded to a soft purple dusk. My crashing heartbeat has returned to normal. I lie on my back in her bed, trailing my fingers through her hair and looking at the poster of Emma Watson in character as Hermione Granger hanging on the opposite wall.

She's dressed in a Hogwarts uniform and brandishing her wand like a sword.

Maddie murmurs, "She was always my favorite."

"Mine too."

I feel her surprise. When I glance down at her, she's staring at me with lifted brows and a look of disbelief.

I shrug. "She's a know-it-all and can be a real pain in the ass, but without her, Harry would've probably been killed off in the first book."

Maddie's mouth drops open. She closes it again, blinking a

few times in the interim. Then she says, "I'm seeing a trend here."

"How's that?"

She glances at the poster of Hermione. "Your favorite character is a short, flat-chested, brainy, pain in the ass brunette."

"Yeah, so?"

She glances back at me. "I would've pegged you more as a Pamela Anderson fan."

"She wasn't part of the franchise."

"You know what I'm saying. Big boobs, blonde hair, unchallenging arm candy."

I smile. "You think I only like you because you're the adult version of Hermione?"

"I think maybe you have a secret weakness for sassy smart girls that you're covering up with a harem of double Ds."

I pretend to be insulted. "A *harem*? Excuse me, but I don't keep a harem."

Maddie thinks for a moment. "Does one keep a harem or have a harem?"

"Hermione would know that. Maybe you're not so brainy after all, Pink."

"Wait. Rewind. You think I'm the adult version of Hermione?" When I nod, she grins. "That might be the best compliment anyone's ever paid me."

"Really? Even though I said she's a know-it-all pain in the ass?"

Maddie shrugs that off. "Nobody's perfect. She's also brilliant, responsible, determined, brave, and always sticks up for the underdog."

Smiling, I press my lips to her forehead. "Don't forget opinionated and bossy."

Maddie quirks her mouth. "And hardworking and compassionate."

"Overly devoted to rules."

"Tenacious."

"Abrasive."

"Powerful!"

I cup Maddie's face and kiss her gently, trying not to laugh. "You're adorable, you know that?"

"Clearly. But I thought we were talking about Hermione."

"Can you stop talking for a second? I'm trying to kiss you."

"If you agree that she's powerful, I'll let you kiss me."

I stare deeply into Maddie's eyes, letting her see everything I feel. My voice husky with emotion, I say, "She's not more powerful than you, little witch."

Her cheeks flush in pleasure. She snuggles closer to me, resting her head on my chest.

We lie comfortably like that for a while, until Maddie glances up at me, her brows knitted. "Is this weird? This is weird, right?"

I sigh, rolling my eyes. "You're weird."

"Granted. But, I mean…"

"If you say one word about me being your client, I'll tickle you until you scream."

"Fine. My lips are sealed."

I snort. "Yeah, right."

"I'm serious. I won't say another word."

"You just did!"

"I meant after that. No, after this."

I press my lips together, starting a countdown in my head. She doesn't even make it to double digits before blurting, "Pink was my mom's favorite color."

Hello, fly ball. But I get the sense this is gonna be important, so I keep my mouth shut and listen, just stroking her hair.

Hesitantly, Maddie goes on. "She thought it was the color of her aura. At least that's what she always said. Her and Auntie Waldine were always going on about things like that. Auras and chakras and astrological charts. I once asked them where church fit in with all their mystical practices, and they said God was an idea that meant different things to different people, but the bottom line was positivity and love. They didn't see religion as being at odds with any of their other beliefs, since the point of all of it was to elevate the spirit."

After a while, when she doesn't continue, I ask, "So you like pink so much because it was her favorite color?"

"Because of the way she described it. All colors have meanings, she said, especially aura colors."

I'm intrigued. "So what does pink mean?"

It's a moment before she answers, and when she does, her voice is quiet. "Unconditional love. Which was her, to a T. She loved everybody. She had such a good heart. She was the best person I've ever met."

She stops abruptly, swallowing hard.

I pull her on top of me so she's resting on my body and tuck her head into my neck. Then I hug her. "She would've been so proud of you."

Maddie makes a strangled sound. "Are you trying to make me cry?"

"Nope. I'm just telling you the truth. I'm sure both your parents would've been crazy proud of you. You're a good egg, Pink. Hey—I bet your aura's pink, too!"

She groans. "Don't let Auntie Waldine know you said that. I'll never hear the end of it."

I stroke my hands down her back and inhale deeply against her hair. I could lie here like this forever.

Right then my cell phone rings, interrupting the blissed-out vibe.

"Ignore it," warns Maddie.

"I was gonna."

It stops ringing, only to start up again a few seconds later. When I still don't answer, it goes to voicemail. Next, there's a chime letting me know someone's left a message.

Thirty seconds later, a text rings through.

I sigh. "It's probably Dick. It could be important."

"An important toupee emergency," she says, smiling. "Go ahead, then." She kisses my cheek, rolls off me, and heads into the bathroom, closing the door behind her.

I dig my cell phone from the back pocket of my jeans, frowning when it starts to ring again. The screen reads *Unknown Caller*. Maybe Dick is calling from someone else's phone?

I pick it up, answering impatiently. "Yeah?"

"Don't think you've won, because you haven't."

It's Bobby. I'd recognize that douchey frat boy voice anywhere.

The evil little robot is tenacious, I'll give him that. His manufacturer must've programmed that into his hard drive.

Then it occurs to me that my number is unlisted. Only a few people have it. I stop rolling my eyes and start growling.

"How did you get this number?"

"The same way I obtained the information about your background: I'm a powerful man."

He's calmer now than when he left, but the smugness is still there. The I'm-better-than-you-and-always-will-be superiority that makes me want to hang him from a tree with his own necktie.

I snap, "Congratulations on being a civil servant with no ethics. I'm sure that will take you far."

"Farther than you'll ever go," he shoots back, his tone poisonous. "Especially when I'm done with you."

The nerve of this prick. Calling me on my own goddamn cell phone to threaten me. My blood starts to boil. "I'm sure you've got a point, dickhead. Make it."

"If you don't stay away from Maddie, I'll go public with everything I know."

My laugh is incredulous. "You think it'll be a big shock to the public that I've got a history of violence? Gimme a break!"

"Oh no," he says, sounding worryingly sure of himself. "I

doubt the public cares about *your* reputation. It doesn't get much more tarnished than that." He pauses. "But perhaps Maddie cares about hers."

Getting angrier with every word that comes out of his mouth, I demand, "What the fuck is that supposed to mean?"

"Let me spell it out for you, since you're too simple to grasp the concept. Perfect Pairings has an excellent reputation in the community. A reputation for professionalism, integrity, and, above all, honesty. How do you think it would look if it came out that its owner was engaged in not only a sordid personal relationship with a criminal with a long history of using women as disposable fuck toys, but also—wait for it—*fraud*."

My mind goes a million miles per hour, matching my racing pulse.

I'm beginning to see the picture he's painting for me.

It's so horrible, it gives me chills.

"That's right." He chuckles softly, pleased by my silence. "We both know a claim that Perfect Pairings was paid to set up a troubled, womanizing athlete in a fake marriage would be disastrous for business. Think of the press coverage! Come to think of it, your sponsors and the owners of your team might not like the idea much, either. I thought I read somewhere that if you had any more problems, you'd be kicked off the team?"

Remembering how adamant Maddie was that she wasn't running an escort service, how I had to give falling in love for real a real chance or she wouldn't match me with anyone, I feel sick.

"She hasn't done anything wrong," I say, hearing my voice as if from far away.

"That's not entirely correct. She took you on as a client. Worse, she *defended* you. Both are epic lapses in judgment, if you ask me."

Grasping at straws, I say, "I'm not her client."

"Really? Hmm. I can't figure any other reason she'd be associated with you. How do you know each other?"

Desperate to put the brakes on this runaway train, I repeat what I told Bettina at church. "Maddie and I met at a charity function."

"Which one?"

"None of your fucking business is which one!"

His satisfied laugh is like nails down a chalkboard. "That's what I thought. And here's some food for thought for you: compared to getting my hands on a sealed court record of a public figure, how hard do you think it would be for me to, say, get my hands on a particular client file from a matchmaking service?" He chortles. "Computer firewalls aren't as secure as they're made out to be."

I feel like I've been punched in the chest.

This fucker has been toying with me.

He already snagged my file from Perfect Pairings.

Which means he knows exactly how much I paid for the service, what my contract says, and everything else, right down to my ridiculous list of requirements.

Even if I denied I was trying to whitewash my reputation by getting married, Maddie would look bad, simply by having me as a client.

Guilt by association.

Then there would be the parade of women coming forward to cry prettily in television interviews about how they were used. All those girls I talked to on the phone before I went to Maddie's office to meet her that first day would crawl out of the woodwork to get their fifteen minutes of fame, cutthroat feminist attorneys who advised them to break their NDAs by their sides.

I can see the headlines now: ***Maddie the Madam Lures Unsuspecting Victims for Notorious Manwhore!***

Still, I can't let myself panic. I can't let this asshole win.

There's steel in my voice when I say, "If you go public with any of that, I'll tell everyone about this conversation, how you threatened me to stay away from her, and that all of this is just a bullshit story cooked up by a jealous ex because she turned down your marriage proposal. You can't prove either of us defrauded anyone. There's no law that says a guy like me can't decide he wants to settle down."

I can almost hear him shaking his head in amusement at my naiveté.

"No one in their right mind would find it credible that the man the tabloids call 'Sexual Chocolate' is suddenly ready to settle down. Far more believable is that you were manipulating Maddie, but either way, the damage will already be done. Her reputation will be ruined.

"And I would never be stupid enough to make the accusations myself. There are plenty of anonymous sources out there who'd happily give the scoop to reporters for free."

He pauses before going in for the kill, his voice as smooth as silk. "But if it did come down to my word against yours, Mr. Spark, who do you think the public would believe?"

I recall with sickening clarity the expression on Maddie's face when she asked about the booty call I supposedly received, the nonexistent booty call concocted by none other than Robert the robot himself:

Doubt.

And if the person who knows me better than anyone with the exception of Dick doubts me, that tells me all I need to know about how my denials of paying Perfect Pairings to set up a fake marriage would look to the public. The fraud tag would stick.

Maddie's business would be ruined.

Everything she's worked for, everything she believes in, the happily-ever-afters she's dedicated her life to finding for everyone else will mean nothing

She'll be the sleazy, unscrupulous, money-hungry matchmaker victimizing hapless women in their quest for true love.

Even though she *isn't*, but she will be.

Because of me.

Bobby says lightly, "Anyway, think about it. And who knows? Maybe nobody will care and you can ride off into the sunset together on your white trash pony." He chuckles. "Then again, maybe they will care. I'm going to check in on Maddie again tomorrow, and if I don't hear from her that you're out of her life, we'll find out which way public opinion swings."

He disconnects, leaving me standing there, naked and checkmated, incandescent with rage.

Which is how Maddie finds me when she comes out of the bathroom.

31

MADDIE

I take one look at Mason standing there with the phone in his hand and know instantly that something's wrong.

"What's up? Was that Dick?"

When I move closer to him, he steps away, looking down. "No. It wasn't Dick."

I stop. The tone of his voice is strange, flat, like he's trying to avoid letting any emotion into it. The oddness of it makes the hair on my arms stand on end.

"Who was it, then?"

When he hesitates, my stomach ties itself into a knot. I reach out and touch his arm. He pulls away quickly, like my touch has burned him. My feeling of wrongness climbs higher.

"Mason? What is it?"

"Nothing. It's just… it's just that I…" He takes a deep breath, closes his eyes briefly, then says, "I have to go."

He bends down to retrieve his jeans from the floor. He pulls them on, one leg at a time, ignoring his briefs, while I stand there in open-mouthed surprise and confusion.

"Go? Now? Where?"

"It doesn't matter."

Heat suffuses my cheeks. I cross my arms over my chest, feeling vulnerable and exposed, and very, very naked. "Excuse me, but it definitely matters. We just made love, and now you're sprinting off with no explanation after getting a mysterious phone call?"

He pulls on his shirt, stuffs his feet into his boots, shoves his phone into his back pocket, and drags his hands through his hair, all while avoiding my eyes. He says gruffly, "I'm sorry. I can't explain right now."

I'm starting to feel queasy. Queasy and unsteady on my feet, like that day I drank three double whiskeys within the space of a few minutes. Shaking with adrenaline, I yank the blanket off the end of the bed and wind it around my body.

"Mason, please talk to me. This feels strange. Is there some kind of emergency? Please tell me what's happening."

"What's happening is that I can't do this."

Everything inside me turns to ice.

My blood stops circulating.

My lungs stop breathing.

My heart freezes to a small, hard lump.

I whisper, "What?"

"I can't do this," he says more loudly, turning for the first time to look into my eyes. He looks panicked, trapped, like a caged animal.

Or like a man filled with regret.

I look at the bed, at the rumpled sheets still warm from our bodies, and something fragile inside me snaps, like a twig underfoot.

I whisper in horror, "Was that… was that another woman on the phone?"

When he doesn't answer, when he just stares at me with wild eyes and a gritted jaw, a small sound of horror escapes my lips.

My voice rising, I say, "Did you just get a booty call, Mason?

Is that what's happening right now? You got a call from another woman *and you're leaving me to go to her*?"

He says, "Would you believe me if I said no?"

"Are you saying no?"

"Answer my question."

"I'm trying to answer your question!"

"No, you're not. You're just asking another question."

A note of hysteria creeps into my voice. "Stop it! Just stop it and be straight with me! At the very least, you owe me that!"

That makes him flinch, as if I've stabbed him in the gut. He moistens his lips, hangs his head, and exhales hard, closing his eyes again.

When he lifts his head and looks at me, it's like looking at a death row inmate right after he's finished his last meal. I've never seen such a total lack of hope on a man's face in my life.

"You're right. I do owe you that. So here it is: I'm leaving. I won't be back. Whatever this was, it's over."

All the breath whooshes out of my lungs. I sit abruptly on the edge of the bed and stare up at him, dying a little more with every painful beat of my heart. "*Why*?"

His Adam's apple bobs up and down. His eyes are glassy, like he's running a fever. "Because I'm not the man for you. I think we both know that."

He's leaving. Some woman phoned him and he's leaving me, not even twenty minutes after he spilled himself inside me, calling out my name.

My voice comes out so faint it's barely a whisper. "I don't believe you. You're not this cruel. There has to be some other reason."

A look of excruciating pain crosses his face. He inhales a long, shuddering breath, then leans down and cups my face, pressing a kiss to my forehead.

"Thank you," he murmurs, his lips moving over my skin. "Please remember that."

He turns and leaves, taking what's left of my heart with him.

~

When the house phone rings a while later, I'm lying on my back on my bedroom floor wrapped in the blanket, staring at the ceiling and trying to decide which emotion I'm most filled with: hurt, fury, or disbelief.

At the moment, disbelief is winning. I feel numb.

I stand long enough to pick up the phone from the dresser, then go back to lying down. My head throbs less when I'm horizontal. "Hi, Auntie Waldine."

On the other end of the phone, there's a short silence. "How did you know it was me?"

I take a moment to ponder that. "Maybe you accidentally projected your astral body over here and it told me."

She says nonchalantly, "Oh, no, I would've known. It takes a boatload of concentrated intent to move the spirit through the astral plane."

"Good to know. Were you calling for some specific reason? Because I'm quite busy at the moment being a soggy lump of existential despair."

She clucks her tongue. "I know. I felt your energy clear across town. I told you things were about to get bumpy."

She did. I have to give her that. "That pesky Mercury."

Snorting, she says, "You think this is bad? Wait until Mars goes into retrograde!"

I sigh, closing my eyes. If things are going to get worse, I might never come out of the house again.

"Listen, child, I know things seem dark now, but it'll all work out in the end."

I say drily, "Really? So the universe is just having a laugh at my expense, is that it?"

"Don't take it personally." She pauses. "By the way, what happened?"

I give her the Cliff Notes version of events, ignoring her interjections of, "No!" and "Oh, my word!" and "That snotty little peckerwood!" when I tell her about Bobby. When I get to the part about Mason and I being intimate and then him leaving, she finally falls silent.

Eerily silent.

Suspiciously silent.

"Auntie Waldine?"

"Still here."

"You're thinking. That never ends well."

"I want you to do something for me, child."

"If it has anything to do with chatting with dead people, I'm out."

"I want you to wait before you decide anything about Mason."

"Wait for what?"

"A sign."

"You don't think him running away in panic after being inside me is a strong enough sign?"

"Oh, it's a sign all right. But not of what you think."

I groan, closing my eyes. "For goodness' sake. The man was in such a hurry to leave, he left burn marks on my carpet! He's probably fiddling with some blonde's big breasts as we speak!"

Sounding exasperated, she says, "You know, child, for such a smart girl, you can be awful dense."

"So I've been told. Are we done with this conversation yet? I hear my major depression calling."

"Oh, shush!" she scolds. "You're not depressed, you're mad as hell. Just listen to your auntie and don't do anything until you get a sign. Promise me."

"Ugh. Fine, I promise."

"Good."

She hangs up, leaving me in worse shape than before she called.

After about half an hour when a tree doesn't fall through the roof and nothing else out of the ordinary has happened, I decide to take a look outside in search of this mysterious "sign."

I peer out the window, waiting for a talking raven to peck on the glass and give me the winning lottery numbers, but that doesn't happen, either. I see no rainbows, shooting stars, or leprechauns. There are no black cats, broken mirrors, or four leaf clovers.

In fact, the only thing I see is my reflection in the glass, looking sadly worse for wear. My face is pale, my eyes are haunted, and my hair has almost achieved the angry goth porcupine look of Mason's on the first day we met.

"Stupid hair," I mutter, glaring at myself. "Stupid man. Stupid *me*, standing at the window looking for omens like a crazy person."

I throw off the blanket and go into the bathroom, where I take a long, hot shower and try to scrub away the memory of Mason's face when he said he wasn't the man for me.

By the next afternoon, my disbelief has given way to the energizing effects of a bright, burning anger.

I channel it into cleaning my office—while Auntie Waldine looks on, shaking her head—and returning Mason's contract fee to the account Dick wired it from, which wasn't nearly as satisfying as I expected.

I should've shredded cash and sent it back to him in a garbage bag like I once threatened. I bet that would've felt a lot better.

Then I call Stephanie and tell her that if we're going to continue to work together, she can't, under any circumstances, allow another man I might match with her to listen in on our phone conversations.

"I take it things didn't go well with you and Mason?" she says, sounding disappointed.

Disappointed! The nerve!

"I'd rather not get into it. But while we're on the subject, lying to me and alluding to a sexual encounter that didn't occur is all kinds of *no bueno*. What were you thinking?"

She pauses, then says, "So you didn't admit you were in love with him?"

My eyes almost pop straight out of my head. "*What*?"

"I told him you were in love with him."

My voice rises to a screech. "*Why would you do that?*"

"Because you are."

I sit frozen at my desk with the phone held in a death grip and my mouth hanging open, contemplating how long it would take me to liquidate all my assets and move to Mexico under an assumed name.

I manage to pull myself together enough to form a severe rebuttal.

"I. Am. *Not*. In. Love. With. Him."

Her lips flap as she expels a burst of air. "Right. You're so not in love with him that you're falling all over yourself to make him happy."

Filled with righteous indignation, I sit up straighter in my chair. "My *job* is to make my clients happy!"

"You know, Maddie, you strike me as someone who's very good at seeing other people, but not so good when it comes to seeing yourself. You've got a blind spot about your own strengths. And about your own feelings. Especially about that. Quite frankly, I don't think you have much self-awareness at all."

If one more person tells me I'm clueless, I'm going to burn down the city of Atlanta.

I say sarcastically, "Maybe I'll get a sign."

"I'm sorry if that hurt your feelings. I'm only trying to be helpful."

Don't you just love it when someone says something that offends you, then tries to backtrack it by saying it's for your own good?

Me, neither.

"Can we just agree that you won't do anything like that again? I don't want to cancel your contract, but if I can't trust you, I'm afraid I'll have no choice."

She gets defensive. "I wouldn't have done it if it weren't in the pursuit of true love."

I collapse face down onto the desk and groan, dropping the receiver on the blotter in the process.

Stephanie's voice comes faintly over the line. "Maddie? Are you there?"

Sighing heavily, I bring the phone back to my ear, but I keep my face on the desk because I have a feeling that by the end of the conversation, I'll want to slam it back here several more times.

"Please hold. Maddie is taking a mental health break."

"You'll be fine."

"Or I'll be entering the witness protection program. Time will tell."

"Do they have televisions in the witness protection program? Because I'm guessing you'll want to watch the news conference Mason scheduled for four o'clock this afternoon."

I bolt upright. "News conference?" I shout, my heart hammering. "What news conference? What's he going to talk about? Have you heard anything? Why would he be giving a news conference at the start of the practice season? Do you think it's bad? Do you think he got hurt? Oh my God, *do you think he's quitting football*?"

Laughing at my reaction, Stephanie says, "Yeah, you're *totally* not in love with him. Not even a teeny little bit."

This whole theme of me being blindly in love is really starting to give me a rash on my butt. "That's ridiculous!"

"Hmm."

She doesn't sound convinced, so I'm forced to provide proof. "If I were in love with him, would I want to kill him with my bare hands?"

"Definitely. It's not really love if you don't Google how to hide his dead body at least once every few months."

"Okay, that's disturbing. What kind of men have you been dating?"

Ignoring my question, she goes on. "I bet you don't fight with him at all, either. Because love is all about rainbows and butterflies and running in slow motion into each other's arms through a meadow of frolicking puppies, right?"

I open my mouth to argue, then close it again. "I mean, that sounds kind of awesome to me."

"Awesome, yes, and also totally unrealistic. If the butterflies were poisonous and the puppies were rabid and the meadow was built on top of a landfill leaking methane gas, it would be more like real love."

"Holy cow. Were you once married to Ted Bundy?"

"No, but I have been in love several times, and there were no frolicking puppies in sight. Real love is more like going to the dentist: painful, but good for your health in the long run. Here's another one for you: I bet he's exactly your type, right?"

"No!" I crow triumphantly. "We're nothing alike! We're total opposites!"

"Congratulations, you just made my point for me. If you had everything in common with a man, you'd be bored to tears within weeks. It's like magnets, Maddie. Opposites attract."

I think of me and Bobby together and deflate. "And to think

I've spent all these years getting couples together based on their similarities."

"I'm not talking about people's interests and backgrounds. That's a great starting point. I'm talking about *chemistry*. No list of commonalities in the world amounts to more than a hill of beans if there isn't chemistry to hold it all together."

We sit in silence for a while, until I say, "I know. Crap."

"Don't sound so hopeless. The night is darkest before the dawn."

"Oh, good, greeting card platitudes. I feel so much better now."

Stephanie laughs. "If I promise not to tell any other men you're in love with them, will that make you feel better?"

"Much."

"Okay, deal. So who else do you have for me to look at?"

I smile. "I think I've got a few serial killers you might be interested in. Very hot and good with their hands. Plus, you won't have to Google how to hide a dead body because they'll already know."

"Sounds perfect."

"Stephanie?"

"Yes?"

"Aren't you going to apologize for telling Mason I'm in love with him?"

She chuckles. "You just keep on pretending you're not magnets, hun, and send me an invitation to the wedding."

She rings off.

I don't have time to dwell on the conversation, however, because when I glance up at the clock and see the time, I have other things to worry about.

It's three minutes to four.

I need to get to a television.

32

MASON

What I needed to do came to me in the middle of the night.

I'd left Maddie and gone home and had been walking around my property for hours. Just wandering around in the dark. Wandering and brooding and, if I'm being totally honest, plotting Bobby's death and dismemberment.

I mean, I've got plenty of acreage and a backhoe I bought on a whim that would come in pretty handy for digging big holes.

Just saying.

Anyway, after the robot-murder urges wore off and the depression set in, I went into the house, poured myself a whiskey, and sat my sorry ass down at my kitchen table. Then, for some strange reason, I said out loud to my empty kitchen, "What the fuck am I doing?"

Then I thought about it.

I really *thought* about it, for a long time.

Eventually, I realized that everything I'd done in my life had led me to this moment. All my fuck ups, all my bad choices, all my decisions about how to handle the things life had thrown my way had led me to sleeping with the woman of my dreams and promptly getting blackmailed by her ex boyfriend, thus losing her.

Yeah. I was in the middle of some pretty heavy existential shit.

But by the time the birds were up and dawn was spreading long golden fingers across my lawn, I felt better. Not happy, because I knew what I was gonna do was not guaranteed to succeed, but calm.

Because it was necessary. And I believed I'd come out on the other end a better man.

"Be the man you think would deserve her," Coach said.

The man I was now wasn't there yet.

So I called Dick and told him to get on the horn with the networks to set up a press conference. Then I called Coach and told him that I wanted to meet with the team first thing before practice. I said I've got something to say to them that they're gonna want to hear.

Then I sat back down at my kitchen table and did something I haven't done since I was five years old.

Prayed.

Not sure if worked or not, but maybe I'll get a sign.

33

MADDIE

I grab Auntie Waldine and drag her across the street to the sports bar. They've got about a thousand TVs in there. Surely Mason's press conference must be on one.

I burst through the front door and quickly scan the TVs, but don't see Mason. So I run up to the bartender, a young man with a goatee and a giant forearm tattoo of the Patriots logo right below Tom Brady's smiling face.

I'm really starting to think God has a perverse sense of humor.

Throwing myself against the bar, I blurt, "There's a press conference on with Mason Spark of the Pioneers do you know what channel?"

The bartender stops polishing the glass in his hand and makes a sour face. "The Pioneers?"

Lord, give me strength.

Composing myself, I say somberly, "I heard their QB is trash-talking Tom Brady on live TV."

The bartender's eyes flare in outrage. He slams the glass down on the bar, snatches up a remote control, points it at the nearest TV, and starts clicking through all the sports channels at a furious pace.

"There!" I shout, spotting Mason sitting behind a table.

The bartender turns up the volume. Then he crosses his arms over his chest and glares at the TV, muttering, "I can't stand this asshole."

I don't want him to turn it off, so I try to project a disapproving air. "Right? He's so…" *Gorgeous. Funny. Incredible in bed.*

"Arrogant," says the bartender. "And selfish. He thinks he's the only one on the goddamn team. I can't wait until he fucks up again and management kicks him to the curb. Their second-string QB is amazing. Nobody will be sorry to see this jerk go."

There's a serrated knife two feet to my left on the bar that someone had been using to slice limes. I'd like to grab it and brandish it in this guy's face, even if he is a Patriots fan.

Beside me, Auntie Waldine says, "Shh! He's talking!"

"…got a prepared statement I'd like to read. I won't take too much of your time."

Sitting behind a table forested with microphones, Mason looks like he's been up all night. There are dark shadows under his eyes, he hasn't shaved, and his hair is… well, it might as well have leaves and twigs in it for how much it looks like he spent several hours rolling around in dense undergrowth.

He's wearing the same clothes he had on yesterday when he left my house.

I press my hand over my heart because of how hard it's suddenly pounding.

He clears his throat and starts to read from the paper in his hand.

"First and foremost, I want to apologize to my team, the ownership and management, my coach, and all the amazing fans of the Pioneers for the way I've conducted myself since I was drafted."

He pauses. In the press room, it's silent except for the whirring of cameras.

The bartender pronounces, "Either he's been fired, or he's coming out of the closet."

At the same time, Auntie Waldine and I hiss, "*Shh*!"

Mason continues, his voice quiet, his eyes downcast. "I have no excuse for my past behavior, except ignorance. I expect many of you won't believe what I'm about to say, and I accept that. I know I can only prove myself through actions, not words."

He stops to take another breath. In his hand, the paper shakes.

"My mother overdosed when I was five years old. It was three days before someone found us. I remember those three days vividly. They're not an experience I would wish on anyone. There were no relatives to take me, so I was placed into foster care. I stayed in the system, moving through more than a dozen foster homes, until I was fourteen, at which time I was convicted of assault and sent to a juvenile detention center."

Fighting tears, I cover my mouth with both hands.

The bartender says, "Whoa."

Mason goes on. "That's where I discovered football. It was the first positive influence I had in my life, the first and only thing I excelled at, and I couldn't get enough. When I got out of juvie, I tried out for my high school team. What happened from there is public record. After high school, I won a full scholarship to Ohio State, and upon graduation was drafted to the Pioneers, where I've remained for the past six seasons."

He pauses again, looking up into the cameras. "And where I've acted like a total ass for the past six seasons."

The bartender chuckles. "Fifty bucks says he's gay."

Auntie Waldine puts her hand on my arm to stop me from picking up the knife.

Mason looks back at the paper and starts to read again. "It took a threat against someone I care about for me to finally realize that my actions have consequences, and that I needed to make some major changes in my life."

"A threat?" muses Auntie Waldine. "I wonder what that's about?"

I don't have to wonder. I already know. My intuition is buzzing like crazy.

The phone call.

Bobby.

I whisper, "Oh God."

Mason says, "So, I've decided a few things. First, my NFL salary for this season is being donated to The Way Forward, a non-profit charity that supports homeless and at-risk kids."

Now the bartender is flabbergasted. "What?" he cries. "That's like thirty million bucks! What a waste of money!"

Another guy a few seats down the bar says, "It's a good tax write-off. He's probably in trouble with the IRS."

I want to stab them both.

Mason goes on. "Second, my seventeen-acre property in Buckhead will now be home to the foundation I'll be forming, Camp Sparky, a year-round sports camp for underprivileged youth."

"Oh, he's lost it," chuckles the bartender. "Next he's gonna give his vacation house to his longtime secret lover, Doug."

"So what if he did?" I say loudly, bristling. "Do you have a problem with gay people?"

He shrugs. "Not if they're Patriots fans."

I'm never setting foot in this stupid sports bar again.

Mason is still talking. "Finally, in partnership with Atlanta's New Day Foundation, I'm going to set up a grant for food and housing assistance benefitting addicts who've completed drug treatment programs. I'm hoping to name the program after my mom, Lauren, but we'll see. I just talked to New Day this morning about the grant, so we're still working out logistics."

"Good for him," says the guy down the bar, munching on beer nuts.

"Yeah," says the bartender sourly. "Now he's only ninety-eight percent asshole."

Then Mason looks up into the camera again, gray eyes fierce.

"The Pioneers have won our conference championship six years running. We've made it all the way through the playoffs, only to lose out on our chance at a Super Bowl ring. I believe that my poor leadership and bad attitude has led to a lack of trust on the part of my teammates, and that breakdown of trust has cost us our ultimate goal. As team captain, I blame this entirely on myself.

"Starting today, things will be different. I can't promise I'll be perfect. I'm a very imperfect man. But I can promise that I'm committed to being a better man. For my team and for the fans, but especially for the person who taught me what it looks like to be good. And that being good is a hell of a lot better than being a selfish idiot."

Someone in the press room calls out, "Who is that person, Mason?"

Mason pauses, swallowing. In a thick voice, looking straight into the camera, he says, "Hermione. If it weren't for her, Harry never would've defeated Voldemort."

At the same time I realize I'm not breathing, the TV screen goes wonky. A weird, fuzzy halo appears all around Mason's head.

A halo colored a very distinctive bright pink.

"Auntie Waldine?" I whisper, wide-eyed.

"Yes, child?"

"Is there something wrong with the television?"

She answers softly, her voice warm. "No, child."

I really wish I were the fainting type, because right about now would be a great time to pass out.

34

MASON

Everyone's shouting questions at me. Cameras flash in my face. But I've said what I came here to say, so I rise and thank them for coming, then get the hell out of there.

Dick is in the hallway outside the press room at the training facility. He's leaning against the wall, arms folded across his chest, smiling. "I'm proud of you."

"Don't be proud yet. Coach signed off on this because he read what I was gonna say, but management might not like it."

Dick waves his hand in the air, pushing away from the wall. "Fuck management. This is great optics for the team. They're gonna cream their jeans when they see you trending on Twitter."

Thinking of it, I shudder. "I can see the hashtag now. AssholeMeaCulpa."

"Don't worry about it. Besides, I've got somethin' more important for you to worry about."

"Oh yeah? What?"

"Coach wants to see you in his office. It's about the new uniforms."

"Why should I be worried about the new uniforms?"

Dick gives me a Mona Lisa smile. "You'll see. I'll be waitin' outside in the car when you're done."

He saunters off, leaving me alone and wondering. I make my way to Coach's office on the other side of the building, knocking on his door when I arrive.

"Come in."

I open the door to find him sitting behind his battered desk, looking like he'd like to rip off someone's head. He sees me and says, "Saw you on the closed-circuit TV. Good job."

Relieved, I take the chair across from his desk. "Thank God. Judging by the look on your face, I thought I was canned."

"Oh no. Not you. But whoever messed up the order on our new uniforms deserves to not only get fired, but shipped off to a work camp in Siberia."

"What's wrong with the new uniforms?"

Coach's laugh is dark. "What's wrong with them? Oh, nothing much. If you're okay with being the laughingstock of the entire National Football League, that is."

He rises, crosses to a rolling garment rack on the other side of the room, and unzips the white plastic cover that surrounds it. Pulling a flap aside, he points at the uniforms hanging from the metal pole.

"Our new uniforms were supposed to be navy and white. What color would you say this is, son?"

Well, I wanted a sign.

Here it is.

I start to laugh and can't stop, not even when Coach starts hollering. I laugh until tears are in my eyes, then I stand and go for a closer look at the new uniforms, which are vibrantly, totally, and quite undeniably the color of unconditional love.

Pink.

35

MADDIE

In a dream state, I let Auntie Waldine lead me out of the bar and back across the street to the office. Once there, I collapse into my chair and stare blankly at the wall.

"You need some chamomile tea," says my auntie, taking pity on me.

"Or something stronger."

"Like what, child?"

"I don't know, but it better not contain eye of newt."

She lifts her brows. "No bat wool or toe of frog either?"

When I realize she's joking, I sigh in relief. "Very funny. If we've got a bottle of tequila hidden away somewhere, that will do."

She pats my shoulder, clucking her tongue. "I remember the first time I saw an aura. I was an eight-year-old child at Disney World and there was this African elephant in the animal experience park with the most *incredible* purple aura you've ever seen. So majestic. I had to go speak with the creature."

When I don't respond but only stare at her, she adds, "We're still friends to this day."

"Of course you are. Tequila?"

"I'll see what we've got." She heads out, leaving me flattened in my chair.

Before I can uncross my eyes and unscramble my brains to try to make sense of things, Bobby comes waltzing through my office door.

Grinning from ear to ear.

Carrying another blasted bouquet of flowers.

I smile pleasantly at him. "Look what the cat dragged in."

If he's taken aback by that, he doesn't show it. He adopts a contrite expression, gathering the bouquet of flowers to his chest like a beauty pageant contestant.

"Madison," he says very seriously. "I want to apologize for yesterday's unfortunate incident."

The great thing about people thinking you're a goody-two-shoes is that they never suspect you might be capable of being more than that.

My cell phone is in the hidden pocket in the side of my skirt. I stand, turn toward the windows, and slip out my phone, pretending to gaze pensively at the street. I tap the icon for the voice memo app, then hit the record button. Then I turn, pulling my arms behind my back, and sit on the edge of my desk. I quietly set the phone down behind me.

I say, "Go on."

Encouraged by my calm demeanor, he tries out a smile. It makes him look like he's in dire need of a restroom.

"Things got a bit heated last night—"

"When I got upset that you'd illegally accessed Mason Spark's sealed juvenile record, you mean?"

His fingers tighten on the bouquet. "I find your infatuation with that person perplexing."

"Is that why you called him yesterday and blackmailed him?"

His eyes go owl round. "He told you that?"

"He told me everything," I lie, making it up as I go along.

"But I wasn't sure if I believed him. Why don't you tell me what happened yourself?"

When he opens his mouth, I warn, "And please, be honest. If I think you're lying, there's no chance for us at all."

I can see his ears prick, though he tries to play it cool. "So there is a chance for us?"

"That's up to you, Bobby," I say, trying my best to look winsome. "If we're going to be together, I'd have to know I can trust you. But you've shown me a different side of yourself lately..." I cast my gaze downward. "A more cunning side. The man I thought I knew would never do something as unethical as circumventing the law."

He steps closer, his voice gaining an edge. "I had to look into his background, Madison. I knew he was bad news, and I was right. But you must understand, I did it for you. For *us*."

I sigh, toying with my hair and channeling my inner Bettina. "So, you called in a favor from someone to get Mason's record? A judge?"

"Yes," he says with exaggerated patience, like you'd say *Duh*. "The point is that Mason Spark has a history of violence."

"Funny you should say that, because he said you threatened him with violence when you called him last night."

"I did no such thing!"

"What did you say to him, then?"

He abandons the bouquet of flowers onto the desk and approaches me with the look of a man on a mission. Grasping me by the arms, he gazes into my eyes.

"I told him he'd ruin your reputation. That he didn't deserve someone like you. That if he didn't leave you alone, I'd..."

"What? You'd do what?"

Bobby's eyes harden. "I'd let the whole world know what a piece of shit he was."

I blink like a crazed ingénue, attempting to look like I'm swooning at the drama of it all. "So you *did* blackmail him."

"Think of it as a strong suggestion."

"Backed up by illegally-obtained court records."

"I'd do anything for you, my darling."

"Including coercion, invasion of privacy, and breaking your oath of office?"

"Of course."

"How romantic."

He clasps me against his chest exactly like he did with the bouquet of flowers, which I now feel very sorry for, and leans in for a kiss.

I shove him aside so hard he stumbles and falls flat on his ass on the floor.

"Bobby," I say, looking down at him as I pick up my cell phone, "go suck an egg." Then I hit rewind on the voice app and replay the conversation.

He screams like a little girl and scrambles to his feet. He lunges at me, attempting to grab the phone. I jerk away, yelping in surprise.

Then something flies across the room and hits him smack on the side of his head.

He topples over and lies flat on the floor, arms and legs splayed out like a stick figure's. He groans once, then falls silent, knocked out.

Breathing hard from the adrenaline coursing through my veins, I look across the office to Auntie Waldine standing in the doorway.

She gestures casually toward Bobby. "I brought your tequila. I hope his skull didn't crack that bottle, it's the good stuff."

I look at him lying there pathetically. There doesn't seem to be any blood leaking from his head, but I don't want to be responsible for an undiagnosed brain injury, so I call the paramedics and tell them to come and pick up the representative from the fifth congressional district off my office floor.

"He tripped and fell," I tell the operator. "I think he might have been drinking."

After examining Bobby and finding him fine except for a bruised ego and a knot on the side of his head, the paramedics left.

So did he, sulking.

"Why do I have the feeling this isn't over?" I ask Auntie Waldine as we watch him peel out of the parking lot.

"Don't worry about him. I'll get the girls together and we'll ask the spirit of his great grand-pawpaw Delmer to give him a visit. That'll scare him straight."

I turn and look at her with raised brows, and she shrugs. "He was a bootlegger and a gangster and a real mean son of a gun, but he wouldn't tolerate any mistreatment of women."

"And you know this how?"

She says airily, "Oh, he's always comin' and goin' during our monthly séances. The man is nosy as can be."

And this is my life.

"Why don't you go on home, now, child. Take a bath. Have a nice glass of wine. You've had a stressful day. I'll close up the office."

"Thanks, Auntie Waldine. I love you, you know."

She smiles, patting my back. "I know, child. We Scorpios are irresistible."

I go home, but I'm a mess of nerves and restlessness. Not even cleaning helps. I decide the only thing that will help is talking to Mason, so I give him a call, biting my nails with anxiety when the phone starts to ring.

He doesn't answer.

"Fine," I mutter, staring at my cell. "We'll do this the hard way."

I send him a text.

Saw you on TV. I know what happened with Bobby. Can we talk?

After a few minutes when the little dots appear indicating he's writing back, I almost pass out from anxiety. Then his text comes through and my anxiety spikes through the roof.

Open your front door.

I run to the door and yank it open. There he is, standing on my porch with his signature glower, looking heartbreakingly handsome. I want to drag him inside and rip off his clothes, but I'm still a lady. So that only happens inside my head.

He says gruffly, "I was only gonna drive by and look at your house, but you sent me that text right when I turned the corner onto your street, so I had to stop. It felt like a sign."

I nod. "It's like the universe is trying to tell us something."

We stand there and stare at each other for a moment, until he says, "I meant what I said. I'm not the man for you."

"No, I get it. The man you are now isn't the man you want to be, and that's the guy you think deserves me. The future you, not the current one."

He blinks. "Yeah. That's pretty much exactly it."

"Don't look so surprised, Sparky. I've got a big brain. We librarians are very bookish, remember? But just for the record, the current you is pretty F-wording great."

His mouth does that twitching thing it does when he's trying not to smile.

"Oh, by the way? We don't have to worry about Bobby anymore because I blackmailed him in return for blackmailing you, and also his dead great grand-pawpaw Delmer is going to pay him a visit."

"I… have no idea what that means."

"It doesn't matter. What matters is that if you ever, and I

mean *ever*, run out on me again after we've made love, I will kill you. And most likely, I mean that literally."

"Deal." He looks me up and down, his eyes drinking me in, then says in a husky voice, "So I hear you're in love with me."

My heart, already pounding, goes totally haywire. "That's what they keep telling me."

"Are you?"

I sigh heavily and throw my arms in the air. "Probably."

He loses the fight with his mouth. The corners of his lips curve up into a smile. Eyes burning, he takes a step closer. "Even though I'm the most aggravating man on the planet, huh?"

"Yes. That's going to be a problem."

He takes another step closer, and now he's only inches away, gazing down at me with that beautiful smile and all that heat in his eyes. "Maybe we should make up some rules, then."

"What kind of rules?"

"Rules of engagement. Like military forces have for governing combat between enemies. The terms of war."

"You know, that might be the most sensible thing you've ever said to me. I'll go first. Rule one: don't be aggravating."

He chuckles, taking my face in his hands. "Rule two: don't be bossy."

"Ha! Rule three: don't start conversations near public toilets."

Very gently, Mason presses his lips to mine. Against my mouth, he whispers, "Rule four: don't ever speak the name Tom Brady near a bed. Or in the entire house. Or anywhere else, for that matter."

"Ooh, that's a toughie. I don't think I can agree to that one. My dear, dreamy, beloved Tom Br—"

He cuts me off with a hard kiss, just as I was hoping he would.

I wrap my arms around the strong breadth of his shoulders and melt into him with a happy sigh. Then he picks me up, kicks the front door shut, and heads down the hall toward the bedroom.

"Rule five," he says. "Stay away from cruciferous veggies and beans."

"What do they have to do with anything?"

He slants me a look. "They're highly gas producing."

I whack him on the shoulder, but can't stop from laughing. "Okay, fine. Rule six: stay away from any pairs of breasts larger than a B-cup."

He rounds the corner to my bedroom and takes us down to the bed, grinning when he lands on top of me. "Silly girl. You should've said, 'Stay away from any breasts other than mine.'"

I give him another smack. "It was implied!"

He kisses me again, this time until I'm breathless. When we come up for air, we're both panting.

"Rule six: only cats in quantities fewer than three are allowed."

He rips open my blouse and starts kissing his way from my neck down to my breasts, pulling aside my bra to lick my nipples. I moan, arching into him.

I breathe, "Rule seven: no booty calls."

He slides his hand up my thigh and under my skirt, flexing his pelvis into mine so I feel his erection. "Rule eight," he says, his voice muffled against my skin. "No robots."

"Robots?"

"Never mind."

I dig my fingers into his full, lush hair and lie back against the pillows, loving the rough scrape of his jaw on my sensitive skin, loving the ragged sound of his breathing, loving how heavy and warm and wonderful he feels on top of me.

Loving all of it, and him.

I whisper, "Hurry. Don't bother getting undressed."

He pulls off my panties, rises to his knees to pull out his wallet, rips open the fly of his jeans, and wraps his jutting erection in a condom so fast it probably set a speed record. Then he positions himself between my spread legs and thrusts inside me without a word, just as desperate as I am.

"Rule nine," I say brokenly, my body aching with pleasure. "Do this every single day."

He rises up on his elbows and gazes down into my eyes. Cradling my head and thrusting again, he says hoarsely, "Every day for forever."

He thrusts again, then again, and then we forget about the rules altogether.

EPILOGUE

MASON

Seven months later

As it turned out, the very next day after my now infamous press conference, Bobby was censured by the Office of Congressional Ethics for multiple violations including solicitation of funds, financial irregularities, and an inappropriate sexual relationship with a young congressional staffer.

Basically, for being an all-around dickhead.

Maddie was more than a little pissed that he'd tried to salvage his reputation by proposing to her. Because, sure, getting engaged to your childhood sweetheart who also happens to be in the business of helping people find their soul mates is great optics when you're in the middle of an ethics scandal, but only if they say yes.

He knew the investigation was ongoing, and he tried to use her as a Band-Aid.

He ended up resigning his position in the House. Last we heard, he was working as an Uber driver and shopping around his memoir.

I seriously doubt we'll be seeing that on any bookstore shelf.

Oh, and his mother didn't die, either. Her imminent demise was greatly exaggerated by Bobby, just another ploy to gain Maddie's sympathy. She's up and around again, gardening and playing lots of bridge thanks to the shiny new stent in her heart.

As for me and Maddie… well, it's going great.

So great, as a matter of fact, that I went out and bought a ring.

I had no idea such a thing as pink diamonds existed, but they do.

And holy fuck, are they expensive.

I've been trying to think of the right time and way to propose, but I don't want to screw it up, so I'm waiting. I want it to be perfect. A perfect fairytale, because that's what my girl deserves.

Maybe I'll get a sign.

"Are you nervous?"

"No. You?"

"Lord, yes. I think I'm having a stroke. I could be dying as we speak."

"If you do, I'd like to bury you in this dress. You look beautiful."

I squeeze Maddie's slim thigh. She's sitting beside me in the back of the limo on our the way to the Hard Rock Stadium, pale and nervous and dressed in a gorgeous royal blue velvet sleeveless dress. She's been adding a lot of blue to her wardrobe lately, branching out from all the pink.

I like to think it's because I happened to mention that blue is my favorite color, but I don't want to say that and push my luck.

"Thank you," says Maddie, glancing over at me with a smile. "I think."

"*I'm* peachy keen, thanks for askin'," calls out Waldine from the other side of the limo.

Sitting next to Dick, she's wearing a skin-tight leopard print onesie and a white jacket that probably used to belong to Liberace. I've never seen so many sparkles and tassels on one piece of clothing in my life.

Compared to her, Dick almost looks conservative in his green-and-yellow plaid suit.

Although it is Miami, so they both fit right in.

"Nothin' to worry about, Maddie," says Dick. "Our boy's played the best damn ball of his career this season. The Pioneers are a well-oiled machine. They're a shoe-in for the big win, that's for sure."

With a squawk, Waldine leans over and raps her knuckles on his head.

"What the hell are you doin', woman?" Dick hollers, batting her hands away.

"Knockin' on wood! You can't tempt fate like that, you big dummy!"

They continue their squabble while Maddie and I look on, amused. Then we're pulling into the stadium parking lot and Maddie starts to hyperventilate.

"Easy, tiger." I pull her over and kiss her temple. She grabs my hand, and hers is ice cold.

"How are you so calm?"

I smile at her gently. "Been here before a few times."

"Super Bowl fifty-four, here we come."

"You gonna be okay in the suite with Dick and your aunt?"

"Oh, sure. We'll just be getting drunk and praying to various deities for good fortune while we watch the game. If you happen to see the spirits of any of your ancestors floating around, ignore them."

Dick says crossly, "I ain't prayin' to no celestial beings, genies, sprites, or fairies, no how. They'd never let me back into Brooklyn."

Auntie Waldine says, "When was the last time you were in Brooklyn?"

"Nineteen-seventy-two."

"Then what in the name of Colonel Sanders are you talkin' about!"

"It's about street cred, somethin' you obviously know nothin' about!"

"Street cred?" She cackles with laughter. "Lord, Dick, if you were worried about that you wouldn't go around dressed like a lounge singer in a second-rate Reno motel!"

"Ha! This from the woman who dresses like the love child of Elton John and Jennifer Lopez!"

Auntie Waldine is about to retort with something smart, but changes her mind. Smiling at him, she pats her mass of red curls. "Actually, that's a beautiful compliment. Thank you."

He rolls his eyes and sighs.

The driver pulls to a stop in front of a private entrance at the back of the stadium and we all get out. We're met inside by a staffer who takes us up to our reserved suite on the club level. It sits just above the thirty yard line and has an amazing view of the entire field.

The stadium is empty now, but game time is in less than three hours, so the seats will soon be filling up.

"This is way too big for just the three of us," says Maddie, looking around the luxury suite in awe.

"Nonsense," scoffs Waldine, throwing her studded purple handbag onto one of the big leather sofas. "Where's the butler? Mama needs a drink."

"I'll send the concierge right in to take your food and drink orders," says the staffer, giving Waldine a little bow.

When she leaves, a grinning Waldine wiggles her eyebrows at Maddie. "Now *that's* service, child. I could get used to this."

"We've gotta get down to the locker room soon," Dick says, checking his watch. "Pre-game meeting in thirty."

"We've got a few minutes."

"Go, please. I don't want you to see me having my nervous

breakdown, anyway." Maddie winds her arms around my shoulders and gives me a hug.

I squeeze her back, inhaling the scent of her hair and smiling.

"Break a leg," she whispers.

I whisper back, "You're only supposed to say that to someone going on stage."

"Sorry. Good luck?"

"I was hoping for maybe one word more than that."

She pulls away to frown at me. "Um… really good luck?"

"No, sweetheart," I say gently. "I was thinking more along the lines of three words you haven't said to me yet."

"I doubt there are three words in the English language I haven't said to you yet. We've been joined at the hip every day for months. You've practically moved into my house."

"But you haven't said three *particular* words in a very *particular* order."

She scrunches up her nose and stares at me like I'm speaking Swahili. I gaze down into her beautiful brown eyes and wait for her to get it.

When she does, her eyes go round and her mouth forms the shape of an O.

"Yeah," I murmur. "Those three words."

She flattens her hands over my chest and pretends to think. "I'm sure I've said those words to you."

"Nope."

"Really?"

"Really."

"Hmm. Now that you mention it, I don't think you've said those words to me, either."

"Really?"

"Really."

"Hmm."

We stand there smiling at each other until Maddie says, "Okay, superstar. Here's three words for you. You ready?"

I adopt a serious face, though my heart is hammering. "I'm ready."

Looking into my eyes, she says calmly, "Let's get married."

I almost topple over onto the floor. "*What*?"

"You don't have to shout at me. You did ask for three words, after all."

I'm so astonished I almost can't from a sentence. "B-but I thought… I meant… I love you!"

She smiles serenely at me. "I know you do, Mason. I love you, too. So much."

"No—I meant I thought you were going to *say* I love you!"

"I know you did, honey, but I figured unless I popped the question first, you'd carry that big pink diamond around for who knows how long before you got around to asking me, so…" She shrugs. "Here we are."

My jaw hangs open. "*You know about the ring*?"

Waldine throws herself onto one of the sofas, props her feet up on the arm, folds her arms behind her head, and grins at me.

"Honey, half of Atlanta knows about the ring. You think you could sneak into a jewelry shop and plunk down millions on a piece of ice in that town and nobody would hear about it? Psh."

I groan. "No! I wanted it to be a surprise!"

"It was a surprise," says Maddie, laughing. "At the time, when a friend of a friend of a friend of the sales clerk called to congratulate me on my engagement. But now it's not. So are we getting married, or what? And where is that ring, anyway? I hear it's huge."

Crestfallen, I say, "I've got it in the safe at the house. I was trying to think of the perfect way to ask you."

"And you did. Well, I did. Whatever. The point is that we're engaged now, right?"

Feeling a little pouty that I didn't get my fairytale proposal, I say, "I don't know. I didn't hear a yes."

Maddie puts her hands on either side of my face and goes up

on her toes to kiss me. "Yes, Mason. Yes. A million times, yes. Except I proposed to you, so you're supposed to be the one saying that."

She looks at me with a cocked brow, waiting.

I feel a swell of love inside my chest, growing bigger and bigger until I don't think my ribcage will be able to contain it. Then I gather her back into my arms and kiss her again.

"Yes, Pink. I'll marry you. And I promise from this day forth to only aggravate you ten percent of the time."

Her eyes shining, she says, "Don't make promises you can't keep, Sparky."

"Okay. Fifty percent of the time."

"I wish. Now go get ready for the game, because I foresee another big ring in your future."

Her confidence in me makes my heart swell even bigger. I love this woman so much, sometimes it gets hard to breathe.

"Okay, but if I see Tom Brady between now and kickoff, I can't be responsible for what happens."

"You're not playing the Patriots, honey."

No, we aren't. They lost to the Titans a month ago, putting them out of contention for the Super Bowl, which was just so, so tragic.

Not.

"I'm just saying. He could be in the stadium. You never know."

Maddie gives me a final kiss, laughing against my mouth, then shoves me gently toward the door. "Go. I'll see you after the game, Sparky. That'll be me running at you on the field, screaming in happiness like a crazy person."

"That's a deal, Pink," I say, my voice husky. "I'll see you then."

Dick and I say goodbye to Waldine, then we make our way from the suite through the echoing corridors of Hard Rock Stadium, headed to the locker room, where the team will gather soon for a pep talk from Coach and our final preparations for our seventh shot at a league championship title.

I know that I've done all I could've over the past seven months to get us closer to that goal. I've worked hard to build bridges, mend fences, and be the best possible man I could be. Some days are easier than others, but deep in my heart I know I've already won the biggest prize of my life.

Nothing's more important than what I have with Maddie. Not money, not fame, and not a football game, either.

She saved me. She's all the best parts of me, all that I could ever hope for, and I'll love her until the day I die.

Three hours later, suited up and ready for battle, my team and I run out onto the gridiron, the deafening roar of the crowd like a thousand jet engines in our ears.

Spoiler alert: we won.

ACKNOWLEDGMENTS

Halfway through writing this book, my mother died. My father died in 2014 when I was in the middle of writing a book, too, so I suppose in a way I was more prepared this time for how everything would grind to a standstill, but nonetheless, the effect on me was profound. I sat with her in her hospital room for the last ten days of her life, watching her die, just the two of us and the most caring, beautiful people on earth: nurses. I want to say a special thank you to the nursing and hospice staff of Adventist Hospital in Simi Valley, California, for their kindness, tact, and generosity, and for making my mom's last days comfortable. You helped us both more than you can ever know.

My mom gifted me with several priceless things, including mental toughness, a dry sense of humor, a deep love of wine, music, movies, and handsome waiters, and a reverence for the written word. Also an appreciation for scotch, but that came later, when happy hour at her assisted living facility was every day at 2pm.

Which reminds me: thank you to the staff and management of The Foothills in Simi Valley. The Jersey Girl really loved you guys.

Her last words to me—her last spoken words to anyone before she lapsed into a coma a few days before she died—were "I love you." I love you, too, Mom. Thank you for everything you and Dad did for me. I've had a beautiful life.

Thank you to my best friend and husband, Jay, for loving me unconditionally. It's rare to be accepted completely without judgment by anyone except cats.

Thank you to Letitia Hasser of RBA designs for your wonderful work and creativity. I always love the covers you design for me.

Big thanks to my PR firm, Social Butterfly PR, and to Sarah Ferguson, PR person extraordinaire. Your help over the past few years has been invaluable, and I can't thank you enough for how you stepped in to handle things when I had a book release the same day my mom died.

Thanks to my wonderful readers for your support! It truly means the world to me.

Big thanks also to my Facebook reader group, Geissinger's Gang, for being so much fun to hang out with and showing so much enthusiasm for these people I create in my head.

Shout out to George Carlin for his classic comedy piece about the usefulness of the F word.

I'd also like to give a shout out to Tom Brady, whom I love deeply, and to Bill Belichick and the entire New England Patriots football team. You're the best and you always will be. Thank you for dominating American football for two decades.

Go Pats.

ABOUT THE AUTHOR

J.T. Geissinger is a #1 internationally bestselling author of emotionally charged romance and women's fiction. Ranging from funny, feisty romcoms to intense, edgy suspense, her books have sold more than eight million copies and been translated into over twenty languages.

She is a three-time finalist in both contemporary and paranormal romance for the RITA® Award, the highest distinction in romance fiction from the Romance Writers of America®. She is also a recipient of the Prism Award for Best First Book, the Golden Quill Award for Best Paranormal/Urban Fantasy, and the HOLT Medallion for Best Erotic Romance.

Find her online at www.jtgeissinger.com

ALSO BY J.T. GEISSINGER

Standalone Novels

Pen Pal

Perfect Strangers

Midnight Valentine

Queens & Monsters Series

Ruthless Creatures

Carnal Urges

Savage Hearts

Brutal Vows

Beautifully Cruel Duet

Beautifully Cruel

Cruel Paradise

Dangerous Beauty Series

Dangerous Beauty

Dangerous Desires

Dangerous Games

Slow Burn Series

Burn for You

Melt for You

Ache for You

Bad Habit Series

Sweet As Sin

Make Me Sin

Sin With Me

Hot As Sin